my

boyfriends'

dogs

DANDI DALEY MACKALL

my boyfriends' dogs

THE TALES OF
adam and *eve* and *shirley*

Dandi Daley Mackall

DUTTON CHILDREN'S BOOKS

an imprint of Penguin Group (USA) Inc.

DUTTON CHILDREN'S BOOKS
A division of Penguin Young Readers Group

Published by the Penguin Group
Penguin Group (USA) Inc., 375 Hudson Street, New York, New York 10014, U.S.A.
Penguin Group (Canada), 90 Eglinton Avenue East, Suite 700, Toronto, Ontario, Canada M4P 2Y3
(a division of Pearson Penguin Canada Inc.) | Penguin Books Ltd, 80 Strand, London WC2R 0RL,
England | Penguin Ireland, 25 St Stephen's Green, Dublin 2, Ireland (a division of Penguin Books
Ltd) | Penguin Group (Australia), 250 Camberwell Road, Camberwell, Victoria 3124, Australia
(a division of Pearson Australia Group Pty Ltd) | Penguin Books India Pvt Ltd, 11 Community Centre,
Panchsheel Park, New Delhi - 110 017, India | Penguin Group (NZ), 67 Apollo Drive, Rosedale, North
Shore 0632, New Zealand (a division of Pearson New Zealand Ltd.) | Penguin Books (South Africa)
(Pty) Ltd, 24 Sturdee Avenue, Rosebank, Johannesburg 2196, South Africa

Penguin Books Ltd, Registered Offices: 80 Strand, London WC2R 0RL, England

CIP Data is available.

Published in the United States by Dutton Children's Books,
a division of Penguin Young Readers Group
345 Hudson Street, New York, New York 10014
www.penguin.com/youngreaders

Designed by IRENE VANDERVOORT

Printed in USA   First Edition

ISBN 978-0-525-42218-1

10 9 8 7 6 5 4 3 2

FOR MY FAMILY:

How blessed with love we are!

thanks

I'm so grateful for my editor and friend, Maureen Sullivan, who has a way of seeing where I want to go and helping me get there. And thanks to Dutton/Penguin for believing in me again.

For my buddy Laurie Knowlton, what can I say? Thanks for encouraging me, for laughing in all the right places, and for praying us both through the process. Tess and Bird, you always come through for me. And Kelsey, thanks for your stories that can't help but spark my imagination.

Special thanks to my wonderful family, headed by Joe, my delightfully crazy boyfriend, who is also my trusty friend and loving husband.

And last—but SO not least—three cheers to all our dogs!

my
boyfriends'
dogs

"MY MOTHER SAYS that falling in love and getting dumped is good for you because it prepares you for the real thing, like it gets you ready for *true* love and all, but I'm thinking it's more like climbing up the St. Louis Arch and falling off twice. Does that first fall really get you ready for the second?" I shiver a little, but it doesn't have anything to do with the idea of jumping off the "Gateway to the West." I admit I've been pretty depressed for the past twenty-four hours, but not *that* depressed. I'm shivering because apparently rain in St. Louis is colder than rain in rural Missouri. Not to mention the fact that my soaking-wet prom dress—and this dress is a fact I'd rather *not* mention—is sticking to me like wet fur.

On either side of me sit my three dogs, still on leashes. Adam, the restless terrier, wags his tail and tries to break free to greet the three strangers I've joined in this dimly lit downtown café.

I glance toward the door, where the sign facing us says OPEN because it says CLOSED to the rest of the world. All three dogs shook themselves the second we stepped inside. Telltale puddles lead across the black-and-white linoleum floor straight to my table. "Sorry about the mess. I'll clean it up before I go. I promise."

The man who let us in, the old man who I think owns the place, pulls down one of the upside-down chairs from my tabletop and sits himself across from me. "Climbing up the Arch to fall off," he repeats in a scratchy voice that sounds like he just woke up, but I'm guessing his voice always sounds like this. "Got to admit I never looked at falling in love in just that way." He gazes out the rain-streaked window as if he's mulling over how many steps there might be in the Gateway to the West. Maybe on a clear day, which this is not, you can see the Arch from here.

I glance at the other two people inside the café, but they don't seem interested in me or my dogs. The big man behind the counter is scrubbing down the coffee machine, and the younger guy at the back table doesn't look up from his newspaper. It's pretty quiet in here, except for the humming of the fluorescent light overhead and the soft groans from the Dalmatian sleeping at my feet. Rain on the roof sounds like somebody's throwing handfuls of pins at us.

When I turn back to the older man, he's staring at my hair, which is still in its prom-night updo.

I reach for the arsenal of bobby pins holding on bravely. As soon as I touch my hair, I discover that massive hair spray plus rainwater equals sticky glue. Nice.

"Just so you know," I offer apologetically, "this isn't how I usually wear my hair." I look over to the counter, but the big guy in a white apron is still cleaning the coffee machine.

I slip the dog leashes off my wrist and start to work un-bobby-pinning my sticky hair. My dogs don't stir, not even Adam. They're pretty worn out from our late-night walk that turned into a run when the downpour started. We must have banged on twelve doors before this one opened.

4   MY BOYFRIENDS' DOGS

The rain picks up and batters the large front window, turning the world outside into a blur of light and motion. Wind makes the whole room creak.

The man across from me keeps studying me as if I'm under a microscope, the most fascinating thing he's ever seen. He has an air of quiet kindness, so I'm thinking he'd be a golden retriever if he were a dog. He's older than my grandfather, with skin darker than my coffee, which is thick and black and without a doubt the worst cup of coffee I've ever tasted. I'm not complaining. It's cold outside, and the coffee shop was closed up tighter than a muzzled pit bull when the dogs and I showed up. This man didn't have to let me in.

"Thanks again for opening up for me and pouring me your last dregs of coffee. I don't even know your name."

"Louie," he supplies. "Just Louie." He smiles, and it takes up half of his worn face.

I smile back. "Louie of St. Louie?"

He nods. "That's the name of this place, Louie of St. Louie's." The way he says it lets me know this café belongs to him and he's proud of it.

He should be proud. Now that I take the time to notice, I can see what a great place this is, old and full of atmosphere. Pockmarked paneled walls, great tables with silver chrome rims right out of the fifties—my mom would go nuts over them—and wooden-backed chairs with round stool seats like you'd see in a classic ice cream parlor.

The guy at the back corner table flips the page of his newspaper, but he doesn't look our way.

I turn back to Louie. "This is a fantastic café, and I'd say that even if you hadn't saved me from being washed away and flushed down the gutters of St. Louis in the middle of the night.

What time is it anyway?" I spot a small round clock on the wall by the coatrack. "Wow. After eleven? I've got to bring my mom back here. During regular hours," I add quickly.

I reach across the table and shake Louie's hand. "I'm Bailey." I thought my fingers were still numb, but when we shake, I can feel every bone in his hand. "I appreciate you letting my dogs come inside, too. If you can just give me a couple of minutes to warm up, and maybe for the rain to let up a little, we'll all get out of your hair."

"Louie!" The big guy behind the counter nods like he wants Louie to join him for a secret conference . . . about me.

But Louie isn't going for it. He leans back in his chair and crosses his legs at the ankles. His worn black boots must be at least a size 14. "You got something to say?" Louie asks the counter guy.

Identity-Crisis Guy. That's what I think when the man at the counter finally faces me. This guy has got to be smack in the middle of an identity crisis. The left side of his head is shaved and beardless. The right half has longish brown hair and a full beard, if you can call half a beard "full." I can't tell what dog he'd be if he were a dog. Some people are like that.

Louie raises his scratchy voice. "I asked if you got something to say to me, Rune?"

"Rune?" I repeat. Rune is a name I've never heard before, but somehow it fits this man, who's keeping that counter between him and me, guarding his distance.

"Rune," I say again, confirming the sound of it.

Louie gives me a tired nod, then shouts back to Rune the Identity-Crisis Guy. "You go ahead and have your say, Rune. My friend here won't mind."

"Your friend?" Rune shouts. "Your *friend*?" He scowls at my three dogs. They're curled on top of each other, being as good as I've ever seen them be. Rune points at us, and the tattoos circling his gigantic arm bulge. He sputters, but no real words come out.

"My new friend," Louie answers calmly, the tiniest grin tugging at the corners of his mouth.

Rune reaches around to untie his apron, then throws it to the floor. "Okay then. Your *friend's* dogs are going to get this joint shut down. You got any idea the kind of fines that health inspector will slap on you for having three dogs—three *wet* dogs—in your restaurant?"

I hadn't thought of that. "He's right, Louie. I'm really sorry." I shove back my chair to get up, but Louie reaches across the table and pats my hand.

"You stay put, young lady," Louie says. "It would be worth a whole heap of fines to hear what such a pretty young woman as yourself, dressed in just about the finest gown I've ever seen, is doing in a café in St. Louis with her three dogs at this time of night."

"Technically, they're my boyfriends' dogs," I admit.

"You steal them dogs?" asks Identity-Crisis Guy. "From your boyfriend?"

"Boyfriends. Plural," I correct.

"She didn't steal these dogs," Louie insists, rushing to my defense. "Do these dogs look stolen to you, Rune?" He turns to me. "You tell him, Bailey."

I glance at the back table, where the younger guy is still sitting alone, studying the *Dispatch* in the dim light of the closed café. When I don't answer Louie and Rune right away, this guy looks over at us, and I think, *Ha! You are so listening.* I'll bet he's been listening all along.

"Well, it's a long story, about the prom, and me being here with the dogs and everything." I'm explaining all this to Louie. Only I'm still looking back at the corner guy, and he's still looking back at me. It feels a little like the stare-down contests Amber and I used to get into in elementary school.

"Long story, you say?" Louie asks. "Well, we got time for long stories at Louie's. Contemplating that storm outside, I'd say a long story might be the best thing on the menu right about now. Wouldn't you say so, Colt?" He hollers this last part to Staring Corner Guy.

"Can't argue with that, Louie," replies Colt the Corner Guy. "But then I know better than to argue with you about anything." He gets up and strolls across to the other side of the room, where he lifts a green sweater from the coatrack. He shakes it out and carries it over to our table. He's almost as tall as Louie, fit as a Lab, but he moves like a greyhound, sleek and confident.

Towering over me, he looks older than I thought, definitely a college guy. He has nice eyes, beagle eyes, round and dark. There's something familiar about him, but maybe it's just those eyes. I love beagles.

He puts the ghastly green sweater around my shoulders. It's ugly, but warm. I stick my arms into the sleeves and sniff my elbow. Faint tobacco and cheap perfume. I start to make a comment about the similarities between this color and pond scum, but I think better of it.

"Whose sweater is it?" I ask, rolling up the sleeves and wrapping the sweater over my gown's glittery bodice, covering hundreds of tiny hand-sewn pearls.

"This sweater has been hanging on that same hook, ruining

8   MY BOYFRIENDS' DOGS

the atmosphere, ever since I started coming here," Colt explains. "I don't think your customer will mind if your new friend borrows it, do you, Louie?"

"I'd say you're right, Colt," Louie answers with an ease that lets me know they're good friends. He motions for Colt to sit down with us.

Colt grabs a chair off the next table and slides it to ours. Before he sits down, though, he grabs another chair and sets it on the other side of the table. If this other chair is for Identity-Crisis Guy Rune, he doesn't take Colt up on the offer.

Colt eases into the chair next to mine, and I try to ignore how boyishly cute he is. Or how he smells fresh like the rain, in a good way. Or how his eyes shine, even in dim light.

This is *so* not the time. I'm still in my prom dress, for crying out loud.

"Go ahead now, Miss Bailey," Louie says, nodding to me. "We're listening."

"Are you sure you want to hear—?" I begin.

But Colt stops me with a raised, just-a-minute finger. "I was hoping we could exchange names first." He reaches down to Adam, my terrier, and scratches the dog right under his chin, the exact spot Adam loves to have scratched. "I'm Colt." He looks over at me, his mouth barely giving in to a smile as he raises an eyebrow like he's asking my name in exchange.

I give it. "Bailey. Bailey Daley."

Identity-Crisis Guy snorts a laugh from behind the counter. His back is to us, and he's wiping the same spot he was five minutes ago.

"I was actually asking for the dogs' names," Colt says, shooting me that dimpled grin again.

I'm pretty sure my face is turning red, but the light's so dim in here, it probably doesn't show. "The dogs' names? Adam and Eve and Shirley."

"Adam and Eve and Shirley?" Colt asks, like I'm making this up.

Rune, still safely behind the counter, groans.

"Which is which?" Louie asks, without a hint of doubting or joking in his voice.

I point to the appropriate canine as I list off the names. "Shirley the Shih Tzu, Eve the Dalmatian. And Adam." Poor Adam has put on so much weight. He used to be skinny. "Hard to believe I've had Adam since I was a sophomore," I say to myself more than anybody else. "Adam was my first."

Adam thumps his rat tail and turns his broad head to me. The dog has no neck, just a bunch of wrinkles around his collar. I stare into the plump white terrier's eyes and see the eyes of his master. Green eyes.

"I had a dog just like this when I was a boy," Louie says, reaching over to pet Adam. "Pure mutt. He loved everybody he met. And everybody sure loved him."

"Tell me about it," I mutter, thinking, remembering.

Louie leans back in his chair and folds his arms across his chest. "No, you tell me about it. How'd that be?"

LOUIE OF ST. LOUIE

LOUIE TRIES TO GET COMFORTABLE as he studies the nice-looking girl in the fancy gown and waits for her to tell them her story. He should have known the second he heard the tap on the door that this was going to be a long night at Louie of St. Louie's.

Truth is, he nearly went on up to bed right before closing time. Rune isn't the best cook Louie ever had, not by a long shot, but the big guy can handle cleanup and closing. They only had one customer after dinner hours, and that was just Colt. The kid has been stopping by almost every night for a couple of months, always for a tall glass of apple juice and the *St. Louis Post-Dispatch*. But he never stayed past closing.

Louie's been living above the café for almost ten years, ever since his Lily passed. He hasn't missed the old house either, not without Lily in it. It wasn't the same house. That's all. And with the boys grown, with grown boys of their own living clear across the country, he doesn't need but the three rooms upstairs.

But he didn't go up to bed tonight. Since the cancer first reached his bones, sleep hasn't been something Louie looks forward to. He feels it in his bones that it won't be too long now before he'll be with his Lily again. That'll be all right.

Then he heard that knocking and opened the door. Finding

a wet gal dressed like a princess standing on the threshold was just about the last thing he expected. But there she was. And here she is.

Here they all are.

"We are all ears, Ms. Bailey Daley," he tells the pretty young girl wrapped in the green sweater. "You want Rune to fetch you something to eat while you tell us your story?"

"Kitchen's closed!" Rune shouts back.

Louie worries that Rune will give himself an ulcer one day . . . or somebody else. How that man stays married to his fine wife is one of life's great mysteries. "Now, now, Rune. We got bread and cold cuts, don't we?"

The girl reaches across the table and touches Louie's hand. Her hand is warm now, at least. The last strand of her coal black hair escapes from the fancy curls she had plastered to her head when she walked in. Now the curls bounce around her face like coils of fine black licorice. She reminds Louie of his granddaughter, Jason's girl.

"I'm not hungry, Louie. Really. Thanks, though." She turns toward the kitchen. "Thank you too, Rune!"

She's something, this little gal in her fancy gown.

"I'm not sure where to start," she admits, shaking her hair so it falls around her shoulders, covering the green sweater.

Colt moves his chair in closer so he can see her face. Louie figures the young fella wants to hear this as much as he does.

"How about starting at the beginning?" Louie suggests.

"The beginning, huh?" Bailey sighs. She reaches down and strokes the old white mutt at her feet. "I guess that means I start with you, doesn't it, boy?"

"Adam, right?" Colt asks.

"Right." The girl settles back into her chair in a relaxed way she hasn't done since walking into Louie's. "It all started with Adam."

the first fall

adam

1

They say there's a line that crosses the middle of the whole universe. They say you can't see that line. But if you step over it, if you cross it, there's no going back.

I crossed that line on March 19 of my sophomore year in high school. And I didn't even realize it—not fully anyway—until the end of May, so of course by then it was too late to do much about it.

The morning began like most school mornings. I woke, showered, and then stood in front of the full-length mirror, my eyes firmly shut while I recited my morning mantra:

"*I am sixteen, with extraordinarily large breasts, a fantastic bod, and hair to die for.*

"*I am sixteen, with extraordinarily large breasts, a fantastic bod, and hair to die for.*

"*I am sixteen, with extraordinarily large breasts, a fantastic bod, and hair to die for.*"

I opened my eyes and studied my reflection. Then I tossed my dog-eared copy of *Teen Mind Over Teen Matters: The Art of Positive Thinking* into the trash, where it belonged.

"Bailey!" my mother hollered up the hall at me. "Hurry, will you?"

"I'm hurrying," I called back, examining the horribly outdated contents of my closet. What *would* a sixteen-year-old with extraordinarily large breasts, a fantastic bod, and hair to die for wear on a bright spring day?

I might have settled for stonewashed jeans and a wrinkly T-shirt, but Amber and I had vowed to hold each other accountable for our last two remaining New Year's resolutions: 1) Dress better, so that we'd 2) Land our first boyfriends.

I'd had zero luck with number two, so the least I could do was try to stick with number one. I settled on a denim mini (Amber assured me they were back) and a gray-and-white-striped rugby shirt.

"Look at this," Mom said as soon as I stepped into the kitchen. She didn't look up from the classifieds. "Three garage sales between here and school."

"Mom," I whined. "Not on the way *to* school. Promise."

Now she looked up. My mom could have passed for my sister, which was sometimes fun, like when we went to Florida and they carded her every time she ordered white wine, which was exactly why she ordered it. Or, not so fun, like when the lifeguard hit on her instead of me. She was shorter than me and could still wear jeans she'd worn in high school. Plus, she had great hair, and great hazel eyes that were now aimed at my semibare thighs. "Bailey, was your skirt that short when we bought it, or did you grow six inches when I wasn't looking?"

I grabbed a bagel. "Isn't it garbage pickup day in Grove?"

"You're right!"

My mother was so easy to distract it almost took the fun out of it. Rich people in the Grove district threw away furniture that cost more than our house.

"We *have* to go there on the way to school, Bailey."

"Grove isn't on the way to school."

"Well, sort of. If Fourth Street were blocked off like it is for parades. And if they were doing construction again on Elm." Mom gulped her coffee.

Me and my big mouth. Mention a garage sale or a garbage pick, and my mom salivated. She'd been renting a stall at one of those antique malls, Aunt Teak's—get it?—for almost a year. I don't think she'd sold anything yet. Our own garage was so filled with the junk she bought from other people's garages that she'd had to park outside all winter. Her real job was as a receptionist in a dentist's office. She got the job because of her great smile. My mom could get any job she interviewed for. Keeping them wasn't that easy, though. She was always ready to move on to something new.

"It'll be great furniture," she muttered. "Heavy. It's good you'll be with me."

"Yeah. Really good." But I knew there was no use arguing with her. "We better leave right now, because Mrs. Weaver will kill me if I'm late for English again."

Mom dashed out of the kitchen, and I cleared the table. When I put away the cereal, I saw that she had cut out the contest entry from the back. Mom loved contests. She'd won more appliances than we'd use in a lifetime, but we always had gifts on hand for weddings.

Mom shuffled back into the kitchen. "Where's my purse?"

"On your arm."

She yawned. "I stayed up for WKMM's Midnight Madness phone-in contest. Worth it, though. I was the twenty-eighth caller. Got us two free tickets to some band named Disaster's Death."

"Cool." I aimed her toward the front door. "Seriously, I can't be late, Mom."

"Late schmate," she muttered with her unique brand of motherly logic.

Once outside, we both headed for the driver's side of the van.

"You have to let me drive, Mom," I insisted, snatching the keys out of her hand. "I'm never going to get my real license if you don't let me practice."

She gave up, and I started the van and backed down the driveway. Backing was my best driving skill. I wasn't too bad going forward. But I kept failing that stupid parallel parking exam. "What's so great about parking along curbs?" I asked halfway across town. "Nobody's parallel parked in Missouri since the Stone Age."

"Left!" Mom shouted when we were still a solid block from our turn.

We spotted the West End vultures, two women from a rival antique store. They revved their engine. "Pull over to the curb so they can't get in!" Mom screamed.

I swerved. My front wheel rolled over the curb in an unorthodox parallel parking maneuver. We leaped out and snatched a table out from under the beaks of the vultures, which wasn't half as hard as cramming the disgusting thing into the van.

"This will look fantastic when I refinish it," Mom declared, shoving the last pockmarked, splintered table leg inside the van and sliding the door shut fast.

"When you refinish it? Like the day after I pass my parallel parking test?"

"Hey! This table is a diamond in the rough, Bailey."

Maybe. But as far as I knew, all of Mom's "diamonds" were

still sitting in our garage, as rough as the day she'd discovered them.

Mom dropped me off at the deserted schoolyard. Everybody was already inside. "Sorry I made you late, honey. Worth it, though. You can have the table when I die."

Great. Clutching my pack, I backed up the sidewalk, turned to run in, then tripped over something and sprawled flat onto the sidewalk. Dazed, I lay on my back and squinted into the sun, hoping nothing was broken and that maybe Mrs. Weaver would count this as excused tardiness now.

"Arf! Arf!" A skinny white dog scrambled out from under me.

"*You* tripped me?"

The dog pranced to my face and started licking. I scrambled to my feet, but he scratched at my bare legs until I picked him up. He had the most gorgeous green eyes, but seriously bad breath. "Thanks a lot, doggie."

He wagged his tail and wiggled, still trying to get at me.

I set him down and jogged over to my fallen backpack, trying to ignore my sore backside and bruised pride. When I turned back around, the dog was gone.

"Fickle, fickle you," I muttered.

2

After English, Amber and I bucked the crowded halls back to our lockers.

"Did you really get knocked down by a giant dog on your way to class?" Amber didn't sound like she believed me any more than Mrs. Weaver had.

"Yeah. Only he wasn't giant."

"Whose dog was it?" Amber asked, as if that were the crucial question here. Not "Are you hurt? Did you get rabies? How will you get Weaver to stop hating you?"

"I've never seen that mutt before," I answered, finally breaking the secret code of my smelly locker, which had smelled even worse before I'd inherited it and filled it with cinnamon sticks. Now it smelled like Christmas vomit instead of regular vomit.

Amber shut her locker. She stood two heads taller than me. In her silky top and lace-up jeans, she could have been a model, and not just because of her height and sleek body. She was more graceful than the rest of us put together. She kept her blond hair short and never looked anybody in the eyes, except me. I'd told her a million times she'd be the one guys would go for in college, after they got over themselves and could deal with a tall woman looking down on them.

"You know every dog in Millet," she said. "Or at least they know you."

I pulled out my tattered science notebook and leaned against my locker. "I'm telling you, Amber, I've never seen that dog before." She was right about dogs knowing me. It was kind of a joke with us that dogs loved me, but guys not so much. Not a very funny joke when you come to think about it.

"Oh . . . my . . . gosh!" This outburst came from Carly, who had the locker next to mine. Carly Fields almost never appeared without a boy attached to her arm.

"What?" I asked, shutting her locker so I could see what the fuss was about. "Did you just notice that you don't have a guy hanging on you?"

She didn't take her gaze off the hallway behind me. "Will somebody please tell me who *that* is?"

Amber and I turned around to see what she was talking about.

And there he was.

He came strolling down the hall as if he were a carnival passing through town—as if he owned every inch of the place, even though he'd never been here before. We could all swear to that. It's hard to explain the way he obviously didn't belong in our school, yet he did belong. Like he was a part of somewhere else in the same way geese are a part of the sky, even though they fly over Millet every season in their crisp, soulful V. But here he was, one lone creature of flight, who had looked down on us, glimpsing Millet from above, and peeled himself from that V, leaving his world for ours.

"Where did *he* come from?" Amber whispered.

Nobody answered.

We watched him stride through the hall. Heads turned. People stopped laughing. A couple of teachers stepped out of the faculty lounge and watched him pass.

Any new kid who moved into Millet, Missouri, population 2,302, was big news. But this kid—with his California tan and his Hollywood body, thick golden hair that brushed his forehead, and a confidence that made him look too old, too cool, for school—he wasn't news. He was a news flash. A news bulletin. A we-interrupt-your-regular-programming-to-bring-you-this-special-announcement event.

Amber, Carly, and I pressed against our lockers, waiting until the absolute last second to face Miss Jones and the Paleozoic era. I, for one, willed him to walk our way.

"Unbelievable! Does anybody know this guy?" Carly tugged down her peasant top and scooted up her mini-miniskirt, which already made my denim mini look granny length. Carly would be the one to end up getting to *know* this stranger. She'd *known* every datable guy in our school. And I'm talking *known* in the biblical sense. True, I couldn't swear to that part. But Carly Fields never bothered to deny the rumors.

"He's coming for me," Carly said, fluffing up her long blond hair.

"Waste a little time, why don't you?" Amber teased. "Might want to let the guy get to his first class before you take him to first base."

Unlike Carly the Home Run Queen, Amber and I were the never-been-past-first-base girls in our group, which explained our New Year's resolution.

Sure enough, Mystery-Godlike Guy changed hall lanes and headed straight toward us like he'd known we were there all along. Like he'd left his flock of geese for us. For this very moment.

For a second, the hall blurred. People moved in slow motion. Sounds and shapes melded into each other, into time and space, sky and earth.

He walked so close I could smell him. Breathe him.

He was moving too fast. He was going to pass us by.

My heart sank. I bit my lip. I held my breath. Think of a cliché, and I did it.

Left, right, left, right. He was in front of us, not slowing down. . . .

Then just as he passed, he turned his head—a head worthy of a spot on a Roman coin, deep-set eyes, strong chin—and he smiled.

At me.

"What was that about?" Carly asked, obviously astonished that Mystery-Godlike Guy had smiled at me. *Me.* She glared at me, her gaze moving up and down like she'd never seen me before and was sizing me up for a new suit.

"What, Carly? What's what about?" But I knew. I wondered if they all knew. Did everybody in Millet feel what had just passed between me and this stranger? Could they hear my heart pounding in sync with his footsteps as he moved down the hall?

"You know this guy, Bailey?" Carly sounded as peeved as she was puzzled.

I shook my head. The bell rang, and Amber and I were scooped into the crowd of last-minute students.

We were so late to science that we ended up in the front row. Amber slumped in her chair and whispered, "He definitely smiled at you."

"Nuh-uh," I answered, not sure why I felt the need to deny it. Because in my mind, I could still see him smiling.

And I was still smiling back.

3

The rest of the morning, everywhere you went people were playing the new-guy guessing game. But by lunchtime, nobody I knew had even learned his name.

Amber and I stared at the menu board. "Why didn't I bring my lunch?" I complained.

Amber groaned. "You're not going to do salad again, are you?" She hated salads and didn't need to like them since she could eat ten cheeseburgers and a gallon of ice cream for every meal and not gain weight.

"So, you come here often?"

I turned and found myself looking into eyes as green as that dog's eyes, the mutt that had knocked the wind out of me only hours earlier. These eyes had the same effect. I nodded, but no words came out.

I felt Amber's elbow in my back, urging me to more intelligent repartee. It wasn't that I didn't know how to talk to guys. Amber said she'd grow two more inches if she could have half of my wit or a fraction of my quick-thinking comeback lines.

But the lines weren't coming back now.

"So, what do you recommend?" he asked, staring at the menu board.

Come on, Bailey, I urged myself. *Calling Bailey's brain!*

Then words kicked in. "That would be . . . BYOL."

He squinted at the menu. "Do you mean BLT?"

"No. Oddly enough, even Missourians can read. Not BLT. BYOL. As in, Bring Your Own Lunch."

"Nice," Amber, my personal cheering section, whispered behind me.

Mystery-Godlike Guy grinned. "I'll keep that in mind. What else?"

"Hamburgers," I answered. "Real beef mixed in with that soy."

"Or . . . ?" His profile showed perfect bone structure (I read that in a romance novel) and zitless tanned skin.

I shook myself back to the conversation at hand. "Or hot dogs. But I'm ethically opposed to any food bearing an animal's name."

"Always nice to meet someone ethically opposed to hot dogs."

"And horseradish. And catsup."

"And chocolate *moose*?" he asked in mock horror.

"Always an exception to prove a rule."

I was standing too close to him. My mouth felt dry. I had to quit while I was relatively ahead. "Well, good luck with lunch." With that, I made my way to the salad bar and piled things onto my plate without really looking at them.

Amber followed me and piled vegetables on her plate, too. It had to be the first time she'd been this close to the salad bar. "You did great," she whispered. We edged through the cafeteria together. "Why didn't you introduce yourself? Tell him your name so he'd give you his?"

"He's not interested, Amber." But she was right. Why *hadn't* I asked his name? Why hadn't I written my address on his arm? My phone number on his forehead?

I plopped down at a half-empty table, which on most other days I might have considered half-full. My backside hurt from the morning's fall.

Amber frowned at her plateful of lettuce and cucumbers. "Want my salad?"

"I can't even eat mine." Somewhere between green eyes and green lettuce, I'd lost my appetite.

"Bailey!" Carly hissed at me from the table behind us. She was seated at the football table between our quarterback and our tight end. I couldn't remember which one she was currently seeing. Apparently, neither could she. Rob had his arm around her, and she had her hand on Kent's knee.

"Who is he?" Carly demanded. "And what's his name?"

This was a first. Carly Fields asking *me* about a guy? I shrugged and turned back to my untouched salad. "*Now* she wants to talk to me?" I muttered to Amber.

Amber was staring wide-eyed over my shoulder. I figured Carly must be doing a number on me at her table.

"This seat taken?"

I looked up, and there he was. Green-eyed, Mystery-Godlike Guy.

I had entered an alternate reality, an alternate universe like I'd promised Amber would be waiting for her at college.

Green-eyes was asking me something. "You're saving it? The seat?"

I stared down at the empty space next to me as if it had magically appeared. Amber kicked me under the table. The guy was still standing, holding his tray.

I swallowed air. "This seat? The one I'm sitting in? It's taken. But this one"—I patted the bench—"is not."

"Is now," he said in a low voice as he slipped in and planted his tray next to mine. Our trays touched, and a shiver shot through me.

I took a bite of salad, but it had zero taste. It might have been because I'd forgotten the salad dressing.

He'd gotten salad, too, but he'd piled on breadsticks. "You don't like dressing?"

"You don't really know me well enough to ask that."

Amber gasped, then covered it with a cough. We both grinned at her.

"This is Amber," I said.

He nodded at her. "Do you do any modeling, Amber? Back in L.A., I knew girls who would kill for a look like yours."

Amber's perfect oval face reddened. She shook her head. Then she grinned and sat up straighter than I'd ever seen her at school, coming to her full height.

I put down my fork and stuck out my hand. "I'm Bailey. Bailey Daley."

He took my hand, but didn't shake it. He held it. His hand was soft and firm at the same time, his fingers twice as thick as mine. "Bailey Daley. Seriously?"

"Very seriously," I assured him, trying to keep my hand from sweating in his. "I come from a long line of very serious people who name people very seriously." I was babbling, but all I could think of was my hand. In his hand.

"You're not making this up?"

"It's Bailey Daley," Amber the reporter-to-be assured him. "You'd have to meet her mother to understand. Big D—that's what her mom lets us call her because she's tiny—she thought it would be a kick to have a kid named Bailey Daley."

I nodded, trying not to let on how acutely aware I was of the intense heat of our hands together. "That's my mom. My dad had nothing to do with my name. Or with me."

"Member of the divorced kid club?" he asked.

"Member in good standing," I answered. "You?"

He nodded. Something passed between us, but I can't describe it. No matter how normal having divorced parents is—I think we're the majority now—I'm not sure we ever feel totally normal. But then who does, right? He squeezed my hand, shook it, but neither of us let go. "Went Smith."

"Well, that puts an end to the Bailey Daley jokes," I said. "How did you get a name like Went?"

His green eyes stopped dancing and turned a full shade

darker. "The day I was born, my father went away and left my mother. That night my grandparents died in a car accident. My mother told the doctor that when I came, everything else went. I guess she could have called me Came, but what kind of a name is that?"

Only then did he let go of my hand. And when he did, I felt like crying. That's how deeply I sensed the loss of it.

4

I filled lunch with witty chatter. But the truth was I didn't know how to talk to guys—really talk—any more than Amber did. Lunch was winding down, and I realized I hadn't learned much about Went Smith. "I still don't know why you're in Millet. I don't know much at all about you, Mystery Guy."

"You will. We've got time."

We've got time. Had anybody ever said a nicer thing to me? It was all I could do not to shake hands with him again.

"Dad and I—and our dog—moved out here so Dad could work in Larkfield at the prison."

"Wait. I thought your dad bailed on you when you were born." I said it before thinking. What was wrong with me? This was too personal.

But he just smiled. "Dad bailed on Mom, but not on me. I did the every-other-weekend thing growing up, but I've been living with Dad since middle school. I guess I got to be a little too much for Mom to handle."

"Where's your mom now?" Amber actually sounded at ease talking to Went.

"St. Louis. So I'll get to see her more often. We could use a second chance." He turned to me. "You and your mom get along?"

"With each other, yeah. With the rest of the world, that depends. Money's always tight in our house. We do okay, I guess. I have *got* to get a job, though."

"Yeah. My dad wants me to get a job ASAP."

"Bailey?" Amber frowned. "You're going to try to get a job in Millet? Man, what's left?" She turned conspiratorially to Went. I loved how he'd put my friend at ease without seeming to try. "Bailey can get jobs. Keeping them, that's another matter."

I shrugged. It was the exact thing I'd been thinking about Mom earlier. Spooky.

Lunch ended, and Went followed us to the dump line. "Don't suppose you have English this hour?" he asked, studying his class schedule. I considered skipping history and going to English again.

"We've got history now," said Amber the Big Mouth.

"Did you get Weaver?" I moved in beside Went so I could read his schedule. He smelled like a California breeze, a sandy beach, the Pacific at sunset. Somehow I knew this even though I'd never been farther west than Nebraska.

"Do you have Weaver *now*?" Carly's strident voice interrupted us, followed by her strident self. She strutted up on the other side of Went. "*I've* got Weaver now!" Carly made this sound like the most amazing coincidence since lightning had struck the same place twice. She slipped her arm through Went's, and they disappeared into the throngs.

Amber and I trudged in silence to history class, a funeral procession in the middle of a circus. "Well, Went was fun while

MY BOYFRIENDS' DOGS

he lasted," she said. "Now that Carly's made her play, we'll probably never get a chance to get to know him."

Know him, *know* him, *know* him . . .

Amber was right. Even with my New Year's resolution, I'd never get a boyfriend like Went Smith.

In history class a dozen kids fired questions at me before our teacher so rudely interrupted with details, details, details about world wars and treaties. The rest of the afternoon people stopped me in the halls to ask about Went. I could have held court in study hall.

I was walking out of my last class when I was accosted by Meagan Bird, our very own head cheerleader. "Bailey!" She blocked my exit with her extraordinarily large breasts, her perfect bod, and her hair to die for. "Went says he's sixteen, but I think he's kidding me. He looks so much more mature than sixteen. We have math together."

Went? Kidding Meagan Bird? In math class? Adding, subtracting, *multiplying* together? I didn't even want to think about it, but my mind was shooting images of them teasing, multiplying. Meagan was a sophomore, like us. Only she was seventeen because her parents had held her back in kindergarten. Twice.

"Pretty sure he wouldn't lie about his age to *you*, Meagan," I said.

"Guess that means he's too young for you, huh?" said Amber My Best Bestfriend.

Meagan acted like she hadn't heard Amber's sage advice. "Went is just so funny!" she squealed.

"In math class?" Amber asked.

"Yes!" she assured us, emphasizing the word with a cheerleading bounce.

"Well, you know how funny numbers can be," I admitted. This whole conversation was giving me a stomachache, or chest pains. But I wasn't about to let her see that. I had a feeling she'd set her sights on Went Smith, just like Carly had. "I need to go to my locker, Meagan . . . if you'll move so I can."

"I smell a Carly-Meagan catfight," Amber whispered when we were out in the hall. "Unfortunately, I can't stick around for the show. Dentist's appointment."

"Say hi to Mom. She's covering reception for Dr. Castor."

"Will do." Amber strode off, her long legs carrying her as gracefully as if she were on a model's runway.

With Amber gone, I felt more alone than ever. All afternoon I'd expected to run into Went. But I hadn't so much as glimpsed his golden locks. Not even once.

And then I did see him.

I was walking to my locker, and there he was. Not at *my* locker, but at Carly's. His back was to me, but Carly saw me. She waved. Went turned around and waved, too.

I ducked into the girls' bathroom. So much for alternate reality. Carly had her hooks into Went like she always did with guys. The universe was back in order.

Alone in the bathroom, I moved to the mirrors. The slap of my sandals echoed like broken applause. The light buzzed. I'd never noticed that before. I waited until Carly and Went—ugh, I hated saying those names together—had time to leave. Then I dashed from the building like it was on fire.

The second I reached the spot of my morning's fall, there was that little white dog. He barked and jumped and whimpered at my heels. I squatted to pet him, and he pounced on me so hard I almost spilled backward again. "Were you waiting for me?"

He jumped up and licked my nose.

"You think that's going to make me forgive you for this morning?" He licked my chin. It tickled. "Oh, all right. You're forgiven."

"Are you trying to steal my dog?" Went Smith was standing over me, grinning, showing two dimples.

"*Your* dog?"

"Can't you tell by the way he likes me better than you?" Went asked. His dog was totally ignoring him. "Here, Adam! Here I am." The dog, still dancing around me, didn't even turn toward Went.

I stood up and gave Adam a little push toward his master, but he bounded back to me. "Don't feel bad. I have this effect on dogs. You can ask anybody."

He leaned down and stroked his dog. "I don't need to."

I looked from Went to Adam. A breeze kicked up, making treetops sway and swish. Silver-tipped clouds sped through blue sky. A tiny flock of geese soared in the distance, their honking so faint I might have imagined it. Then everything came together. This green-eyed dog, Adam—this dog that had knocked me off my feet in the morning—belonged to this green-eyed boy, Went—the boy who'd been knocking me off my feet ever since.

And that's when it happened. I think the instant I'd seen Went strolling up the hall of Millet Central, I must have stepped one foot over that invisible line, the line that circles the whole world, the line of no return. And now, meeting Adam, hearing the geese, and gazing into Went's knowing eyes, I lifted my other foot and crossed over that line of my own free will.

I was going to make Went Smith my boyfriend, my first real boyfriend. And there was no going back now.

5

A new confidence spread through me as I faced Went. "Come with me. I'll give you a free tour of Millet, Missouri." I took a couple of steps. Adam followed me. Went did not.

"I . . . uh . . . " He glanced toward the drop-off and pickup lane.

"Is your dad picking you up?"

"Not exactly. Carly offered to give me a lift."

The old Bailey Daley would have stared at her feet and felt like an idiot. She might have pulled out a funny line or two, but she would have escaped as fast as she could. Not the new Bailey. "Adam doesn't want to ride with Carly."

Went laughed. "Adam said that?"

Carly's black Mercedes was edging through the mass of cars. The Mercedes was used, but still. It was a Mercedes. She honked the horn. Went squinted over at her.

I took hold of his hand. "Are you coming with Adam and me or not?" I held my breath. I'd crossed the line. *No going back. No going back.*

Went broke into a smile. "Let's get out of here."

We took off running up the sidewalk, away from the parking lot, away from school. Adam barked at my heels. I laughed so hard I could barely see where we were going—through the back lot, across the street, weaving through lawns.

Went was laughing as hard as I was. He didn't let go of my hand, or I didn't let go of his, or both. Adam ran circles around us, nearly tripping me twice.

"Where are you taking my dog and me?" Went shouted as we dashed through an overgrown playground with two broken swings and no kids. We slowed to a jog. Hands on hips, he leaned forward, like he was trying to catch his breath.

Maybe I was in better shape than I thought because I wasn't even breathing hard. Or maybe air was thicker over the line, in the alternate universe. "We're going job hunting. You said you needed one."

"Actually, I think I said that's what my dad wanted."

"It'll be fun," I assured him. "Thrill of the hunt and all that." I led Went to the only cinema in Millet. "Ta-da! The Millet Movies, where I had my first real job!" Even in sunlight, the old theater looked dark inside and out. The sidewalk out front suffered from jagged cracks.

"They still run movies here?" Went frowned up at the prewar marquee.

"Only on weekends. But we run two movies—count 'em, *two* movies—in different rooms at the same time. Actually, it's more like one big room with a thin wall down the middle. The advantage of this architectural design is that you can see one movie and listen to the other. Two for the price of one."

Went squinted up at the marquee. "I get it. It's retro, right? Old movies?"

I could tell he was serious. "Nope. First-run only. Are you saying you've already had these movies in Los Angeles, California?"

"Not for a long, long time."

"Huh." I stroked Adam's ears, and he groaned with pleasure.

Went cupped his hands to peer in. "Think they're hiring? I take a mean ticket."

"I'm sure you do, surfer boy. But the owner, Big Barry, takes all tickets. Hey! Maybe he'd let you put handprints out front the way they do in Hollywood."

Went sighed and faced me. "So how did *you* get a job here?"

I considered how much of the story I should tell my first real boyfriend. "I sang."

"You what?" He was doing a terrible job of trying not to laugh.

"I'd been hounding Big Barry for a job. Then one night he was showing a musical."

"So you sang?"

"Not onstage. See, Big Barry sits behind that table inside and sells the tickets. Only he weighs three hundred pounds and moves so slowly that the line got long, and people got grouchy. So I came to the rescue. I took over and moved people through fast. But I had to do something more to prove to Big Barry that I was indispensable."

"So you sang?"

"They'd come for a musical, right? So I gave them one. When I made change, I sang—like, 'Give me a twenty. I thank you, sir. Now here's the change, but I'll give it to her.'" I sang this so Went would get the idea. "We sold out of popcorn when I sang popping songs at the refreshment counter."

"Impressive. So he hired you on the spot?"

"On the spot. Same spot he fired me on two weekends later when the musical was replaced by a war movie."

"Show business," Went said sympathetically.

We moved on to Main Street Millet. A couple of freshman girls spotted us and waved like they were landing planes. "Hi, Went!" He waved back.

The muscles in my neck and shoulders knotted. "You sure do get around," I commented, ready to shove those freshmen into oncoming traffic if need be.

"I do. And in very good company."

I felt my muscles relax. "Thanks."

"I was talking about Adam."

We laughed and kept walking. I reached over and took his hand. I had never done that. I mean, I'd held hands with guys before. But I'd always waited for them to make the first move. Too big a chance of rejection. This time it was different. I'd crossed the line. Went's fingers wrapped around mine, then interlocked. A shiver shot up from each hand, electrically charged. I wondered if he felt it, too.

Went broke the silence. "So, what other job opportunities are there in Millet?"

"Oddly enough, all the ocean lifeguard slots are taken."

He chuckled. "Probably would have been a long commute anyway."

"Eight hundred miles, give or take." It struck me that I hadn't had this much fun in a long time. Maybe never. And all we were doing was job hunting in Millet.

No wonder everybody wanted boyfriends if this was what having one felt like.

Went and I strolled along Main, Adam prancing between us. We'd come to the end of the old part of town when Went tackled me and shoved me into the bank alley drive-through.

"Hey!" I cried, struggling to get free.

He put his hand over my mouth and jerked his head toward Main Street. I stopped struggling and looked. Carly Fields was cruising Main. Went let me go, and we flattened our backs to the bank's brick wall like we were bank robbers hiding from the cops.

"I *thought* I saw a Mercedes back at school," Went whispered. "But I didn't believe anybody in Millet would have one. Is it her dad's?"

"Nope. He drives a big one. He owns this bank we're holding

up. Carly got her Mercedes on her sixteenth birthday. She does admit that hers is used." A twinge of jealousy, or maybe fear, invaded me. What if Went wished he'd waited for Carly?

Went was staring at me, his face close to mine. "What were you thinking?"

"I was thinking about Carly's Mercedes," I admitted.

"What about it?" he asked softly.

I stared into those green, green eyes. No way I could tell him what I was really thinking. I didn't want him to think I was the jealous type. "I was feeling sorry for Carly. *My* mom never gives *me* used gifts on my birthday."

Went laughed hard. Then he tiptoed out and peeked down Main Street. "Coast is clear. On with the job hunt."

We ruled out applying to Carly's dad's bank and continued up Main. The street jogged, then shot uphill to the highway. The town changed as sharply as the road curved. Behind us lay a tiny bridal shop, an ancient pharmacy, a photo shop, a used-book store, and a candy store. Ahead lay twenty-first-century America. Fast-food joints lined both sides of this stretch. Gas stations sprang up faster than a blinking stoplight.

"Now this looks promising," Went commented, "if a little crass."

"I heard that," I said. "And second it."

We struck out in every fast-food joint, but not because of Went. He charmed each manager. But when they refused to re-hire me, Went told them we were a team. It was the same story everywhere we went. At Millet Markets, Went had the owner eating out of his hand. "More than anything, Mrs. Hales," Went said, concluding his job pitch, "I really want to get to know the people of Millet. And what better way is there than working in the heart of the town, the center that meets people's basic needs?"

"We could use a few more like you around here," Mrs. Hales said.

Went smiled over at me. "Great! Then you have room for my friend, too?"

Mrs. Hales frowned at me so hard I took a step back. "Bailey?"

"Afternoon, Mrs. Hales," I chimed in, wishing I'd stayed outside with Adam.

She turned back to Went. "You, yes. Bailey, no."

I understood. She liked me. She just hadn't liked my bagging methods. I'd gotten so bored after a week bagging items exactly the same way that I mixed things up for fun—yellow with yellow, red with red. It wasn't my fault strawberries and tomatoes had to go with canned tomatoes and red meat. "It's okay, Went," I whispered.

"Mrs. Hales," Went said, "if Bailey can't work here, *I* can't work here."

Without the slightest hesitation, Mrs. Hales said, "Nice meeting you, Went."

Outside, I kept apologizing, but Went laughed it off. Our last stop was Grady's Gas and Snack. Halfway there a dachshund, Bertha, waddled out of a bush and ran to greet me. Adam tried to get between Bertha and me.

"So you're, like, the Pied Piper of Dogs?" Went asked.

"Something like that." I sent Bertha on her way. But before we reached the top of the hill, two more dogs fell in behind me.

Grady's Gas and Snack looked like a million other quick stops—red awning over two rows of pumps, a handful of parking spaces out front, and a one-room snack shop inside. Sarah Jean

Kinney was sitting behind the counter reading the *Millet Messenger*. She'd gone to school with my mom. If there were "good ol' girls" the way there were "good ol' boys," Sarah Jean was one.

She looked up at us, then folded her paper. "Well, look who we got here. How you doing, kiddo?"

"Fine, Sarah Jean. How are you? How's Rudy?" Her son, Rudy, was still in elementary school. He'd been born with some kind of syndrome that kept him from holding on to skills he learned. Everybody loved Rudy.

"That boy's got it into his head he wants a horse. It's all he talks about." As if she'd just noticed I wasn't alone, she turned to Went. "Who's your friend?"

Went introduced himself and explained that he needed a job. "I guess I'd like to show my mother I've changed since she moved to St. Louis. Before I see her again—it's been two years—I'd like to be able to tell her I have a good job." He smiled at Sarah Jean. "I'm sorry. I shouldn't have gone on like that. You're just so easy to talk to."

By the time he was finished, I thought Sarah Jean might quit her own job just to make a place for Went at Grady's. She promised to talk to the owner.

When we left, I wasn't sure what to say to Went. "Listen, I'm sorry about things with your mother. I'm sure she'll be really happy to see you, no matter what."

His forehead wrinkled. "Are you talking about that job stuff? That I need a job to prove myself to Mom?" He laughed and put his arm around me. "Bailey, I just made that up. I saw Mom last week. We're cool." His arm tightened around my shoulder. "You're pretty cute, you know that?"

I wasn't sure I understood what had just taken place in

Grady's, and I didn't really care. Went's arm was around me, he thought I was cute, and all was right with the world.

6

I had no idea what time it was when Went and I strolled up Ukulele Lane toward home. I'd lost track of time. Maybe there was no such thing as time on the other side of that universal line I'd crossed. To me, it felt like Went had been my boyfriend forever.

"I thought you were kidding when you said you lived on Ukulele Lane," Went said when we walked under the green street sign.

"Didn't you notice Guitar Drive and Harp Road when we crossed them? We're a very musical neighborhood."

"I see that," he agreed.

Music blared from the corner house, where the four Johnson kids lived. I used to babysit for them, the worst job of my career. Our street was nothing to brag about. The houses were all small, like ours. Nobody paid much attention to lawns, not like they did in Amber's neighborhood.

"Ukulele Lane," Went repeated for the fourth time. "So that makes you—" He cracked up, unable to finish the thought.

I confirmed it. "Bailey Daley of Ukulele Lane. I know. I sound like a Dr. Seuss story. Amber says that with this name, I have to be a songwriter when I grow up."

"Or a stripper," Went added helpfully.

"I hadn't thought of that." But I liked thinking of Went thinking of Bailey Daley of Ukulele Lane as a potential stripper. What if my boyfriend was thinking of me as a sex object? Too cool. I could hardly wait to tell Amber.

Mom's van was parked in the driveway, and I spotted her inside it, wrestling with the garbage-pick table we'd scrounged that morning.

For a second I wanted to keep on walking past our house. It was pretty early in our relationship to have Went meet my mother. But sooner or later, a boyfriend has to meet his girl-friend's mother. "Hey, Mom," I called, turning up the drive.

"Bailey!" she cried from inside the van. "I need help. Hurry!"

Went and I ran to the rescue. Mom was stuck between table legs, and the table was lodged in the van door. "Get me out of here, Bailey." She tried to duck under the table, but even my tiny mother couldn't fit.

"How did you get in there?" I asked, thinking what goes in must come out.

Went brushed me aside and put one foot inside the van, under the stuck table. Grabbing the tabletop in both hands, he said, "I'll lift it, and you can duck out."

True to his word, my boyfriend lifted the table.

Mom, in her bright-green-and-teal pantsuit, rolled under the table legs and out of the van. "I'm free!" she cried, lifting her arms to the heavens.

"You okay, Mom?" I wondered how long she'd been caged by the table, but I didn't ask.

"More or less." She leaned in and whispered, "So that's Went."

"How did—?" Then I remembered Sarah Jean at Grady's. "Man, news travels fast around here."

"Where do you want the table?" Went asked, backing out of the van.

"I sure hope you didn't scuff it," Mom said.

Went let go fast and stared at the table. "Wow. I'm sorry if I—"

"She's kidding, Went," I explained. "Have you gotten a good look at that table? It's all scuffs."

"Yeah," Mom said. "How on earth did you manage to scuff up the whole thing in such a short time?"

Went's grin was a match for Mom's. "It's a family secret." He stuck out his hand. "Went Smith."

Mom shook his hand. "I know."

"And you're Bailey's sister?"

I rolled my eyes. "Sorry, Went. She gets that all the time."

"But it never gets old," Mom admitted.

"Apparently, neither do you."

Mom laughed. "Where did you find this boy, Bailey? Honestly, my daughter has been bringing home strays her whole life."

As if on cue, Adam barked from inside the van.

"Adam?" I ran to the little dog's rescue. Somehow he must have jumped inside while we were rescuing Mom. I picked him up, and he licked me in great thanksgiving. "Poor baby," I murmured. "Mom, this is Adam. I've known Adam longer than I've known Went."

"That long?" she quipped. "I don't know about you guys, but I'm starving. Went, would you like to stay for dinner? What do you think, Bailey? Pepperoni and extra cheese?"

I could have hugged Mom for inviting my brand-new boyfriend to dinner. This is how it was meant to be. My boyfriend and I, my boyfriend's dog, and my mom, all having dinner together. "What do you like on your pizza, Went?"

His cell phone rang.

"Fancy California boy," Mom commented when Went pulled out a slimline iPhone with enough bells and whistles to launch satellites.

My old-fashioned cell had three more weeks of probation remaining from the cruel and unusual punishment meted out by my equally old-fashioned mother, simply because the poor, hard-working cell phone had put in overtime—about one thousand minutes of overtime. Our phone bill, said my mother, the only witness and the hanging judge, equaled the national debt of half a dozen Third World countries. Man, I missed my phone.

"Okay." Went said this loud enough into the phone to bring me back to the present. "I said I'd be there. Yeah. . . . Soon as I can, Dad." He slid it back into his pocket.

Mom closed her eyes and touched her forehead like she was getting a vision. "Wait, wait. I see an angry father wondering where his wandering son is. I see two women—who look like sisters instead of mother and daughter—eating a whole pizza by themselves." She opened her eyes.

"Sorry. Dad wants us to have dinner together. Thanks for the pizza offer, though. And the séance."

"Anytime," Mom said.

"Want me to walk with you?" I volunteered. I couldn't have cared less that his place was at least a mile away. I would gladly have forgone pizza and walked with him to the top of Mount Everest.

"I think I better run," he said.

"Need a lift?" Mom asked.

"Almost forgot." Went rushed to the battered table. "Speaking of lifts, where can I put this?"

"We can get it, Went," I assured him.

"No problem." He lifted that big table as if it were a surfboard. "Just show me where you want it."

Mom hopped to the driver's side of the van and poked the garage door opener. The garage door lifted, revealing piles and piles of furniture.

Went didn't even make fun of the mess. He dashed straight for one of the few openings and set down the table. When he came out, he brushed his hands together. "If you want to refinish it, I'd be glad to help."

"You're kidding," Mom said. She turned to me. "Is he real, Bailey?"

I nodded. "I'll walk you to the corner."

"Bye, Mrs. Daley of Ukulele," he called over his shoulder as we walked arm in arm, Adam tagging along behind us.

"I'll take you up on that refinishing offer!" Mom shouted after us.

"She's great," Went observed.

"All the Daley women are."

At the corner, Went stopped and turned to me, his green eyes intense. I knew it was time for him to go. It was only for the night. We'd see each other in school the next day. But I didn't want him to leave.

Adam sat down behind me. "I have a feeling you'll have to carry Adam home." I picked up the little dog, kissed his head, and held him out to Went.

Instead of taking Adam from me, Went didn't move. I pressed the dog to Went's chest and smiled up at him. "Here you go."

"No," Went said softly, "here *you* go." He placed his hands on my shoulders and leaned down, Adam smushed between us.

ADAM   43

And he kissed me.

The kiss couldn't have lasted more than a second, but I could still feel his lips when he took Adam from me and stepped back. "See you tomorrow, Bailey Daley of Ukulele Lane." He turned and ran, with Adam tucked under one arm like a football.

I watched until I couldn't see even the shadow of Went Smith. As I floated back down the street, I was shouting on the inside:

I am sixteen, with extraordinarily large breasts, a fantastic bod, and hair to die for.

I am sixteen, with extraordinarily large breasts, a fantastic bod, and hair to die for.

I am sixteen, with extraordinarily large breasts, a fantastic bod, and hair to die for.

And for the first time in my life, it felt true.

7

I got to school early the next day and waited outside for Went. Amber arrived, looking amazing in a pink-patterned top and orange cargos, tied together with this funky orange-and-pink belt. She waited with me for a few minutes. "Maybe he's not coming."

I shook my head hard, discarding that outrageous impossibility. "He promised he'd see me at school. Went wouldn't break a promise."

Amber frowned. "You did hear yourself, right?"

I glared up at her. She didn't understand because she didn't have a boyfriend. "Maybe he's already inside."

We walked to our lockers, and there was Went, talking to Carly by her locker. Carly gave me a prom-queen wave.

Went turned around, beaming. "Bailey! Morning." He came over to my locker. I messed up my combination because I couldn't think with him standing over me, his breath on my neck. "How's your mom?" he asked.

"Good," I answered. "Your dad?" I hated being so formal. It was as if the day before had never happened, as if I hadn't crossed the line, as if there had been no kiss. Carly was calling him. I jerked open my locker, and three books fell out. Before I could get them, Went picked them up. I held out my hands, but he wouldn't give me my books until I looked at him. "Save me a seat at lunch?" His green eyes were soft and deep.

I nodded.

He handed over my books, and the bell rang.

I watched him walk up the hall with Carly. He stopped and said something to Meagan. He exchanged greetings with the Marlowe twins, gorgeous freshmen who could have passed for juniors.

"Come on," Amber said. "We're going to be late."

We were in our back-row seats before either of us spoke again. "You know," I began, trying to be reasonable, "it's not Went's fault if Carly flirts with him."

"That depends," Amber said.

"On what?" I snapped.

Amber's eyes grew big. She and I never argued about anything except music. "Never mind."

I didn't see Went until lunch, when he was friendly and wonderful to both Amber and me. We'd all packed our lunches.

"Where do you buy your clothes, Amber?" he asked. "They're great."

"Thanks." She bit into her sandwich. He waited for more, but she didn't give it.

I didn't like that Amber was retreating again, so I jumped in. "Amber makes almost all her own clothes."

"You're kidding." Went opened his bag of chips.

Amber nodded, but didn't say anything.

I changed the subject. "Where's Adam? He didn't attack me this morning. I missed that."

"Adam sends his greetings. He whimpered all night. I think he missed you." Went set down his chips and touched my wrist. "I know I did."

Amber choked. "Sorry. Too much mustard. I'm having trouble swallowing it."

I kicked her under the table. "Do you have a yard for Adam?" I asked Went.

"This whole dog thing isn't working out that great. There's no fenced-in yard. And Dad refuses to let the dog have the run of the house when we're gone."

I pictured sweet Adam. I really liked the dog. After all, he was the one who had led me to Went. "So what did you do with him?"

"Dad bought a kennel. It's not very big, though."

"A cage?" Amber asked.

Went shrugged. "I don't like it either. I'm hoping Adam will sleep all day."

"Went, you can't leave Adam caged up every day," I said.

"I can't let him out. He'll wander off." Went crumpled the empty chips bag. "I don't like it, but there's nothing else to do with him, except kennel him all day."

I couldn't stand it. "Adam could stay at our house."

"Bailey?" Amber said. "Your mom doesn't even like dogs."

"She just says that." Mom's heart's the size of Wyoming. She'd never turned away a single stray I'd brought home. Once, we had three cats, a really old and smelly dog, and a bird with a broken wing. "Mom will love Adam once she gets to know him."

"Are you serious? That would be great, Bailey."

My mind was spinning overtime. It *would* be great. I tried not to act too excited about the implications. "You could drop Adam off every morning," I said. *Which means we would have to walk to school together.* "He'd be fine at my house all day while we're in school." *And then you'll have to come home with me to get your dog!*

"Sounds good," Went agreed. "Check with your mom and let me know. Did I give you my cell phone number?"

Yes! "I don't think so," I answered.

Amber rolled her eyes. I would have kicked her, but she'd scooted out of range.

Went wrote his phone number on his napkin and handed it to me.

I folded it carefully. "I kind of lost my cell," I explained. "I'll find it in a couple of weeks. But my home number's in the book. And if you don't have a phone book yet, all Millet numbers are the same except for the last four digits, and my last four numbers are all fours. And seriously, don't worry about Mom. She'll love Adam like I do. So, bring your dog by tomorrow morning, and—"

"*My* dog?" Went stuffed his trash into the brown bag. "Hey, if we share the work, we share the dog."

"You mean it?" I hadn't had a dog since old Brownie died.

Went grinned at me. "I mean it. From now on, Adam is *our* dog."

I couldn't believe it. Twenty-four hours ago I didn't even have the hope of a boyfriend. Now I had a boyfriend, and *we* had a dog.

When school let out, I couldn't find Went anywhere. And believe me, I looked. I even checked—with my eyes shut—the boys' locker room. "I don't get it," I told Amber. "How could he leave without saying goodbye?" I wasn't mad at Went, just baffled. "I admit this is the first time I've had a real boyfriend, so I might not—"

"A what?" Amber interrupted.

"A first real boyfriend," I continued. "I mean, you can't count Brian or Jason."

"Bailey, you—" She stopped and slammed her locker.

"What?" I could tell she'd been dying to say something to me all day, and I suspected it was about Went.

She sighed. "Nothing. I'll walk home with you." She shot me a grin, but it felt fake. "I want to catch Big D's reaction when you tell her about your new dog."

Amber and I didn't have much to say on the way home. I couldn't remember ever feeling awkward like that around her, but something had changed. I had a boyfriend now, and she didn't. I'd stepped over the line and left her stranded on the other side. "Amber, what's the deal with you and Went?"

"What?"

"I mean, you acted like you liked him yesterday."

"No I didn't! I was just being friendly, Bailey!"

"I didn't mean *like* like. I know you don't *like* like him."

Her whole body relaxed. "Okay then."

"I just meant that you guys seemed friendly yesterday, and today you didn't." I fumbled for the right words. "I want you to know that you'll always be my best girlfriend, even though Went is my boyfriend now."

"Shut up," she said, grinning.

I smiled, too. But I determined to be more thoughtful around my friend. The last thing I wanted to do was to make her feel bad now that I felt so wonderful.

Mom was home, so I did the rip-off-the-Band-Aid move and told her about Adam.

"Bailey, what were you thinking?" she shouted.

"Told you," Amber said.

"What's the big deal, Mom? He's a dog, not a serial killer. He's housebroken." *I hope.* I hadn't actually asked Went about that, but Adam was no puppy. "Adam's a sweetheart. And he smells a hundred times better than Brownie did."

"Brownie? A skunk smells a hundred times better than that dog did."

"And yet, you and Brownie bonded. You cried for days after that dog died."

"My eyes were still watering from the smell," she said. But I could tell she was remembering. Toward the end, Brownie became more her dog than mine.

"Went will come get him after school. You'll hardly even know the dog's around."

She groaned and walked off to the kitchen. It was as good as a yes.

After Amber left, I went to my room and took out the napkin with Went's phone number. He had wonderful handwriting. Exotic even. His 7 had one of those little European lines through it so nobody could mistake it for a one. Very classy.

This was his cell number. And I was his girlfriend. I could call him. Nothing weird about that. He *gave* me his number. Maybe he was hinting that he wanted me to call him. Why hadn't I thought of that before? There was so much about being a girlfriend that I had to learn.

I dialed the number. It rang and rang. Then a voice came on. "Hi, this is Went. Leave a message, man. Talk to you later." He sounded so friendly. I'm not sure I'd appreciated his mellow voice before. There was a beep.

"Uh . . ." I couldn't think of a thing to say, so I hung up.

That was stupid. How was he supposed to know it was okay for him to bring his dog, *our* dog, over in the morning? I hit redial and waited for his voice mail. I could have dialed all night just to listen to his voice. But this time, I managed to use my own. "Hi, Went, Went's machine." I laughed like an idiot. "This is Bailey Daley of Ukulele Lane." I sang that part, and I'm not a bad singer, if I do say so myself. "Anyways, just wanted to tell you that we're all set with Adam. Our dog is more than welcome at the Daley household. So bring him by in the morning, okay?"

A beep sounded, and I was disconnected. I didn't even get to say goodbye.

The rest of the night I stayed close to the phone. I tried to study, but I'm only human. How was I supposed to care about the Paleozoic era when my mind was tied up willing the phone to ring? Where was he? Why didn't he have his cell phone? Isn't that why people had cell phones? So their girlfriends could reach them wherever they were?

8

The next morning I changed clothes three times before settling on a red tank dress, rope belt, denim jacket, dangly earrings, and my funky platform runners. I ate a bagel with cream cheese, packed my lunch, and then sat at the kitchen table and helped Mom fill out contest entries. "What are we doing this one for?" I asked her to take my mind off the kitchen clock's second hand.

"A cruise to Aruba—first prize. Second prize is another vacuum cleaner. But third prize is a year's supply of oatmeal, which we could use for cookies, right?"

"Umm-hmm." The second hand hadn't moved, I swear.

"Bailey, when is that boy supposed to bring that dog here?"

"*Went* is bringing *Adam* before school," I explained. "I'm going outside to wait." The sky was gray and cloudy, a little threatening. I was glad I'd opted for a jacket. I heard the garage door open, and Mom walked out, heading for the van.

Then I saw him. He came jogging around the corner with Adam right behind him.

"Went!" I shouted, waving.

Adam poured on speed when he heard me. He passed Went and jumped into my arms. "I missed you too, Adam. You're going to love it at my house."

"Sorry I'm late." Went looked like he'd just rolled out of bed— hair disheveled, wrinkled white T-shirt, khaki shorts, sandals. He was adorable.

"No problem. We can get Adam settled and still have time to walk to school." I wanted to walk with Went to give us more time alone.

Mom backed the van down the drive, then stopped. "Went," she said coolly.

"Hi, Mrs. Daley. Thanks for letting my dog stay here. I haven't forgotten about refinishing that table for you."

"Neither have I," Mom said. "Bailey, do you want a ride?"

I took Went's arm. "No thanks. We're good. Bye, Mom."

Mom revved the engine and drove off.

"Come on. I'll show you both around." I couldn't help wondering what Went would think of our little home. It was eclectic. That's what Mom called it. The whole house was furnished with her garage-sale finds or treasures from garbage picks.

Went and I walked through the living room, past end tables loaded with antiques and knickknacks.

"What a cool room," Went said.

All the tension drained from me. "You like it?"

"I love it. I wish we had time to look at everything. Is that a real war helmet?"

"World War Two. There's one from Vietnam down there." I pointed to a triangular wooden table in the far corner. "I'll give you the tour after school if you like."

I showed Adam his water dish and makeshift bed. Then I kissed him goodbye. Went didn't say goodbye to our dog, probably because Adam was so into me. We slipped out the door fast, leaving the whimpering Adam on the other side. As we walked away, I heard the *scratch, scratch, scratch* on our wooden front door.

There had never been a better walk to school than the one Went and I had that gray morning. Sometimes we held hands. Sometimes Went put his arm around my waist or over my shoulders. I barely knew what we were talking about, but I was acutely aware of every movement of Went's body next to mine. I prayed cars would drive by. I wanted everyone to see us.

"Hey," he said when we were almost to school. "Sorry I didn't call you back last night. I didn't see your message until it was too late."

It had taken all my willpower not to ask him about that, but I hadn't wanted to appear needy, the kind of girlfriend who phones her boyfriend two dozen times to hear the sound of his voice on voice mail. "No sweat."

"Cool."

I waited for him to tell me where he'd been, but he didn't.

It wasn't until lunch that I learned at least part of the story. The minute Went sat in the seat I'd held for him, Darius and Dave and some of their crew plopped down with us. They were the most popular guys in the school, and they got in the most trouble. Amber glared at me, like it was my fault these guys were sitting with us. She should have been grateful. Most girls in the cafeteria would have killed to be sitting where we were.

Darius rubbed his temples. He and I used to be in the same Sunday-school class when we were kids. "I should have stayed in bed. You hungover, Went?"

"Nah. I'm good."

Maybe I should have been shocked, but I'd been to parties where guys did shots and most girls drank whatever they were handed.

The rest of lunch was dominated by the Dave Crew. Amber bailed halfway through and sat with some of our other friends. I acted like I was part of the gang. Guys had to be guys. And at least Went hadn't been with Carly.

The next days were wonderful. I had a boyfriend. We walked to school together, or rode in Mom's van if he got to our house too late for us to walk. Van rides were never as good as walks. Mom generally ranted the whole way as she detailed Adam's list of sins, crimes, and misdemeanors. Turned out the ol' dog wasn't very housebroken. Plus, he loved chewing on furniture, scratching doors, and destroying shoes. Otherwise, Adam was a sweetheart. I couldn't sit down without having the little terrier spring into my lap.

Usually after school, one of Went's new buddies would drop us off at my house, where Adam would greet me for five solid minutes. Then Went and I would walk Adam together. I was never ready for them to leave.

Weekends were different. I barely saw Went. It must have been my third week as Went's girlfriend that the weekend loneliness hit hard. I called Amber to complain. "Why doesn't he ask me out on the weekend? I've dropped enough hints to fell a good-sized elephant."

"You know he goes to Dave's parties." She sounded tired of this conversation.

"I know."

"So, it's the twenty-first century, Bailey. If you want to go out with Went, *you* ask *him*."

Amber was right. I talked her into coming over for moral support while I made the big call to Went. She watched while I dialed. "You've got his number memorized, I see," she observed. "You must be the girlfriend."

"You're not helping." The phone rang once. "He probably won't answer." Twice. "Maybe I should text him instead." Three times. "I told you he—"

"Yeah?"

"Went?" My heart pounded. Amber moved in closer and nudged my arm.

"Hey, Bailey." He sounded really glad to hear from me. "What's up?" In the background I could hear music and voices. Somebody laughed, a guy.

"I called because I just had an idea," I said.

"Okay." He said something to somebody there. It sounded like, "Not now. I'm talking." Something like that. "So, what's this idea you just had?"

"Well . . ." I was starting to back down. Maybe I could make up an idea that didn't involve me asking him for a date.

"Do it!" Amber whispered, elbowing me again so hard it hurt.

I took a breath and let it go. "I was thinking it would be fun for you and me to go out tomorrow night because it's Saturday and people around here consider Saturday date night, which is why I was thinking it would be a good idea if we went on one." I'd said it so fast I didn't know if Went could possibly have understood me.

He laughed softly, but it didn't feel like he was laughing at me. "Sure. But I'm not going to Millet Movies."

Relieved, I smiled at Amber and gave her the thumbs-up sign. "Don't tell me you've seen both movies already?"

"No. But I rejected both movies already, like two years ago. Besides, Big Barry creeps me out. What else is there to do around here?"

I looked to Amber. She was smushed next to me, her ear to the phone. What *was* there to do in Millet besides go to a movie?

Amber swooshed her arm in front of her. She did this until I realized she was mimicking bowling.

"I guess there's a bowling alley, but I'm really lousy at bowling."

"No bowling. If my buddies back in L.A. heard that I'd gone bowling, I could never return to California."

That made me want to bowl with him. No way I wanted him returning to California. "Hey!" I was getting another idea. "You like animals, right?"

"Don't tell me you want us to walk Adam on our big date."

I ignored that. "Any chance you could get your dad's car?"

"I think so. What's in that pretty little head of yours?"

Pretty little head? I liked that, coming from Went. "The zoo. There's a zoo in Larkfield. It's not L.A. or San Diego, but it's fun. Went Smith, would you go to the zoo with me tomorrow?"

"Bailey Daley of Ukulele Lane, it would be an honor."

"Yes!" Amber exclaimed, jumping to her feet and doing a little dance.

"What was that?" Went asked.

"Nothing. So, we're on?"

"I'll be by for you tomorrow morning. Night, Bailey."

When he said that, I melted inside.

9

"You were never *this* excited when I took you to the zoo," Mom observed. She was still in her penguin PJ's, worn in honor of my zoo date.

"Was too excited about the zoo when you took me." But I knew she was right. I'd been up since 6:00 A.M.—on a Saturday. I glanced at the clock—again. It was almost 10:00. "What time does the zoo open?"

Mom kept cutting something out of a magazine, probably

a contest. "I can't remember, Bailey. Maybe ten? When did Went say he was picking you up?"

"We just said morning." Which was idiotic. Why didn't I nail down the time? Clearly, I needed girlfriend practice.

An hour and a half later, I was a wreck. I'd worn a path by the window, watching for Went. I'd changed clothes twice and shoes once. Mom hit garage sales and came back to find me eating cereal out of the box, a nervous habit I'd developed in third grade.

"Call him," Mom pleaded. "If you don't, I will."

"He'll be here. It's still morning, right?"

Finally, at ten minutes past noon, Went drove up and honked.

"About time," Mom muttered.

I hurried out the door and ran to the blue Buick. I thought about giving Went a piece of my mind for making me wait all morning. I thought about tearfully explaining how hard it had been on me to wait and wait. But when I saw him behind the wheel, his muscled arm sticking out of a white tee, all I could think was how grateful I was that this hunk was mine. My boyfriend.

Went's tanned face lit up when he saw me. "Hey, Bailey! Ready to party with the animals?" He reached across the front seat and opened my door.

I slid in and kissed him. The kiss kind of missed and landed on his chin. "On to the orangutan!"

He revved the engine. "Hip, hip, hippopotami!"

I buckled my seat belt. But if the Buick hadn't had bucket seats, I can't say how close I might have gotten to my boyfriend. All the way to Larkfield we sang animal songs, resorting to "Old

MacDonald" when we ran out of pop animal lyrics. By the time we pulled into the parking lot, it had already been the best date I'd ever had.

At the entrance gate, I dug in my purse for my wallet.

"My treat," Went said, putting his hand over mine.

"I can pay for me," I offered. "After all, I asked you to the zoo."

"I'd like to buy the tickets, Bailey." He put his money on the ticket counter, then turned back to me. "Unless it's a big feminist rights thing for you?"

"Thanks, Went. I'll buy our snacks."

He laughed. "Deal. And man, did you get the short end of that stick."

Larkfield Zoo was tiny compared to the St. Louis zoo, where Mom used to take me. I hoped Went wouldn't think it was boring. I headed for the water animals first. "They don't have penguins. Can't afford a cold house."

"Penguins are overrated," Went said. "Give me a good, solid seal any day."

I couldn't believe he'd said that. "Seals are my favorite!" We took off running, and when we reached the seal and otter area, we were both out of breath. The seals swam in a pool about twice the size of the school gym. "I named every seal in this place."

"When?"

"When I was five."

Went laughed. "And these are the same seals?"

"Of course."

"So tell me their names." He gripped the metal bar that kept people from sliding down the pit into the water.

I pointed to the big seal sunning herself on a rock. "That one's named Bailey."

Went raised his eyebrows at me. "Bailey? Interesting name for a seal. Where'd you get it?"

I ignored him and pointed to two seals swimming side by side toward the zookeeper, who was dangling fish above the water. "Bailey and Bailey. They're brother and sister."

"Both named Bailey?"

"I was five," I reminded him.

A seal lumbered out of the water and slid onto the sunning rock.

"Let me guess," Went said. "Bailey?"

"You guessed it! I had no idea you were so clever."

Went slipped his arm around my waist. We watched the seals together while the sun beat down on us, and scratchy music played from a speaker somewhere, and all the seal Baileys ate fish tossed to them by the zookeeper.

When the seals were finished, Went glanced around. "Is there a water fountain around here? I'm thirsty."

"Ooh. I don't know. But there's a shaved-ice stand right back there. I'll run get us each one. Name your flavor, and guard the seals. I'll be right back."

It took me a while to find the shaved-ice stand. It wasn't where I'd remembered. I ordered two grapes and waited while the kid shaving the ice did his thing. The zoo wasn't busy, which must have been this guy's cue that he didn't have to rush.

When I got back to the seals, Went wasn't there.

I circled the seal pool and found him a few yards away at the otters. He was talking to a redhead I recognized from school. She'd graduated from Millet Central and was probably a senior at Tri-County, where I'd go next year. Tanya or Toni, something like that. She was holding the hand of a little girl who looked like a miniature of herself.

I plastered on a smile and strolled up to them. "Here's your ice, Went."

He took it from me. "Thanks, Bailey. This looks great." He sipped at the grape juice melting in the paper cone. "You and Tahlia know each other, right? This is her little sister, Amy, who loves otters."

I nodded at Tahlia, then focused on the little sister. "Hi, Amy. So you're a big otter fan?"

"I like penguins better," she said.

"Wrong zoo for you, huh?" I commented.

"We better get back," Tahlia said. "See you around." This she said directly to my boyfriend.

Went and I moved on and explored the recesses of the Larkfield Zoo. Everything was fun with Went. I felt like I'd never seen camels before Went and I saw them together. Or monkeys or elephants. He made everything better.

But wherever we went, the Tahlia scene was repeated, only with different players. By the monkey cages, Went ran into someone named Cheri, who acted like she and Went were long-lost friends. A backpacker with one long braid down her back struck up a conversation with my boyfriend while we were waiting for the lions to come out of their cave, and the girl had never met Went before. There was a freshman from Millet at the elks' pen, a sophomore from Larkfield at the picnic tables, and a perky zoo worker at the petting zoo.

The afternoon grew hotter, so we ducked into the reptile house to cool off. An older man was there, talking to a pack of

Boy Scouts and giving anecdotes about the reptiles. Went and I tagged along and listened to the life cycle of the rattlesnake and the mating habits of the cobra.

Then we came to the geckos. "Now, this is a Madagascar day gecko," the old man explained. "Unlike other types of geckos, the Madagascar day gecko mates for life. If his wife dies, like this guy's here did, the poor fellow wanders around for the rest of his life, a dejected widower. He's a one-woman gecko."

I moved in closer so I could see this loyal, loving gecko. It was a light green lizard, with reddish-brown spots that made a thin line down his back. He didn't have eyelids, so his eyes looked sad and surprised, like he was constantly searching for his dead wife and horribly surprised when he couldn't find her. If I'd run across this poor gecko out in the free world, I would have scooped him up and taken him home with me.

We followed our Boy Scout troop back to the snakes and listened to our guide tell tales of the poisonous cottonmouths. When the group moved away from the water moccasins, Went slipped his arm around me and drew me with him around the corner and into a dark recess where we were by ourselves.

I looked up at him, his face a shadow. "What are you—?"

He held his finger to his lips. "Shh-hh." Then he touched my lips with his finger and moved in closer. We faced each other, and Went smoothed my hair, his hands tracing the line of my scalp, then moving to my neck, then my shoulders. My whole body trembled as his fingers trailed down my arms. His arms closed around me, wrapping me in himself. I didn't breathe. I couldn't. Slowly, he lowered his head until our lips were touching. He kissed me, like he'd done several times before. Only this time, he kept kissing me, his lips pressing harder, moving against mine.

And then tongue. Lots of tongue. At first, I didn't get it. But then I did. I really did. And his hands. I wasn't sure how you score it, but I think I was being taken to second base.

When we stopped, Went was grinning.

I was glad it was dark in our little nook. I must have looked like a gecko caught in the headlights. A Madagascar day gecko, a one-man gecko who had found her man.

10

"I adore geckos." I was curled on my bed at midnight, recounting to Mom my zoo day with Went.

Mom had brewed herb tea for us and brought it to my room. She sat cross-legged on the foot of my bed. "Geckos. So you've said."

"Did I tell you they mate for life?"

"You did." She sipped her tea. "You really like Went, don't you, honey?"

I thought about Went, his strong arms pulling me to him. His smile. His kiss. "Mom, I think I love him."

Mom choked on her tea, spilling some on my bedspread. She dabbed at it with the hem of her nightgown. "Bailey . . ."

Mom and I had always been able to talk about everything. "Be happy for me."

"I am. Honest. I think it's great that you're getting to know Went. You haven't known him very long, though, right?"

"How long does it take to fall in love?"

Her gaze flew to the ceiling. She was quiet for a full minute. "I guess you're right. It doesn't take very long to feel like you're in love."

I knew she'd understand. Mom and I didn't just look like sisters. We could talk like sisters, like friends. "Were you thinking about my father?"

She nodded, then reached over and sort of stroked my hair. "You have his hair, you know. Your father was something else, Bailey. Probably still is. But there's a lot more to real love than feeling like you're in it." She sighed and stared into my eyes. "Your dad and I felt it all right. Maybe that's why I want you to be careful."

"Mom. We're not doing anything we have to be careful about, okay?" She and I had had "the talk" more than once. Mom had a way of saying what most mothers probably say to their daughters—don't have sex until you're married. But the way she said it made it sound like a "do" instead of a "don't," like sex was handcrafted by God. And if I used it the right way, then sex would be this beautiful thing waiting for me to share with one man for the rest of my life. So I shouldn't waste it on anyone else. That way, I'd live happily ever after with my husband—like Madagascar day geckos.

"I didn't mean *that*—although I do mean that, too," she added quickly. "The no-sex rule is still in play."

"Agreed."

She stared into her mug as if she could read tea leaves. "I'm just saying . . . it won't be easy since you feel like you do, but you need to be careful with love, Bailey. Once it gets physical—you know, kissing . . . touching—it can take over and take you where you weren't planning to go. That's all." She gulped her tea. "I don't know about you, but I'm going to bed."

I didn't hear from Went Sunday, so when he came over with Adam Monday morning, it was all I could do not to fling myself into his arms. We fell into a steady routine after that, beginning with our glorious walks to school. On Thursday it started raining halfway to school, and we ran, hand in hand, laughing while rain drenched us. Before we got there, Went stopped and held me. We kissed in the rain and could have been starring in our own romantic movie. My times alone with Went were magical.

It was just that other people got in the way. Once we were at school, I had to share my boyfriend. Even though Went and I were clearly together, it didn't stop Carly and Meagan and a dozen other girls from playing up to him.

"I hate the way he ignores you when Carly or the Dave Crew come around," Amber complained. It was Friday, and we were eating lunch with Went, but he'd moved to the end of the table to talk to Dave. Carly just happened to be there, too. They were all so loud the cafeteria police kept giving them the evil eye.

I leaned across the table so Amber could hear me. "He can't help it if people like him so much." I glanced at Went. He looked hot in jeans and a yellow polo shirt, with this wooden-bead choker necklace that only he could have gotten away with in Millet, Missouri. "Can you blame them for wanting Went?"

"Nope," Amber answered. "But I can blame *him* for cutting you out like this. Soon as those guys are around, he treats you like he could take you or leave you, and he chooses to leave you."

"He's not like that, Amber," I insisted. "He's different with me." I whispered across the table, "Amber, he loves me." He hadn't said it, not in those words. Neither had I. But when we were together, that's what it was. Love.

Amber fixed me with her big blue eyes. "Bailey, you know he sees Carly. And Meagan. You have to know that."

I tried to swallow, but the peanut butter stuck in my throat.

I'd heard rumors about Went and Carly. I hadn't heard about Meagan. "Don't believe everything you hear."

"Have you asked Went about him and Carly?"

I shook my head. "I trust Went." What we had was so full, so deep. He couldn't possibly have had that with anybody else. "Love is about trust."

Amber shoved her trash into her bag. When she looked at me again, I could tell she was struggling to control her words. "So, tomorrow's Saturday. Do you and your boyfriend have a date?"

I grinned, doubly pleased that I had a good answer. "We do."

Amber looked surprised. "Seriously? Well, good. Good for you, Bailey."

"We're refinishing a couple of Mom's tables for her. It was Went's idea. He feels like he owes Mom for taking care of Adam." Turned out Adam couldn't hold it during a whole school day. Mom had been coming home to walk the dog during her lunch hour. "She asked me to ask you to come, too."

"Me? Why me? I've never refinished anything."

"Yeah, but you're artsy, and we're not."

"True." Amber had seen Mom and me fail at enough decorating and fashion attempts to know the Daley girls had missed out on the art gene.

On Saturday, Mom forced herself to abandon the garage sales and work on refinishing what she already had. Amber showed up before we finished breakfast. She and I went to work in the garage sanding the old table Mom had salvaged from Grove while Mom drove to the hardware store for stain and varnish. When Mom got back, Amber and I were still sanding, with the music blaring. Went still hadn't shown.

"He better get here soon," Mom warned. "I don't know how to stain that thing."

"Thing?" I repeated, wiping sawdust off my forehead with the back of my hand.

"Masterpiece," Mom corrected.

"It's a cool table, Big D," Amber said. "I was thinking I could stain these grooves a darker color, here around the edges."

Mom inspected the scrolls carved into her prized table. "Great idea, Amber. I hadn't even noticed that etching. A dark stain would really bring it—"

"Hey, everybody!" Went called, squeezing sideways between two dressers to get into the garage. "Don't tell me you started without me."

Seeing Went still electrified me. I loved the way he looked in his old jeans, with paint splatters and holes in the knees. "You made it!" At the sound of my voice, Adam barked and made a run at me. I stopped sanding and greeted the little dog. I missed him when he was at Went's.

Went strolled over to our work area. "Mrs. Daley, this table is sweet. You must have a great eye for antiques. Can't believe anybody would throw this away."

Mom brightened. "You like the table? Really?"

"Are you kidding? When we're done with it, you'll be able to sell this baby to the highest bidder." He squatted down by Amber and examined the table leg she was sanding. Amber backed away. "We ought to fix this leg first, I guess."

"This leg's wobbly, too," I pointed out, wanting to be part of this operation.

"Do you have a Phillips screwdriver? I might need glue, too." He sat on the garage floor and wiggled the table legs.

Mom got out the toolbox. "Take your pick." She smiled at him, a real smile—maybe for the first time since he'd been coming to our house.

It meant a lot to me for my mom and my boyfriend to get along. "We really appreciate your help, don't we, Mom?"

"Bailey's right. Thanks, Went." Mom put her hand on his shoulder.

Went smiled over at her. "My pleasure, Mrs. Daley."

"He can't keep calling you Mrs. Daley," I objected.

"Some of Bailey's friends call me Big D." Mom elbowed Amber, who was silently sanding. "You'd have to ask Amber where they came up with the name, though."

Went shook his head. "I don't think I could call you *Big* D. How about 'D'?"

The rest of the day, it was "D" this and "D" that, as Went fixed the broken furniture. He stained the garbage-pick table, two other tables, and an oversized dresser. We worked and talked and listened to the radio count down the top singles.

Mom dashed into the house and came out with her own CD player. "My turn," she announced.

"Not the Beach Boys, Mom," I complained. Her player held five CDs, and four of the slots always went to the Beach Boys.

"Are you kidding?" Went put down his rag and wiped his hands on his jeans. "I love the Beach Boys!"

"Makes sense," Amber commented. "Very California."

"I wore out my *Pet Sounds* album," Went said.

"No way!" Mom punched on her first CD—*Pet Sounds*.

"Go to track seven," Went commanded.

Mom did. After two notes, she shouted, "'Sloop John B'! I love this one." Mom started snapping her fingers and tapping her feet. Went danced up and took her hand. Then, as if they'd rehearsed it, they broke into this cool rock 'n' roll routine, with Mom twirling under Went's arm, then both of them making a bridge and spinning under it.

"Go, Big D!" Amber shouted.

I clapped. Adam barked. Our neighbors across the street looked up from lawn trimming to see what was going on. Went and Mom danced the whole song, finishing with a dip that had Mom inches from the floor.

"Whoa," Mom said. "That was fun. But it used to be a lot easier."

"You are one terrific dancer, D," Went said, shaking his head. "It was a privilege to rock with you." He bowed and went back to refinishing. But they both sang along with the Beach Boys for the rest of the album.

Mom brought out sandwiches. Then we went right back to work and sanded or stained all afternoon. Finally she called it quits. "Step away from your brushes. I've had it for today. I can't believe what a terrific job you guys did."

Amber stretched. "I think I'll call Mom to come get me. I'm pretty beat."

"I'll take you home, honey. It's the least I can do." Mom turned to Went. "Went, you were a huge help. I really appreciate it."

"Always a pleasure to help out another Beach Boys fan." He glanced around the garage. "Where's Adam? I better get Dad's car back before he has a fit."

I was lodged behind the dresser with the little dog sleeping peacefully on my lap. "Adam's here, Went. Are you sure you have to go? We could order pizza."

"Tempting. But I told the guys I'd hang tonight." He called our dog. "Adam!"

Adam didn't budge.

"Why don't I keep Adam overnight? You won't be home anyway."

"Fine with me." Went walked over and kissed me goodbye on the forehead. I got to my feet and carried Adam toward the house. "Bye, Went," I called again.

"Bye, Bailey," he called back. He was still talking to Mom.

I couldn't help watching the two of them together. If you hadn't known better, you could have thought *they* were boyfriend and girlfriend.

I set Adam down by his water dish and let him drink. Then I hurried back to the garage, in case Went was still there. I got there just in time to see Went whisper something to Mom. And as he did, his hand slipped around her back for a little hug.

I was sure there was nothing to it. This was my mother we were talking about. But I stayed where I was, out of sight, until Went got into his car.

Mom turned, looking dazed or puzzled, and walked back to Amber. "Amber, am I crazy, or did that boy just hit on me?"

Amber's answer came like a flash. "You're not crazy. He's hit on me, too."

11

"Amber! Went hit on you?" Mom sounded shocked.

Adam scratched at my leg. I picked him up and retreated farther, one foot in the kitchen, one in the garage.

"More than once," Amber admitted. "Almost as soon as he showed up, after Bailey was already into him. A couple of times since then, too."

I couldn't see Mom's expression, but I could imagine it. "Did you tell her?"

"Are you kidding?" Amber said. "She's crazy about him, Big D. I couldn't do it."

I buried my face in Adam's furry neck. Tears pressed behind my eyeballs, but I wouldn't let them out. I didn't want to know that part of Went. That wasn't *my* Went.

I breathed in Adam's earthy scent. Then I made a noisy entrance to join Mom and Amber in the garage. It took all I had to pretend I hadn't heard a word.

I pretended a lot after that. I pretended not to hear the rumors about Carly and Went, and Meagan and Went, and Went and Whoever at Dave's parties. I pretended not to mind if Went didn't ask me out on the weekend. I pretended it didn't matter that he'd started leaving Adam at my house night and day. I was glad to have Adam around. But it meant Went and I spent less time together.

Still, the time I did spend with my boyfriend was sweeter than ever. He couldn't have been more caring or more loving when we were alone together. Some nights we sat outside or in the empty amphitheater at Millet Park and watched the stars. I lived for those moments, when he'd hold me and tell me how beautiful I was, when he'd kiss me and make me feel things I'd never felt before.

Each minute with Went was a new experience, even our make-out times—which I would never call them because it meant too much to me, and to him, too, I was sure. One night he'd kiss my ear and breathe softly into it, and I could have melted into the soft spring grass. The next time he'd kiss my neck and send off tiny explosions through my nervous system. I was falling deeper and deeper in love. And I was willing to do whatever it took to stay there.

A few weeks before school let out for summer, Went got himself a car. It wasn't much to look at, but it was his. He picked me up for school every morning. I missed our walks, but riding to school with Went and walking in with him had to make it clear to people like Carly and Meagan that Went Smith was taken—by me.

Sometimes at night we took long drives and parked on country roads. We'd sit together, close on his not-bucket seats, and kiss. Or we'd climb up on the hood of his car and lean back against the windshield. Those were the times when things got tense. We didn't come out and talk about "it," but I knew Went wanted to steal second base, race past third, and slide home. And he knew I didn't. Or wouldn't. Eventually, he'd get frustrated, and so would I, and he'd drive me home in silence.

Things were getting pretty frustrating at school, too, especially in the cafeteria.

"Bailey, can't you tell your boyfriend to tell Carly to eat somewhere else?" Amber complained. "I'm so tired of having the whole Dave Crew, plus Carly, invade lunch." She grinned at Darius, who was sitting next to me. "No offense, Darius."

Darius laughed. "None taken." When Darius laughed, I could still see through the shaved head and arm tatts to the kid who'd sat by me in Sunday school. "Don't let it get to you, Bailey."

I wasn't sure what he meant by "it," but watching Carly with Went, I had a good idea. "They're doing it, aren't they, Darius?" I whispered.

He shrugged. "It doesn't mean anything to either of them."

"How could sex not mean anything?" I whispered back. I could see Amber straining to hear us.

"See?" Darius said. "That's why he has sex with Carly and not you. It would mean too much to you."

"That doesn't make any sense!" I said it too loud. Amber's eyes got huge, and Dave looked over at us. But Went was too busy talking with Carly to notice.

"Makes perfect sense," Darius said, like we were talking about math problems. "Look, a guy's got needs, right?" This time he lowered his voice and leaned down so we were eye level. "And you're a virgin, right?"

I felt my face heat to blood red. "Darius!"

"I'm just saying. Carly supplies *that* need. You supply the rest. No big deal, girl."

But it *was* a big deal. It was a huge deal. I guess I knew in my heart that Carly and Went were . . . I couldn't even say it to myself. Suddenly dizzy, I got up from the table.

"Bailey? Are you okay?" Amber's voice mixed with the buzzing in my head.

"I have to get out of here." I ran out of the cafeteria, leaving my lunch, leaving Went there . . . with Carly. I couldn't live like that. I couldn't share my boyfriend. And now that I knew—really knew—what was happening, what was I going to do about it?

When Mom got home from work, she found Adam and me curled into a fetal position on my bed. She sat on the bed with me. "What's the matter, honey?"

I shook my head. I wanted to tell her. I wanted to talk to her. She was my best friend, even more than Amber was.

MY BOYFRIENDS' DOGS

"You can talk to me, you know?" she said. "Something tells me this has to do with Went."

Tears flooded my cheeks. Poor Adam was wet from the spillage.

"Did he do something to you?" she demanded.

"No!" I sat up. "He *didn't* do something to me. That's just the point."

She got up and paced the room, then came back to the bed and tugged me to my feet. "Come on, Bailey. I always think better when I'm saling."

"You want to go to a garage sale? Now?" It wasn't even a weekend.

In minutes we were trolling the streets of Millet in search of garage sales. Neither of us said anything about Went for at least fifteen minutes.

"There's one!" Mom slammed on the brakes like we were on a safari and had spotted our first tiger. She wheeled into a driveway with a GARAGE SALE sign stuck in the lawn. Nothing was set up outside. The sign looked old, and the garage door was shut.

"Mom, they're not even open."

"They will be." She shut off the engine and got out.

"I'll wait here."

"Coward," she muttered. Mom ran up to the front door and rang the bell.

After a minute the door opened, and a woman appeared. Mom pointed to the sign. The woman shook her head. Mom begged. Finally the woman disappeared inside the house. Mom gave me a thumbs-up sign, and the garage door opened.

In a few minutes she walked out with a giant, gaudy picture

frame and a bright yellow wicker shelf that would have been perfect in a hut in the South Pacific.

She waited until we were in the van and cruising again before she started prying. "Okay, Bailey. So what's up with Went? Is he pressuring you to have sex? Is that it?"

"No. He's never asked me that."

"And he knows you're a . . . that you haven't . . ." She glanced at me and didn't even seem to notice the GIANT GARAGE SALE! sign on the lawn we were passing.

"The whole world knows I'm a virgin, okay?"

"Don't say it like it's a disease. It's a gift." Her voice softened. "And you only get to give it once."

"I know. But I love him, Mom. I've never felt like this."

Her fingers tightened on the wheel. "You may love lots of guys before you find *the* guy, Bailey. Are you going to have sex with all of them?"

"Some people do," I muttered, thinking of Carly.

"You're not one of them," she said simply.

"Well, maybe I wish I were."

Her head snapped around. "Bailey Daley, you don't mean that! Do you want to go around leaving pieces of yourself with every guy you think you're in love with? Is that what you want? Because that's what happens." She made a sharp U-turn and headed back toward home.

"Maybe I don't know what I want."

"Well, I know what you want!" She was getting crazy. This wasn't "Big D." She was screaming at me like regular moms—and I didn't like it one bit.

"You *don't* know what I want!" I shouted back. "How could you?"

"I know that you want to be happily married. I know—"

"I'm not talking about marriage! I'm sixteen. I'm talking about keeping the only boyfriend I've ever had. I'm talking about doing what everybody else is already doing."

"Bailey!" Mom screamed. "Do you hear yourself?" She almost missed our street and had to turn so sharply the tires screeched.

"Yeah. I hear myself. And it's a good thing because nobody else in this van does."

She pulled into the driveway and slammed the brakes. "Bailey, don't you dare have sex with that boy! Wait until—"

But I didn't let her finish. "*You* didn't wait, but you want me to?"

"Bailey!"

"Well, it's true. So what gives you the right to tell *me* to wait?" I stumbled out of the van before she had the engine off. I should have known better than to think she'd understand. She wasn't my sister or my friend. She was just my mother.

The next few days, Mom and I were painfully polite. I apologized for the crack about her not waiting to have sex. She'd always been straight with me about "having to get married," but she'd never let me feel like I'd been an accident or a regret. She'd convinced me that I was God's gift to her, no matter what the route.

But even my apology and her acceptance couldn't wipe out the tension between us. Something had changed. Maybe it had changed the day Went walked into my life, the instant I'd stepped over that invisible line and convinced him to run away from Carly with me.

And now, I couldn't help but think that there was another invisible line I had to cross to keep Went away from Carly.

12

Sunday night with only a week of school left, Went and I sat on the hood of his car, a thick blanket beneath us and a blanket of stars above us. His arms locked around me, we melted into each other, into our own world. I leaned back against his chest and listened to his heart beat. "Went?"

He pressed his cheek to mine and stroked my hair. "Hmmm?"

"Could we do something this weekend?" The last two Saturdays I hadn't even seen him. He'd hung out with Dave's crew . . . and Carly, although he never mentioned her when he gave his brief reports on his weekend activities.

"Why? Did Big Barry get a new movie in?" he teased.

"We could go into Larkfield," I suggested, snuggling even closer. The night had grown crisp, but I felt warm in his arms. I could have stayed like this forever.

"Sure. We could take in a Larkfield flick Friday night."

My chest tightened. *Friday* night. "If we went on Saturday afternoon, we'd get a discount. Then maybe we could go to the zoo. We should celebrate the end of school."

"I told Dave I'd go with the guys to Cairo Saturday."

Everybody knew there was nothing in podunk Cairo except free-flowing, no-ID-checking beer. Most of the rumors I'd heard about Went and Carly involved that slimy excuse of a town. I turned and faced Went. His green eyes glowed in the moonlight, and I almost couldn't stand how handsome he looked. "Went, don't go there."

"It's no big deal, Bailey. We can still do Larkfield on Friday. We could leave right after school lets out and—"

"Carly will be there, right? In Cairo. That's where you and

76   MY BOYFRIENDS' DOGS

Carly meet, isn't it?" I sounded so calm, even to myself. But inside stars and planets were exploding.

Went took my face in his hands. "Bailey, that doesn't have anything to do with you and me. It's not a big deal."

"Making love—or having sex, or whatever you call it with Carly—that's not a big deal?"

"Babe, it doesn't mean anything."

"Would it mean something . . . with me?"

He sat up straight. "Whoa. I didn't see that coming."

"I know."

"What are you saying here, Bailey?"

I looked into his eyes, and a calm passed over me. "I'm saying that I don't want you to be with Carly. I want you to be with me."

His eyes narrowed. "Let's be clear here. By 'be with me,' you're saying . . ."

I laughed. "Have sex! Make love! Do the deed."

He put his hand over my mouth. Then he took it away and kissed me, hard and deep, soft and gentle, a kiss filled with passion and promise and love.

Neither of us wanted my first time to be on top of a '95 compact car. Went said he was going to make this something I'd always remember, *we'd* always remember.

The last week of school, Went ignored Dave and Carly and everybody else. On Tuesday, he was waiting for me when I walked into the cafeteria. "We need to talk."

Amber took the hint. "If you two will excuse me, I'll go see if they've got anything good at the salad bar . . . like brownies and ice cream."

"Thanks, Amber," I whispered as she took off. She and I had

avoided the topic of Went Smith since that day in the garage. It had cut down on our conversations, but saved our friendship. I turned to Went. "So, what's going on?"

"I've got a plan for this weekend." He looked like he could burst into song. "Are you free? Saturday and Sunday?"

"Let me check my date book." I mimicked paging through an imaginary book.

"Bailey, I'm serious here!" Went gripped my shoulders and peered into my face. I don't think I'd ever seen him like that, as excited as Christmas. He reminded me of Adam when I'd been gone too long and finally came home to him.

"I don't have anything going on this weekend, Went."

"You do now. It's all worked out. I want you to go with me to my mom's in St. Louis. We can even go to Six Flags if you want to."

I hugged him. "That's a great idea! I love Six Flags."

"You think your mom will let you go?"

I thought about it. "Mom has to work this weekend." I knew she wouldn't care if I went to Six Flags. I'd done that with friends before. The overnight thing was something else, though. "She'll probably want to talk to your mom about having me spend the night. But I don't think she'll have a problem with it."

His head dropped. Then he grinned at me. "Bailey, Mom won't be there. That's the whole point."

I got it.

"She's going away on business, and I have a key to her apartment. Mom doesn't mind if I stay there when she's gone. We'll have the whole place to ourselves, babe. It will be perfect." He threw his arms around me and hugged me.

"Whoo-hoo! PDA!" somebody shouted.

We un-hugged and stared at each other.

"You still want to do this, don't you?" He looked like a little kid, afraid he was going to be let down.

"Of course I do, Went." I kissed him and said it again. "I do."

"What's the big deal?" I was arguing with my mother—again. Poor Adam trotted between us like he was chasing tennis balls. After school, I'd waited for Mom to get home so I could hit her with Went's St. Louis proposal. Well, not *all* of his proposal. So far, things weren't going well, and all I'd said was that I wanted to go to St. Louis Saturday . . . and come back Sunday. "It's not like I've never been to Six Flags with a bunch of kids before," I insisted.

"You've never stayed all night, though, Bailey. That's the part that worries me."

"When we didn't stay the night last summer, you worried because we had to drive home so late," I reminded her.

"I know." She might have been thinking it over.

"It's really safer to stay the night," I pressed.

"So who all's going?"

"You want a signed invitation list, Mom? I'm sixteen, not six."

"That's also what worries me."

Here is where it would get tricky. I didn't want to lie to her. Lies of omission maybe. But not outright lies.

"Is Went going?" she asked.

I tried not to react. "Yeah. I told you a bunch of kids were going. Males and females. Six Flags was coed last time I checked." All true.

"I don't know, Bailey. I need details. I need to know where

you'd stay. Whose mother invited kids to spend the night there?"

I was hoping she wouldn't ask that question. I'd told her, truthfully, that one of the moms had a place for us to crash. I'd just withheld the name of that mom in order to protect the so-far innocent. "Mrs. Smith," I muttered.

"Went's mother? No wonder you didn't happen to mention that little detail."

"Because I knew you'd be like this! And it's not fair that you'd judge her because she's divorced and Went's living with his dad. He used to live with her, you know. And now they've moved so he can spend time with his mother. And she wants to get to know his friends. And so she does this nice thing and invites us to her home, and what do you do? You automatically prejudge her that she's unfit to chaperone." Words were coming to me at warp speed, and I was spitting them out just as fast, even though I knew as I said them that part of my speech stretched the truth so thin even Adam could see through it.

I stopped talking and picked up Adam. He felt heavier than when he'd come to us. Tears were leaking down my cheeks. I wasn't sure where they'd come from or why, but holding that terrier never failed to comfort me.

Mom walked over to Adam and me. She petted the dog for a minute. Then she put her arms around me. "I hate fighting with you, Bailey. Man, nothing wears me out more."

I cried harder, but no sound came out. "Me too."

She sighed. "You're right. As soon as you said it was Went's absentee mother, I got this image in my head of a wasted, mini-skirted, leather-skinned bleached blonde, a cigarette in one hand and a can of Schlitz in the other. I'm sorry. That was wrong."

I forced myself to look at her. "Went says she's great."

Mom looked like she was trying out for the Face Olympics. Her lips forced a weak smile that wouldn't stay up. "I'm sure she is. And I know I can trust you, Bailey."

I turned to her, not sure I'd heard her right. "Are you saying . . . ?"

"I'm saying *please* be careful. I love you too much for you not to be."

"I can go?" I still couldn't believe she'd come around. I thought . . . well, I wasn't sure what I'd thought. "I can go to Six Flags on Saturday and stay over?"

She laughed a little. "Yeah. But you better get out of here before I change my mind."

I threw my arms around her. "Thanks, Mom." Tears flooded my eyeballs again. I didn't know if they were part of the relief, the surprise, the excitement, the guilt, or the reality. I was going to St. Louis with Went to cross that next line.

13

Time either crept by like woolly worms crossing the highway or flew like eagles. There was nothing normal in my life—not time, not anything. On the last day of classes, Amber and I sat in study hall, but there was nothing to study. All I could do was stare out the window and try to imagine what was about to happen.

"So do you want to talk about it, or what?" Amber asked.

"Talk about what?" I knew she had to know. A few kids I didn't even like had come up and asked me about my St. Louis trip.

Amber raised one eyebrow. "I can't believe you didn't tell me about St. Louis, Bailey." She sounded hurt, not angry.

I felt lousy for hurting her. "I'm sorry. I wanted to, Amber. I've missed talking to you. I mean, I know we've talked. But not *talk* talked."

She shrugged. "Yeah. Not talking about Went kind of sliced the topics, huh?"

"I know you're not crazy about Went." She didn't deny it, so I went on. "I didn't feel like I could talk to you about him. But you have no idea how much I wanted to."

The study hall monitor walked by and gave us a dirty look. Too bad. It was the last day we'd ever spend at this school. What could they do to us now?

Amber smiled at me like the old Amber. "I'm sorry. You should be able to tell me anything, and you couldn't. That was my fault." She scooted her chair closer. "So, tell me everything. Are you really going to St. Louis with Went?"

I nodded, giving her a look I figured was a cross between excitement and panic.

"What's Big D say about all this?"

"Mom's been pretty great. I mean, she doesn't know it will just be Went and me."

"Or that you're planning to do it."

"Right. But she knows we'll be staying the night at Went's mother's."

Amber frowned. "And Went's mom is cool with this? So, what? Like, she'll show you to the spare bedroom and go back to hers?"

"Eeew! No! She's not going to be there."

"Ah." Amber nodded. "Are you sure you're ready for this, Bailey? I thought you wanted to wait until you were married."

"I thought so, too . . . until Went."

"Are you sure you're not just doing it for him, though?"

"What do you mean?" I guess I raised my voice, because the monitor glared over at us.

"Don't get mad," Amber whispered. "You'd be asking me the same question if I were the one about to round third and head for home."

We laughed, and then Amber got serious again. "You know that when people say everybody's doing it, it's not true, right? You're not weird or immature or anything else if you don't have sex. Nothing says you have to go through with this."

"I want to do this, Amber." And I did. Maybe not for all the reasons I'd always thought I'd want to have sex for the first time. I'd pictured that moment often enough. I'd be wearing a beautiful white wedding dress and carrying a bouquet while my new husband carried me over the threshold, both of us eager and crazy in love.

"Well, I'm here for you," Amber said finally. "You know that, right?"

I hugged her and felt those tears trying to leak out again. "Hey," I said, shoving us apart and trying to joke us both out of it. "I'm not going away forever, you know. I'll be back Sunday."

But the thought that raced through my head, and probably through Amber's, too, was—what would I be like when I came back on Sunday? What would Bailey Daley be like after crossing *this* line?

"Meet me in St. Louie, Louie!" Went and I belted out together as we left the city limits of Millet and turned onto the Interstate. Neither of us knew the real words to the song, so we sang whatever lyrics we felt like. We rolled down the windows so everybody in the state would know how happy we were.

Adam sat on my lap and stuck his head out the window. Went's dad had made us take the dog to his ex-wife's for the weekend. He said she needed a real taste of what it was like to raise a family. I didn't mind at all. "Doesn't your dad like Adam?" I asked when we'd run out of St. Louis songs.

"Dad hates Adam. The dog may be housebroken at your house, but not ours."

"You're kidding. Adam hasn't blown it at home for ages." I got eye to eye with the little guy. "Adam, you'd better behave at Went's, you hear?"

"You got that right. Dad's threatening to dump Adam at the animal shelter."

"He can't be serious!" I hugged Adam closer.

"He's serious. You don't know my dad."

"Don't you worry, Adam," I told him. "I won't let it happen."

Went put his arm around my shoulder. "Come here, you."

I undid my seat belt and slid to the middle, where somebody had conveniently installed a middle seat belt. From there, it was easy to lean my head on Went's shoulder. The day was perfect, sunny but not too hot, blue sky with artful wisps of white floating through. Went kissed the top of my head. "I love you, Bailey Daley." It was the first time he'd said it. I'd known it was true. I knew how he felt. But he'd never said the words.

My throat closed. Those tears sprouted in my eyes again. But this time, there wasn't a bit of sadness in them. Only sheer, perfect joy. "I love you, too, Went Smith."

We pulled into Went's mother's apartment complex around noon. The grounds reminded me of a Club Med vacation commercial—kidney-shaped swimming pools, couples hanging out poolside, guys shooting hoops. And the whole thing was walking distance from Six Flags. You could see the top of the roller coasters from the parking lot.

"This is nice," I observed. I'd pictured a run-down, semi-scary apartment in downtown St. Louis or a dingy building with crackheads passed out in the stairwells. I guess I was as bad and judgmental as I'd accused Mom of being.

"Wait till you see the apartment." Went snapped on Adam's leash, then led me by the hand up a flight of stairs—totally free of crackheads—to a big wooden door with "203" on it. The name above the doorbell was Waslynski, not Smith.

"Are you sure you've got the right apartment?" I tapped the gold nameplate.

"Mom went back to her maiden name." He glanced both ways and then reached behind a bush and came up with a key. "Remind me to put it back when we leave."

He unlocked the door and returned the key. Then he turned to me with his best Went-smile, the one that took up his whole face and moved down his gorgeous tanned neck. "Come on. I'll show you around."

My heart sped up as I followed him into the apartment. Went and I hadn't gotten this far in our talks about the weekend. Most of our planning had been taken up with the details of getting us there. The logistics and the timing of when we were going to do what—that, we hadn't discussed.

"Isn't it great?" He swooped his arm like a showman unveiling his prized sculpture. "She's a designer. I mean, professionally. She designs and decorates people's houses. That's how she can afford this place. Do you like it?"

The room we were standing in was all white except for dabs of red—a red vase with a single rose on a glass coffee table, a red satin pillow on a stuffed chair, also white. On the walls hung canvases of modern art, white with broad red stripes or funky circles.

"Wow!" I picked up Adam because he hadn't done his business on the walk in, and I didn't want him doing it now. I didn't think I could have lived in such modern surroundings. I would have been afraid to touch anything. But I could still appreciate the beauty of the room. "It's gorgeous, Went."

One of the paintings was long and narrow, occupying a good third of the whole wall. I stepped up for a better look and read the signature: *Waslynski*. I turned to Went. "Nuh-uh. Did your mother paint this?"

Went nodded. "She's got two paintings in a gallery right across from the Arch. "Come on. I'll give you the tour."

I held Adam as Went led me from the kitchen and breakfast nook to his mom's bedroom, her office, and an entertainment room with a giant television and a pool table.

"This place is too big to be an apartment," I observed.

"You ain't seen nothin' yet, kid." Went slipped his arm around me. "I saved the best for last."

At the end of the white-carpeted hallway was the spare bedroom. Went touched the door, and it opened to a room that had to be twice the size of my bedroom at home. Unlike every other room in the house, this one had color. The blue bedspread matched the curtains, and oranges, blues, and greens blended throughout, with live plants giving everything an outdoor feel. It was as if the color from the rest of the house had drained into this one room. "I love it," I managed to say.

Went took Adam from my arms and set him on the carpet. Then he leaned down and kissed me. The kiss started out soft as butterflies, then grew harder and more intense. I kissed back just as hard, losing myself in him.

I felt his arms around me, moving up and down, making my whole body tense, then mush, then tingly, then light. With one movement, he swept me up into his arms. We didn't stop kissing while he carried me into the bedroom and laid me on the bed. I closed my eyes and felt him on top of me, surrounding me, kissing me. His hand slid under my shirt.

"Arf!" Adam barked and barked. Then he pounced onto the bed.

As if I'd been wakened from a trance, my eyelids flew open. Sunlight streamed in through the open curtains. I bolted upright, forcing Went off. His shirt was unbuttoned. My heart was pounding so hard I thought I might have a heart attack. I fought for words. When I could catch my breath enough to speak, I said, "Went, let's go to Six Flags."

"Now?" He stared at me in disbelief.

I nodded. "Could we, please?"

He took a deep breath and let it out. Then he sat back on his heels and started buttoning his shirt. "Now."

"I just . . . well, I thought it would be dark. And I have this little nightie thing in my bag that I spent my life's savings on. Plus, I don't want Adam to watch us."

Went burst into laughter that drained all the tension out of the room. He finished buttoning his shirt, then picked up the little dog. "Thanks a lot, Adam. You and I are going to have a man-to-man talk about this later." He set Adam down and helped me up.

"Is it okay?" I asked, afraid that I might have wrecked everything.

"It's okay." He hugged me to him, wrapping me in his arms so I felt safe . . . and loved, like I could do it. I could give myself to Went Smith.

14

"You're sure you're not mad?" I asked Went for the tenth time as we dodged traffic to get to Six Flags. We had to leave Adam in the apartment and hope for the best.

"Bailey, I keep telling you. It's better this way. I want everything to be perfect. So, wait until dark, expensive nightie, and no dog."

Went had said all the right things. He understood, and it only made me more excited about our night. This was a guy I could be happy with for the rest of my life.

Once in the park, it felt like we were inside a snow globe, with the rest of the world shut out and unable to do anything but watch us. Paths were lined with souvenir shops and food stands. Carnival music played. We passed a mom and dad with two kids, all of them stuffing themselves with cotton candy. I imagined Went and me years down the line, walking this same path with our own kids. I slid my arm around Went's waist.

"Where to, Captain Bailey?" he asked.

"To the merry-go-round!" I knew the way blindfolded. The Grand Ole Carousel had been my first ride every time I'd come to Six Flags.

When we got there, I pointed out the big black horse. "That's *my* horse."

"He is, huh?" Went asked as my trusty steed spun out of

sight, ridden by some elementary school impostor. "Don't suppose that horse's name is Bailey?"

We laughed and scooted in as soon as they opened the gate for the next round of riders. This was about the only ride without long lines.

"You can ride Brown Beauty," I said, climbing onto my black horse and introducing Went to the lesser brown model next to me.

Went started to climb up, but someone on the other side of him said, "Excuse me." It was a girl about our age, wearing shorts and what could have passed for a bikini top. "I don't suppose y'all could give me a lift up on this little ol' white horse?" Her Southern accent was thick enough to smother an alligator.

"Sure." Went moved to the other side of Brown Beauty and stood behind the girl. "How do you want to do this?"

She laughed and smiled back at him. "That's the question, isn't it?"

No. The question is, what do you think you're doing with my boyfriend? There were empty saddles all over the merry-go-round—horses, tigers, chariots, all without riders. Why did she have to pick the horse next to ours?

Before I knew what was happening, Went had lifted her up and set her in the saddle. His hands stayed too long around her bare stomach. "Are you all set?" he asked, like he was afraid she'd fall off if he let her go.

"Fantastic, thanks to y'all." She stuck out her sweet li'l hand. "I'm Jessica."

Went shook her hand and nearly bowed. "Went Smith. Pleased to meet you."

The merry-go-round started up, and Miss Jessica squealed

like it was her first ride on the Screamin' Eagle, instead of a kids' merry-go-round.

"Went, you better mount, cowboy." I said this while flashing a fake smile at Li'l Miss I'm-Too-Much-of-a-Girlie-Girl-to-Mount-a-Merry-Go-Round.

Went finally climbed aboard Brown Beauty. "Yahoo!" he cried, holding on with one hand and acting like he was rodeo riding.

A Southern laugh sounded from the other side of my boyfriend, and I saw Went give his full-court smile . . . to her.

As soon as the ride stopped, I yanked Went off his horse and led him to the exit. "On to more manly rides!" I cried. "How do you feel about roller coasters?"

We started with the easiest coaster and worked our way up. I'd always loved roller coasters. I remembered Mom bringing me to Six Flags and coaching me to stand on tiptoes when we reached the you-must-be-this-tall-to-ride signs.

Went and I were halfway through the long line waiting for The Boss, working our way to Mr. Freeze, my personal favorite in the roller-coaster category, when my gaze landed on two people who looked older than my grandparents. They were sitting on a bench and eating from the same ice cream cone. One would lick, and the other would laugh. Then they'd change roles. They watched each other with such profound love that I wondered what had brought them to Six Flags. Their fiftieth wedding anniversary? A birthday? Or did they come here every Saturday? I wanted that to be Went and me in fifty years, laughing and sharing an ice cream.

I turned to Went to point out the old couple, but he wasn't there. I looked around until I saw him pressed against the side ropes half a dozen people behind me. He was talking to some girl who looked college age. I started to shout at him, but I didn't. I stared at this great-looking couple smiling and talking together. Anyone would have thought *they* were boyfriend and girlfriend.

How could he look at her like that? I could never look at any guy the way he was looking at her. *That's just Went,* I told myself. *He doesn't mean anything by it.*

The line kept moving forward. Went and I kept moving farther and farther apart.

I waited for him to catch up with me, and we rode rides all over the park. I lost myself in the thrill of every minute spent with Went. I loved having him to hold on to when the roller coaster made that jerky climb right before the big drops. I loved his laughter when I screamed on the high-speed turns.

But then I'd lose him—for seconds or minutes. I lost him when I went for Cokes and found him, like I knew I would, talking to a stranger, a girl who looked like she'd won the lottery. Sometimes I lost him when we were only inches apart, like on one ride where we had to share a train car with two girls from Illinois. I wasn't the only one hugging my boyfriend during the scary turns on that ride.

We ate dinner at a theme restaurant while cartoon characters roamed the aisles like they did all over the park. One minute I felt like the luckiest person on earth, so much in love with Went that I couldn't wait to get back to that apartment and show him how much I loved him. And then I'd catch him eyeing a girl at another table, or he'd flirt with our waitress, and I'd have to excuse myself and go to the john so I wouldn't cry.

When we walked outside, it was that magical time when day

fights with night and slowly lets night have its way. Went took my hand. "Look at that sky, Bailey. It's perfect. For us." Orange-tinged clouds danced in the sky, and the setting sun winked at the horizon. The park lights winked, too. Nothing in the park was slowing down. People milled around in mini-packs. Theme-park characters handed balloons to crying children and posed for pictures with honeymooners. Went leaned down and kissed me. "Let's go back."

I nodded, a thrill flashing through me. This was it. This was all that mattered. Went was never going to see the other girls at this park again. Only me. We headed for the exit. After a few steps, the heel of my right foot ached. I couldn't help limping.

"What's the matter?" Went asked.

"I guess I must have a blister. It's no big deal."

"You sure?"

We walked on, but I couldn't come close to a normal walk. I had to slip my heel out of my stupid shoe and scoot the thing forward with my toes.

"Bailey, let's take a look." Went guided me to the nearest seat. Wooden benches were scattered around an octagon of bright pink flowers. It was one of the best places for kids to get their pictures taken with Bugs Bunny or Daffy Duck.

I plopped down on the bench, and Went kneeled at my feet. Gently, he took off my shoe and lifted my foot to examine my heel. "Ugh," he said, still holding my foot in his hands. "No wonder you were limping. You've got a king-sized, broken blister."

"I'll just keep my shoe off. I'll be okay." I started to get up, but he still had my foot.

"No way. Don't suppose you have a Band-Aid?"

I shook my head.

He released my foot, set it down so tenderly, then stood up and glanced around. "There's got to be a first-aid station around here. I'll get some ointment and a Band-Aid."

"Went, don't," I protested. "I can walk. This is silly."

He grinned down at me. "No. What's silly is having me carry you out of here. And that's the only other option."

"I'm sorry." I felt like crying, and not because of the stupid blister.

He bent down and kissed my forehead. "Take it easy. I'll be back with Band-Aids."

There was nothing to do but lean back and wait. I watched two little girls, who had to be twins, get their picture taken with Bugs Bunny. A group of high school guys and girls formed a chorus line with Taz and Daffy while a woman snapped their pictures with everybody's cameras.

I hadn't worn my watch, but it felt like Went had been gone forever. I hoped he hadn't had to walk too far. The orange clouds faded into the sky, leaving a gray-blue mix that blotted any left-over sun. Still I sat and waited. My thoughts bounced back and forth between what could have happened to Went and what was about to happen with Went and me. I didn't want all of this time to think.

It was getting ridiculous. Went could have invented Band-Aids by now. I stood up, one shoe on and one shoe off, and looked in every direction.

Then I spotted him. He was standing on the other side of the flowers, leaning against the wall of a noisy arcade. But he wasn't alone. Went was laughing with Tweety Bird, or with the no-doubt hot girl who was dressed up as the theme park's Tweety. The big yellow head made her as tall as Went, but there was no denying her tiny waist, in spite of the giant hands and feet. It would have been funny if I hadn't known what was going on . . . if I hadn't known Went.

I fell back onto the park bench. Then I burst into tears. I cried and cried. I couldn't stop crying. I covered my face in my hands, my elbows on my knees, and I sobbed. Every emotion came out with those tears—anger, hurt, pain, guilt, love. I didn't look up. I didn't want to see children staring at me, happy people keeping their distance.

When I finally emptied myself of every tear, I had to catch my breath in little pieces that jerked my shoulders. I needed Kleenex.

And then a tissue appeared.

Startled, I looked over to see Goofy sitting beside me. Just me and the lop-eared Goofy. He was staring straight ahead, not at me, but he held the tissue right under my nose.

I took it and blew. Another tissue appeared. And another.

"Thanks," I managed, stuffing the used tissues into my pocket.

He didn't say anything.

I glanced over at him. I'm not sure I'd realized before that moment that Goofy was supposed to be a dog—a goofy dog with no tail. His costume was pretty worn and patched. There was a round, grated opening below the dog's snout. When I was a kid and discovered the park characters weren't the real cartoon characters, I'd investigated every costumed star I could get close to. I'd figured out that the opening was where the person's head went. I used to try to get Bugs and Sylvester and Taz to talk, but they never did. Mom said it was a Six Flags rule so characters wouldn't say anything they shouldn't. I never remembered seeing Goofy there, though. "So when did Goofy come to Six Flags?"

He didn't answer, of course.

"I know you can't talk," I told Goofy. That made me sad enough that tears threatened again. Goofy handed me another tissue.

I dabbed at my eyes. When I looked up, Goofy was leaning in front of me, his palms up and shoulders raised in the universal "What? What's wrong?" gesture.

I shook my head. "It's a long story."

He leaned back on the bench and crossed one giant paw over the other as if he had all the time in the world.

And so I gave him my story, the shortened version, about Went and me and why we'd come to St. Louis, and how I loved Went and I'd thought he loved me, but he kept talking up other girls and I didn't know if he could ever be a one-woman man the way I was a one-man woman. I had to squeeze my eyes shut so I wouldn't cry again.

I felt Goofy's big arm come around my shoulder, but I didn't look at him. I soaked in the comfort of that caring, canine, furry arm around my shoulders. We sat like that for a couple of minutes, neither of us talking. I thought of Adam and the comfort dogs always gave me.

Finally, I leaned forward until I could see Went, still talking to Tweety Bird. He was trying to peek through the grated hole of the costume. He was laughing and being Went. I pointed them out to Goofy. "There. That's my boyfriend. My boyfriend is hitting on Tweety Bird. Tweety Bird! I was never even sure Tweety was a girl. And yet, there's my boyfriend, hitting on Tweety."

I stood up and faced Goofy. "I am not the kind of girl who

can share a boyfriend. And Went can't be the kind of guy who doesn't hit on other girls. I was just one of the girls to Went, even if he did like me best most of the time. But I'd never be *the* girl. I'd never be the only one for him. He might never have only one—that's just Went.

"But it isn't me. And it isn't enough."

Goofy leaped off the park bench, one fist raised high in the air.

"I'm a gecko, Goofy! A Madagascar day gecko. When I mate, I'm mating for life!" I hugged the big, furry guy, and he hugged me back.

"I'm going home." I picked up my shoe and began hobbling toward the exit.

Goofy jumped and waved with both hands. He blew me kisses.

After a few yards, I turned back to see if Goofy was still there. He was there, watching, his hands, or paws, clasped in front of him.

"Just so you know," I shouted back, "I've always loved Goofy best!"

I FINISH THE STORY, but when I smile across the table at Louie, I can tell he doesn't think the story's over.

"How did you get home?" he asks.

"Called my mom and had her come get me at the apartment. She was mad, but she's my mom. We got over it."

Rune has listened the whole time from a stool by the counter. Now he storms across the room, pulls up the empty chair at our table, twirls it around, and sits backward. "I'd like to teach that guy, that Went, a lesson." He makes a fist, and his tattoos—a hula girl and a snake—dance. "Give me two minutes alone with that loser."

"You never saw Went again?" Louie asks.

"I saw him. That summer he came around, wanting to get back together with me."

Rune pounds the table. Shirley the Shih Tzu barks. Eve the Dalmatian trots over to check out this big, loud human. "The nerve of that guy!" Rune glares at me. "You didn't do it, did you? You didn't go back to that creep?"

I shake my head. "Mom said that going back to an ex-boyfriend was like buying your own garage-sale junk after the sale's over. Somebody else may think your old stuff is gold, but you know better. It's not golden for you."

"I like your mother," Louie says.

"Yeah." I grin at him. "She knows a lot about garage sales."

"But you kept the dog." The cute guy, Colt, says it like a fact, not a question. Somewhere during my story, Adam ended up on Colt's lap, where the dog is still sleeping peacefully, snoring even.

"I couldn't leave Adam in that apartment. It wasn't hard to find the key behind the bush. Adam was ready to go. Nobody ever asked for the dog back. In the end, Went went, and Adam stayed." I reach over and scratch Adam. He doesn't stir.

Louie sighs deeply and turns to stare out the rain-streaked window. The aroma of coffee has died out, leaving the smell of rain to take over. Louie's back is as straight and still as the chair. I get the feeling he's a million miles away. "All these years," Louie says so low the rest of us grow quiet to hear him. "All this time, and I never knew."

Colt and I exchange shrugs. "You never knew what, Louie?" Colt asks.

Louie's back is to us, so we can't see his face. He answers so slowly that it feels like each word carries the weight of a thousand memories. "Never knew I was a Madagascar day gecko."

It's a line that should have made us laugh, but we don't. Colt and Rune stare down at the table or their hands. I know I'm missing part of Louie's story, but I don't ask. Instead, I reach over and put my hand on his shoulder.

Without turning around, Louie reaches back and covers my hand with his.

"Wait a minute," Rune says, breaking the uneasy silence. "That still doesn't explain why you and them dogs of yours—your boyfriends' dogs—come in here going on midnight in a dress like that there one."

"Nope." I grin at him. The big guy's growing on me, identity crisis or not. "That's because Went was just my first love. And Adam was only my first fall."

"Adam," Louie says, turning back to the table. "Now that's a mighty fine name for a dog that's a first fall, I'd say."

Eve has settled next to Rune. She stretches out her neck and lays her head on Rune's big thigh.

"She likes you, Rune," I tell him, pointing to the Dalmatian. "You should feel honored. Eve doesn't warm up to everybody." I turn to Adam, still curled on Colt's lap. "Unlike some dogs I know."

Colt keeps petting the little terrier. "So what do you think, Louie? Shouldn't we be hearing about that second fall?"

"I tend to agree with you, Colt," Louie says, shifting around in his chair so that it makes me wonder if his whole body doesn't hurt. "I'm not going anywhere." He nods to the window. "Neither is that rain by the looks of it."

"What I want to know," Rune says, Eve's head still resting on his leg, "is where'd you get *this* dog? What boyfriend in his right mind would let go of a dog like this here one?"

"Not to mention a fine young woman like our Bailey there," Louie adds.

"Bailey," Colt asks, "are you sure nobody's waiting on you anywhere? Like . . . your date maybe?"

The question takes me by surprise. "I guess I'm not sure, to tell you the truth." I'm not carrying my cell. I glance at the clock. It's tomorrow already.

"Could I borrow your cell?"

Colt hands his over, and I text Mom to let her know I haven't been kidnapped and I'm safe and warm. I pass the phone back to Colt. "Thanks. I guess that does it."

"Well, then," Louie says. "I guess you better get started on that story of yours."

"And this story is about Eve, right?" Rune asks, making sure.

"Right." Looking at the Dalmatian brings back a flood of memories. "This is about Eve."

RUNE THE IDENTITY-CRISIS GUY

RUNE CAN HARDLY BELIEVE this spotted dog likes him so much. Every time he strokes her smooth, white head, she thumps her tail on the floor. He never had a dog when he was a kid. He asked his old man for one once and got slapped down for it. "You think I want another dog eating me out of house and home?" his dad had yelled. "One dog is enough." He'd meant Rune because they'd never had a dog. Rune thinks he was about six at the time.

Fran, Rune's wife, has nagged him for years to get a pet for the boys. She and Rune fought about it last week, he's pretty sure. They fight about so many things it's hard to keep track. More times than not, Fran and the boys, Miguel and Stefan, end up crying, and Rune slams the door on his way out, the way he did tonight. That's why he volunteered to close for Louie. He wasn't looking forward to going home for another round with his wife. He doesn't know how many more rounds either of them can last.

He's afraid to move his leg. He doesn't want to disturb the dog.

That girl in her party dress clears her throat, like she's finally going to get going on Eve's story.

"What kind of a host am I?" Louie says. "Here you're doing all the talking, and you don't even have a glass of water to show for it." He starts to get up.

"I got it," Colt says, beating the old man to it. The kid carries that white mutt with him to the kitchen.

"Good thinking, Ace," Rune calls after him. "Now the health inspectors will really come down on us."

"Sorry, Rune," the kid calls back. He shifts the dog under one arm and brings back a glass of water that he sets in front of the girl, Bailey. "There you go."

Rune doesn't know much about the kid, except that he always orders apple juice and hogs the newspaper. He reads that paper like he's looking for clues. Rune never saw anybody read a paper like that. Colt's not a bad guy, though. And he tips more than the cost of the juice.

"So?" Rune presses. It surprises him that he wants to know about this dog as much as he's wanted to know about the girl in the party dress.

"So," the girl, Bailey, says. "Eve. Looking back, I guess my second fall all boiled down to a case of mistaken identity. But I'm getting ahead of myself."

the second fall

eve

1

The thing about having a first boyfriend is that most of us girls—whether or not we realize it at the time—sign a Declaration of Dependence. Now don't get me wrong. We'd never admit this to you guys, or even to other girls usually. Maybe not even to ourselves. But from that first boyfriend on, in varying degrees, we become addicted to boyfriends.

For me, everything changed after Went. I had crossed the line. I had been a girlfriend with a real boyfriend. So after we broke up and I vowed I would never get back together with Went Smith, I felt an emptiness I hadn't felt in my boyfriend-less days.

My friend Amber tried to help. "Bailey, you are so much better off without Went. *No* boyfriend is better than a *bad* boyfriend."

Only from where I stood, across the invisible universal boyfriend line, Amber was simply wrong.

It was midsummer before our junior year, when we'd be herded to Tri-County High, in Freemont, with all the other juniors and seniors in a sixty-mile radius. Amber and I were soaking up the sun's cancer rays at the pool in Freemont because I didn't want to drive to Larkfield and risk running into Went. And yes, I said drive. The only good thing about my summer so far had been that I'd miraculously passed the parallel parking test, astounding the license examiner as much as it astounded Mom and me. We all knew it was a fluke, but we took it.

I rolled onto my back for some equal-opportunity tanning. A guy and girl strolled right by my beach towel. They were holding hands. Boyfriend and girlfriend.

"Amber," I whined, "why can't *I* have a boyfriend? I miss having someone to hold my hand like that and gaze at me like he thinks I'm wonderful."

Amber sat up on her towel, looking perfect in her two-piece. "Didn't you learn anything from breaking up with Went? Get real! You wanted a boyfriend so much that you wore blinders the whole time. He hit on Big D, for crying out loud."

I sat up to face her. "I know. And this time, no blinders. I promise. Plus, I'm holding out for a gecko, who only has eyes for me. See? I have, too, learned from my Went relationship." I plopped back down on my towel. "Which is why I am *so* ready for a mature boyfriend."

I tried. I really did. But my junior year turned into a blur of short-term, no-dog boyfriends. Short-term, because I meant it when I told Amber that from now on, I was a Madagascar day gecko. The boy I'd choose to love had to love me back—just me. No longer would I overlook the transgressions of a player. I deserved better.

So when No-Neck, my first football boyfriend, got too friendly with a Tri-County cheerleader, I dumped him. It almost felt good. Truthfully, it had only taken one date for me to realize that No-Neck couldn't talk coherently about anything except football, and not so much that.

No-Neck was followed by Switch, as in Switchblade, not because he carried one, but because he looked like he could. He was almost as sexy as Went . . . and about ten times as stuck on himself. When I refused to have sex with him—after the second date!—he broke up with me and found his solace in good ol' Carly.

I'm pretty sure King Hairy came next—don't ask. He was definitely single-minded, though not about girlfriends. He would have been perfectly happy to have a dozen girlfriends simultaneously. His single-mindedness was on the subject of sex—he wanted it. I really don't think he had any other hobbies, goals, or interests.

My relationship with Mom seemed to get worse with the passing of each dogless boyfriend. I blamed it on Mom's having totally lost her cool. Before and after my dates, she'd give me the third degree of stock questions, and I'd dutifully supply her with stock answers.

We didn't fight all the time. But we did fight a lot, and most of the fights could have been prerecorded:

Mom:

"Bailey, where do you think you're going?"

"What do you think you're doing?"

"What *were* you thinking?"

"I've had just about enough."

"I've had all I can take."

"How could you do this to me?"

Me:

"Nowhere."

"Nothing."

"No one."

"Not my fault."

"You don't understand!"

The last few months of my junior year, I had dated Mediocre Mark, whose sole purpose in life was to find the easiest classes and sleep through them. Amber didn't like him because he never spoke in complete sentences. But I saw his potential, and I went for it. Mark, who, as it happened, was head-turning hot, proved to be my biggest challenge. I wore him down with a series of ego-booster tactics culled from *Cosmo*, including one about asking for a man's help. Mark's help in my intro to creative writing class brought down my grade from an A- to a C+, but it was worth it—for a while. I had a loyal boyfriend, a potential gecko. We did everything together. We even took our PSATs together, and I pretended not to notice when he copied my math section.

It was because of Mark that I enrolled in the "College Now!" summer school program at the University of Missouri. Amber, of course, signed herself up for the AP course in writing and journalism the day we heard about it. Going to summer school my last truly free summer of my life—because I couldn't count the summer before college with all that impending stress—appealed to me about as much as attending reform school before going to prison. But Mark was going to Mizzou to get out of working at his dad's car wash all summer, so what choice did I have? Mizzou it was.

Three days before school ended, Mark brought up the subject of sex. It wasn't that we hadn't discussed it before. Usually, Mark lacked the ambition and follow-through to make a big issue out of it. But this time it was different. We were parked in my driveway after having sat through the worst movie I'd ever seen, in which at least seventeen teens got slashed to death. Mark loved it. "You are so sexy, Bailey," he said, his hand grasping for second base.

"Mark," I began, removing his hand and scooting back a few inches on the clean plastic seat of his dad's car. Mark looked so good. True, the boy had lousy taste in movies. But he was loyal and never looked at another girl, as far as I could tell. "We need to have a serious talk about the Madagascar day gecko." I proceeded to explain to him the concept of a lifelong commitment to one person.

"Know what else I found out about the gecko?" I'd done a report on geckos for my science class. "Scientists at the University of Akron are working on a superglue based on gecko feet. They're studying the incredible way geckos can hold on to anything with their feet."

Mark said, "Huh?"

Once again, I explained to my boyfriend the high concept of mating for life. "Sex is a lifelong gift," I concluded. "It's because I think sex is so great that I've decided to wait until I'm married and mate for life, like the gecko."

Mark's forehead wrinkled. "You mean you're not gonna have sex with me?"

"No, Mark," I answered.

"No sex?" he repeated.

I reduced language to primitive gesture and shook my head. "Ever?"

I repeated said gesture.

"Why didn't you say so before?" Mark asked, right before he broke up with me.

———

Mom drove Amber and me and a van filled with our stuff to Columbia for Mizzou's "College Now!" orientation. I'd tried to back out of it, of course. But it was too late to get our money refunded. Unlike Amber the Great, I didn't have a scholarship. What I did have was a summer job at Grady's Gas and Snack in Columbia, which Mom's friend Sarah Jean had pulled strings to get me. There was no backing out. I was doomed to take a precollege French class, which I'd signed up for simply because Mark was supposed to be in it and he thought French sounded sexy.

Amber and Mom were so psyched about this "college experience" and getting a head start that I chose to ride by myself in the backseat, where I stared out the window and brooded and wondered if everyone in summer school would already have boyfriends.

"I still can't believe we're actually on our way to college!" Amber exclaimed, as enthusiastic as she was annoying. She and Mom talked about college all the time. It wore me out. How could I make up my mind where I wanted to go to college? What if I signed up for Mizzou and then got a great boyfriend who was going to KU? People have to think ahead about these things.

Amber planned to go to Mizzou and become a journalist. That's why she was here at the great J-school of the Midwest. I, on the other hand, had signed on because I'd wanted to be with my boyfriend, who was now my ex-boyfriend.

I knew my deep sadness wasn't all about Mark. I think I missed Went more than Mark, really. In the middle of the year, I'd heard that Went and his dad had moved back to California. Without saying goodbye. Now, staring out the dirt-smudged window, I thought that if Went hadn't moved away, I just might have overturned my vow about not shopping at my own garage sale. I missed having someone.

"Amber," Mom said cheerfully, ignoring the fact that her own daughter was sniffing back tears in the backseat. "I'm so proud of you for getting that scholarship. You'll be hitting the ground running when you enroll here."

"Thanks, Big D. And thanks for the ride, too. You don't think Bailey and I have too much stuff, do you?"

"If you do, you can always have a garage sale," Mom advised.

Mom stopped at two garage sales and one roadkill funeral before we made it to campus. Mom always stopped and buried roadkill. She was the only person I knew who did, except for Amber and me. We even carried a shovel in our van, and we had a special blessing to say over the makeshift grave. But this time, I sat in the car for the event.

Mom stopped twice for directions before we found the "high school" dorm. Couples were everywhere—strolling hand in hand, sitting on dorm steps, lounging under trees. A lot of them were obviously college students, although why *they* would go to summer school was beyond me.

"Well, we'd better get started moving you two college girls in," Mom said, winking when she said "college."

Our dorm room was on the fourth floor, and we had to take the stairs because the elevator was broken. "Great start," I muttered, lugging my biggest suitcase up eight flights. "This is brutal."

Mom and Amber grunted and groaned as we carried up everything we could conceivably carry, but they didn't complain. Finally, Mom peered into the back of the van at the TV, a trunk of Amber's books, and two unmarked boxes of bricks. At least that's what it looked like when Mom tried to lift one. "That's it for sweating the small stuff," Mom announced, swiping at the sweat pouring down her neck. "Nothing but the big-ticket items left."

"Bailey and I can take it from here, Big D," Amber volunteered. "Bailey, grab that side of the TV, and I'll get this one."

We managed to wrestle the thing out of the van, but no way could I walk with it. I was already sweating right through my antiperspirant. "I can't hold on any longer," I warned.

Suddenly, just like in the movies, a tall, dark, handsome stranger came jogging up to us. And I mean *tall*. "You ladies look like you could use a hand." The guy took the TV out of our struggling arms and carried it like it was a pillow. "Where to?"

"Seriously? Thanks!" I gave Hercules our dorm room number, and we trotted along behind him to the stairwell.

"I'm Steve," he said, aiming this news flash at Amber.

Amber smiled, but she didn't introduce herself.

"Thanks for the help, Steve," I said, giving my friend a little nudge. "I'm Bailey, and this is Amber."

"I'm in for the basketball training camp," Steve informed Amber. "How about you, Amber?"

"Journalism," she answered.

"Cool. I've heard good things about that program. You planning to come here in the fall and major in journalism?"

"One more year," said my friend-of-few-words.

Ask him about his plans! I wanted to scream it up to her, but she and Steve must have been in way better shape than I was. They'd moved half a flight ahead of me, and Steve was carrying a television.

"For now, I guess I'll be majoring in basketball," Steve went on without any encouragement from Amber.

"Can you do that?" she asked.

He laughed. "Not forever, I guess. I thought about taking a journalism or creative writing class this summer, but basketball takes up too much of my time."

"You could always quit basketball," Amber suggested.

He laughed again. I, on the other hand, was pretty sure Amber wasn't joking.

Steve helped us carry up the rest of the junk from the van while Mom waited in the dorm room and started unpacking boxes. "Hey, thanks a million for the help, Steve," Mom called over to the doorway when we were done. "Don't know how we would have made it without you."

I seconded Mom's motion. "Seriously, thanks a lot."

Steve nodded at Mom and me. Then he turned a big smile on Amber. "I've got to run to practice. But there's a social, a dance thing, in the Union tomorrow night if you want to go." He was adorable, all flushed-face shy. "Anyway, I could come by here for you. Like at seven?"

Amber shrugged. "Sure."

Steve's smile broadened. "Cool!" He jogged backward, not willing to take his eyes off Amber. "I'll see you then. Before then maybe. I'll call you. Or see you. Or both."

Amber waved. She was grinning, too, now. "Okay."

The second Steve was out of sight, Mom hustled Amber inside the room with us. She whisper-counted to ten. And then she and I went crazy. "Amber's got a date! Steve loves Amber!" Mom and I sang various versions of this ditty until Amber managed to strategically place her hands over our mouths.

"Stop it!" she pleaded. "He'll hear you." But she looked as excited as I felt. Our Miss Amber had a real live college date with an extremely cute, almost-college jock.

Mom stayed for a while and helped us figure out where to put our lamps and clothes and stuffed animals. "I have to get going," she said finally. She grabbed both of us in a group hug, and we hugged her back as if we'd never see each other again.

Turned out Steve wasn't the only guy who wanted to date Amber. My Amber-prophecy about guys getting over themselves and appreciating all that Amber had to offer was coming to pass. And she wasn't even officially in college. Not just the basketball players either. I faithfully e-mailed Mom details about Amber's many suitors.

In return, Mom sent Amber and me cutesy cards in the mail. She phoned every day and e-mailed. But she said she wanted us to get *some* mail that didn't demand we buy magazines at a giant student discount. I, personally, believed she had other reasons for writing. Her first card to Amber read:

Tall guys, small guys,
You attract all guys!
Amber has her pick of winter, spring, and summer, fall guys.

My first note said:
When a dog gets pregnant, then their babies we can sell.
When a girl gets pregnant, then she's on her way to . . .
(Just kidding! God loves babies. He just wants girls to wait until they're married so everybody can live happily ever after.) Love, Mom

Poor Mom. If she'd only known. She didn't have a thing to worry about. Bailey Daley was coming up empty in the boyfriend department. Two weeks into summer school, and I hadn't had anything that even slightly resembled a date. A couple of guys flirted with me in the cafeteria and in my French class, but they flirted with other girls, too. And I refused to put on blinders. Not this time. I'd learned my lesson with Went.

But I still wanted a boyfriend.

"You're obsessing over this boyfriend thing," Amber told me one night as we lay in our beds in the dark and tried to get to sleep. Somebody on our floor had rap blaring from speakers the size of North and South Dakota.

"You think? Well, guess what. I'm done obsessing about having a boyfriend."

"You are?" asked my obviously skeptical friend.

"Yep. From now on, no obsession. Only action."

Amber groaned. "I already don't like the sound of this."

I ignored my abundantly-dating roommate's careless comment. "I've had a lot of time to think about this. I'm about to launch a new Bailey Boyfriend Plan." I explained my plan's main objectives: to land a boyfriend who only had eyes for me, and who had eyes for more than my body and what his body might do to mine. "I admit this hasn't been a huge problem lately, but one must be prepared," I continued. "After all, *I am seventeen, with extraordinarily large breasts, a fantastic bod, and hair to die for. I am seventeen, with extraordinarily large breasts, a fantastic bod, and—*"

My mantra was interrupted by a pillow to the head. I picked up my own pillow and skillfully defended myself. When we stopped pounding each other and laughing ourselves breathless, we fell back into our beds. After a couple of minutes of silence—if you didn't count the blaring rap in the background—Amber said, "Bailey, there's more to life than having a boyfriend."

"There *is* more," I agreed. "I'd just like to experience it all with a boyfriend."

MY BOYFRIENDS' DOGS

2

Although my job at Grady's drastically cut into my boyfriend-hunting plans, by the second week at Grady's Gas and Snack of Columbia, I loved my job. Sarah Jean would have been proud.

Saturday we were crazy busy. Wanda, my manager, made me work the cash register. Once I got the hang of it, I liked it. I even started humming to myself between customers. Then before I knew it, I was singing.

"Girl, I like that song," Wanda said, shouldering me from the register so she could ring up her customer.

"Sorry. I didn't realize I was singing it out loud." I couldn't have named the song if I'd been on trial for it. I felt like I'd been caught singing in the shower, which was about the only other place I sang since the unfortunate event at the Millet Movies.

Wanda turned to me and stared hard. She outweighed me by a hundred pounds and was still beautiful. Her brown skin glowed, and her eyes sparkled like she knew wonderful secrets about everybody but just couldn't tell us yet. "You have a nice voice, girlfriend. Sing it out next time!"

Wanda was my boss, so I obeyed. Each day I grew a little braver, and by the end of the following week, I'd become the singing Grady girl. Depending on the age and mood of the customer, or the type of purchase, or maybe the weather, I had a refrain for everybody who came in. Thanks to my mom's unusual musical tastes, I knew songs and lyrics from every era.

Gas-only customers usually got a Beach Boys number (Mom would have been proud), like "I Get Around." Truckers loved country, but sometimes at night you would have been surprised how long they stuck around for blues or jazz. I didn't work off stereotypes for my customers—I tried to get a feel for the person.

For our older customers, I'd sing something from the forties with lots of heart and memory. One grouchy old man, who had the face he deserved, was about to storm out of Grady's one morning, swearing that the doughnuts weren't fresh. But when I started singing "I'll be seeing you in all the old familiar places"—I'm not sure what the name of that song is, but I know the lyrics—he stood in the doorway as if frozen. He stayed that way through the whole song, three verses. And when I stopped singing, he turned around with tears streaming down his face, and he thanked me.

Groups of high school or college guys got purchase-appropriate rock. Hand-holding couples earned "I Want to Hold Your Hand." It was fun. And could Wanda dance! Her favorite songs were blow-the-roof-off gospel. Sometimes, with the old spirituals, Wanda would join me singing. She couldn't help herself, even though customers usually headed for their cars at that point. Like I said, Wanda was a great dancer. I would have worked at Grady's for nothing just to hang with Wanda.

It was usually light when I walked back to the dorm after work. But one Friday night I volunteered to stay late and close so Wanda could keep her big date. When I left and walked up Broadway, the stars were already out. I hadn't gone far when I got the feeling someone was following me.

Bailey Daley, you are imagining things, I told myself. But I didn't believe me. My heart sped up, and my legs moved faster. I definitely heard footsteps behind me. I shouldn't have been out alone that late. I should have called campus security to walk me home. I could have asked Amber and Steve to come get me.

I ducked up a side street and fumbled for my phone, hoping I'd lose whoever was following me. Heart pounding, I pressed my back against the brick wall until I heard the footsteps pass. Suddenly, I remembered Went that first day when I'd snatched him out of the jaws of Carly and she'd come looking for both of us. We'd hidden by the bank, pressed against a wall just like this.

My thoughts spiraled backward. *Went.* My first real love. I fell so hard, and I hadn't fallen that hard since. I could still see him, tanned, smiling, so at ease in every situation. I remembered how excited I'd been on that drive to Six Flags, how passionate Went and I were at his mother's empty apartment. I hadn't felt that way since Went. What if I never did again?

The pain came back, too—not as sharp, but there, like a shadow. I closed my eyes, and I was back on that wooden park bench, crying my eyes out, with kind Goofy sitting silently next to me, his furry arm around my shoulder.

At least I'd gotten Adam out of the deal.

All at once, something rushed out at me.

"Help!" I cried, not sure whether to run or stand there and pray myself invisible.

A big dog came bounding out of nowhere. It galloped straight at me, then lunged. Its giant paws landed on my shoulders. I opened my eyes and stared into the face of a king-sized Dalmatian. "Easy, boy," I said. "Or girl. Sorry. Too dark to tell." The dog licked my face. "You're just a sweetheart, aren't you?" It felt so good to be with a dog again. Only a dog could greet me so wholeheartedly.

I managed to get the dog's paws off me so I could check around for its owner. "Show me where you live, big guy." We moved on down the side street until I could read the big sign over the brick-arched entry: FIRE STATION 11.

"Dotty!" A man came running out of the firehouse as if it were on fire. He looked left, then right, until he spotted us. "Dotty! There you are." He jogged up and grabbed the dog by her collar. "Sit!" he commanded. Dotty sat. "Bad dog," he scolded.

"Dotty's okay," I said, scratching the dog's ears. "She's beautiful."

"I can't believe she ran off like that. That's never happened before." The man looked a lot older than my mom. He was short, stocky, balding, and cursed with the longest chin I'd ever seen on a human. He wore an armpit-stained white T-shirt with tan pants and suspenders that made him look like a fireman.

"Is Dotty a real firehouse dog?" I asked.

He patted his dog's spotted back. "She's more of a mascot, aren't you, Dotty ol' girl?" He frowned over at me. "Still can't believe she went for you like that." Dotty stretched her neck toward me, but kept sitting.

I reached over and scratched her. "I do love dogs. I miss mine."

"You a Mizzou student?" he asked.

"Only for the summer." We introduced ourselves, and Larry and Dotty walked me back to the dorm, even though I told them I'd be okay.

"Thanks again," I told Larry as he tugged on Dotty's collar. The sweet girl didn't want to leave me.

"You come back to the station and hang out with Dotty anytime you like," Larry called over his shoulder.

I stopped in to visit Dotty a couple of times after work. It helped me not miss Adam as much. Meanwhile, I tried to work on the dress-for-success part of my Bailey Boyfriend Plan. I didn't have the cash to buy new clothes, and Amber's didn't fit me. But she taught me the power of accessories—belts, scarves, ties, jewelry. Thanks to her, I was growing into a semi-funky style all my own—part retro, part fun.

The first Saturday I didn't have to work at Grady's, Amber had promised to watch Steve's basketball game and go out with him afterward. "Are you sure you don't want to come with us?" she begged. "Or I could break my date with Steve, and you and I could do something. Steve would understand."

"You are too good for your own good," I said, checking out my semi-funky self in the mirror—denim Capris with the perfect braided leather belt, two neon camis layered strategically under a V-necked, shirred black top, and a beret. "What do you think?" I turned to Amber for fashion approval.

Amber tilted her head and gave me two thumbs-up. "Funky. Love the high-tops, by the way." Amber wasn't afraid to tell me when I missed the fashion mark, so I knew she meant it. "You could at least go to the game with me."

I shook my head. "Not in the plan. I've decided I want a brooding, deep-thinking boyfriend who will challenge me intellectually, and not physically." Amber laughed, but I ignored her. "So, I'm off to Beaman's Musical Instruments store. I walk right by there after work all the time, but I've never gone in."

"Could it be because you don't *play* a musical instrument?" asked Amber the Smart Aleck.

"Exactly. But that doesn't mean I wouldn't like a boyfriend who does. I've always wanted to go with somebody who played the guitar, or maybe the sax."

"I played clarinet in middle school," Amber offered.

"Have fun with the bouncing-ball boys, Amber. I'm off to

find a deep, sensitive boyfriend." I tipped my beret and strolled to the music store. It was the perfect day for finding a gloomy boyfriend. A dark gray sky promised a rain that refused to fall. A few sun-dried leaves tumbled to the sidewalk, too eager to give up their lives to wait for autumn.

I rounded the corner, straightened my beret, took a deep breath, and practiced my opening line in my head: *Do you think the world will ever see another Lester Young?* I really did listen to jazz, and I loved Young and Coltrane and Miles Davis. So I wasn't being a fraud. I could hold my own in music conversations, even though I couldn't play anything myself. So, one might ask, what was I doing in a store that sold musical instruments? I had my answers at the ready: *I keep thinking I have to learn to play the guitar sooner or later, because I play it in my head constantly.* Or *I just like being around drums. Doesn't everybody?*

I was crossing the street to Beaman's when I saw the Dalmatian sitting out in front of the store. I walked over to her, and she wagged her spotted tail. "Dotty, what are you doing here? Where's Larry?" Something about the big dog didn't seem quite right. Maybe she was lost. Maybe it was the dark, threatening storm. "You wait here, Dotty." She wagged her tail and danced around, ready to follow me. "Sit." It always worked for Larry, but apparently not for me. "Stay?" I tried.

I slipped inside the music shop and looked around for Larry or one of the other firemen. The store was crowded, and I couldn't help noticing a nice array of guys scattered throughout the three rooms, and not a single girl in sight. "Larry?" I called.

A few guys frowned over at me, then went back to stroking drums and guitars.

I had to get Dotty back to the fire station fast and return

to this boyfriend mecca. I dashed out of the music store as the owner was heading my way. The man probably thought I'd shop-lifted something, although I couldn't imagine what.

The Dalmatian greeted me heartily when I came out, almost knocking me down.

"Come on, Dotty. I've got to get you home. Larry will be worried about you." The dog trotted along beside me as I back-tracked up the street and finally down the little road to Fire Station 11. I took hold of her collar in case she decided she didn't want to stay in the firehouse. Larry would have to start tying her if this kept up.

"Larry!" I shouted as soon as we were inside the building. Still holding the dog's collar, I shouted again. "Hey! Somebody! I found your lost dog."

Out of nowhere, in a blur of fur and spots, came another dog, another Dalmatian. She lunged at the one I was holding. They growled at each other. I let go of the collar. The dogs faced each other, teeth bared, low growls coming from both of them. Crouched with their front halves low and rear ends high, they were mirror images.

"What the—?" Larry came running up behind me. Two of the other firemen followed him. "Where did *that* come from?" Larry demanded, pointing to the dog I'd led in.

"I thought it was Dotty," I confessed. "I kind of took her from the music store and brought her here."

"Well, you better kinda take her back, Bailey," Larry said. "You just took the dog? Without telling anybody?"

I nodded, panic seeping into my veins.

A couple of the guys laughed, but I didn't see anything funny. What if the owner was already reporting a stolen Dalmatian?

Even Larry looked like he could burst into laughter at any minute. "I'm not kidding, Bailey. You'd better get this dog back to where you found her before they throw you in the clink for dog theft." He turned back to his firemen buddies. "They don't still hang people for dog thieving in this state, do they?"

"That's horse thieving, boss," somebody answered.

I knew they were just teasing me, but it didn't help the panic ready to cut loose inside of me. I had just stolen somebody's dog. "I didn't mean to do it," I said to Larry, or the guys, or maybe to this poor dog who wasn't Dotty. "It was a case of mistaken identity."

3

Without releasing my grip on the unidentified dog's collar, I raced back to the music store. How could I have thought this dog was Dotty? True, it was sort of dark out. And the dogs' bodies matched. But now that I'd seen them together, this one's face was smooth, not like Dotty's angular face.

I half expected patrol cars and crime scene tape waiting for me at the music store, but everything was quiet. Normal.

"Stay!" I commanded. Then I changed my mind. I couldn't let go of this dog until I found her owner. Together, Mystery Dog and I stepped into the music store.

"Nice dog," said a guy at the drums, who looked like he'd have been more at home in a biker bar.

"Thanks. I don't suppose you've seen this dog around here before?" I ventured. Mystery Dog wanted to explore, and it was taking all of my strength to hang on to her collar and keep her wagging tail from knocking over the guitars.

"No dogs!" The little man who'd tracked my exit earlier came charging at me. "You can't bring your dog in here."

"She's not mine."

"You can't bring anybody's dog in here."

"I know." I switched my grip on the dog's collar to my left hand. I couldn't afford maiming my right. "Do you know whose dog this is?" I asked Angry Skinny Music Man.

"Me? How should I know whose dog you bring into my music store? Get him out of here."

"It's a female," I corrected.

"Out!" He pointed toward the door, just in case I hadn't noticed where it was when I walked in through it.

I glanced around the shop. "Hey! Does this dog belong to anybody?"

"Out!" yelled Angry Skinny Music Man.

"Anybody know whose dog this is?"

"Out, out, out!" Angry Skinny Music Man made shooing motions with his long-fingered, bony hands. I bet he was a piano player. Wagner, most likely.

"Okay, okay. I'm going. Only if somebody comes looking for this dog . . ." I stopped. What? What if somebody did come looking for this dog? And what if nobody came? I couldn't just leave the poor thing on the streets to starve. What if it stormed? Surely the owner would come back to look for her when he discovered his dog was no Lassie and hadn't found her way home.

"Go!" shouted Angry Skinny Music Man.

"Right. I'm going. Only tell anybody who asks about the dog that they can find me in Jones Hall, fourth floor. Bailey Daley." I gave him my phone number, but he didn't write it down. He was too busy shooing Mystery Dog and me out of his store.

"You won't forget, right?" I asked from the front step as the door shut in my face. "Bailey Daley, fourth floor Jones."

It wasn't easy sneaking Mystery Dog into the dorm. I waited at the back entrance until somebody came out. "Hold the door, please!" I shouted.

A redhead who looked college, not high school, held the door for me. "Nice dog," she said, as if we all had dogs in this dorm.

"Thanks." I had to pull the dog in with me. She obviously had never seen a dark stairwell before, and she didn't like it. We didn't pass anybody on the stairs. I shoved open the door to the fourth floor and peered down the hall. The coast was clear. "Come on, Mystery Dog."

The dog pranced along beside me, her toenails clicking on the hall floor. I had my door unlocked and had almost made it home free when the door across the hall opened and somebody said, "Is that a dog?"

It was Yvonne, one of the girls who lived across the hall from Amber and me.

"This?" I shoved Mystery Dog into my room. "Nah."

Yvonne and her roommate partied every night. We had no idea what summer school program they were supposed to be in, but I don't think they ever went to class. Too hungover. I figured there was a good chance Yvonne might end up thinking that the spots before her eyes were in her imagination.

Once safely hidden in my dorm room, Mystery Dog and I had a serious talk. "You're too well fed to be a stray." She wagged her tail. "I guess we could put up 'Lost Dog' signs with your picture on them." She pawed my leg until I rubbed her chest. "You'd like that, wouldn't you—your fifteen minutes of fame?"

Mystery Dog and I hung out in the room until Amber got

back. I loved having a dog around. When I sat on the floor and leaned against my bed to read over my French verbs, she curled next to me as if we did this every day.

It was an hour before curfew when I heard a key in the lock. Then the door cracked open. "Thanks again, Steve. I had a wonderful time." Amber's dreamy voice sounded like she was telling the truth.

"Me too," Steve said, equally convincing.

"I better call it a night, Steve. I'm going to early service in the morning. Besides, you're going to miss your curfew if you don't get—"

Amber's voice was interrupted by kissy noises. I scooted around for a better look. All I could see was Amber's back, but it wasn't an entirely bad view. Steve's hands moved up and down my roommate's back as they kissed.

Amber and I didn't kiss and tell—okay, I hadn't even kissed since I'd become an almost-college coed. But I knew she and my mom still totally agreed about keeping sex in marriage. Steve, on the other hand, might have had other ideas, the way his hands were moving and—

"Arf!"

"Shush!" I scolded Mystery Dog.

"Do you have a dog in there?" Steve asked.

"No," Amber insisted. "It did sound like a dog, though." She opened the door a little wider and called in, "Bailey? What are you doing in here?"

I scrunched behind the bed and pulled Mystery Dog with me. "I'm listening to a tape from Mom. She recorded Adam and some neighborhood dogs. I'll be out in a minute." It was the best I could come up with on such short notice.

They both seemed to buy it. "Ah," Amber called. "So that's what the bark was." She turned back to Steve. "Night, Steve. And thanks again."

The second Steve was gone, Amber stomped into the room. "Okay. Where's the dog?"

Mystery Dog broke loose and trotted over to my roommate.

"Bailey! Do you want to get both of us both kicked off campus? They don't even allow lizards and goldfish in this dorm. What do you think they'll do if they find out you're housing a dog? A big dog? A big spotted dog?"

When she calmed down, I explained the whole case of mistaken identity to her. "So I didn't even get to try out my boyfriend plan," I said, winding it up and going for sympathy. "Instead, I come home with a dog." I gazed at the Dalmatian stretched over my feet. "She's sweet, though, isn't she?"

"Very," Amber admitted. "But we can't keep her, Bailey."

"I know. Maybe you could put an ad in the paper. Or we could make signs that—"

There was a knock at the door. Amber and I stared at each other like we were surrounded by the FBI. I considered hiding under the bed.

Amber got up. "I'll get it. Nobody knows you have a dog in here, right?"

I shrugged and threw my arms around Mystery Dog. They were going to have to go through me to get to this dog. No way I'd let them haul her off to the animal shelter.

Amber opened the door to a guy I'd never seen before. He had dark, sunken eyes and a handsome face carved with lines that must have come from pain. Square chin, broad forehead, wavy brown hair pulled back in a ponytail that worked for him. This guy was fine.

"I hear you've got my dog," he said, sticking his hands deep into the pockets of his baggy pants. He wore a white T-shirt under a flannel shirt a couple of sizes too large for him, but he was a good-sized guy and could look Amber in the eyes. "Are you Bailey?"

I stood up. "I'm Bailey."

His Dalmatian trotted over to him, and he squatted down to pet the dog. "Hey, Eve. What's up, girl?"

"Eve?" I asked. "You named her Eve?"

He stood up and locked me with those coal black eyes of his. "Eve," he repeated in a voice that was mellow and melancholy at the same time. "The first woman. The first cause. Anyway, what's in a name?" His eyes were deep-set, like bullets shot into his face. I couldn't look away.

Amber slid past him out the door. "I'm going downstairs for a soda. You guys can work this one out without me." She left us alone.

The dog came trotting back to me. I walked to the door, and Mystery Dog—Eve—stayed behind me. "How do I know you're this dog's owner?" I asked, crossing my arms in front of me. I didn't really doubt that he was the owner. The dog seemed to know and like him. I just didn't want either of them to go yet. "I mean, anyone could walk in here and claim this dog belonged to them, right? Why didn't you look harder for her when you didn't see her at the music store?" I had a hundred other questions for him, like if he played the guitar or the drums, if he went to Mizzou, if he had a girlfriend.

The guy studied me. His brow furrowed, and I could see how those pain lines must have formed. "I don't *own* Eve."

"You don't?" Now I really was confused.

"Nobody really owns anybody or any thing," he explained.

"If we all *got* that, really got that, there'd be no war or starvation in the world. The classes wouldn't be divided into the medieval feudal system we have in America, with oil companies on top."

He was blowing me away, this guy. I'd had boyfriends who didn't even know what medieval was.

He looked at his dog. "If Eve chooses to live somewhere else, who am I to stop her? I mean, when you get down to it, we all own everything and everything owns us."

I wasn't sure I got it, but I knew I'd never met anybody like this. I grinned at him, but I think the state of the world weighed too heavily on him for him to grin back. "I'm Bailey." I didn't stick out my hand or anything so mundane. "You want to come in?"

"Mitch," he said, walking over and sitting on Amber's bed. The name fit so perfectly, he could have made it up.

I had an idea that conversation starters were going to have to come from me. "Are you a student at Mizzou?"

"Summer school," he answered.

We both petted Eve to fill the silence, or at least I did. I had a feeling that none of my prepackaged sports questions would work with this guy.

"And they let you keep your dog in your dorm room?" I was already trying to figure out how I could sneak Adam to *my* room.

Mitch shook his head. "I'm living off campus. Above a bakery. It's better for my work."

"You work at a bakery?"

"No. My *real* work. The theater."

"Cool."

Silence again. Long and awkward.

"So are you taking AP acting classes this summer?" I tried.

He made his frowny face, deepening those pain lines. He looked so cute I wanted to kiss him and make him smile. "Not acting. I would never act. The passion of film originates behind the camera. Directing. That's where change can begin."

"Really?" I imagined e-mailing Mom about my boyfriend, the director. We'd go to galas and openings. He'd work on location, and I'd always go along because he couldn't do his best work without me. "And they have directing classes here?"

He didn't answer.

"Have you gotten to . . . to direct anything?" My questions were getting dumber and dumber.

"I've done some directing, although nothing you would have seen."

"Ah." I wasn't sure if that was a slam on me—as in, *nothing you would have seen because you obviously only go to Disney movies.* Or maybe he was opening up to me, admitting that he hadn't done work anybody ever watches.

"Did you always want to be a director?" I asked, as if the most hated question on campus weren't the two hundredth time someone asked for your major and if you'd always wanted it.

"Last summer settled things."

I was afraid that was all I was going to get. I was right. "So, what's your directing class like?"

"We're in teams, and we'll produce a film and have a showing at the end of the summer."

"That's so cool!" I said. "Can anybody come see your film? Could I, for example?" *On your arm? As your girlfriend?*

It took him forever to answer. "I don't think you'd appreciate the film I've been producing in film class."

Now I was getting a little offended. Maybe I smiled too much. "You don't know me well enough to say that," I replied, smile-free.

He shrugged. "That's true. One more proof that the world is heavy with judgment and prejudgment. I apologize for succumbing to the prevailing worldview."

I was pretty sure that was an apology. Sort of. "That's okay," I muttered.

He stood up. "I should go."

No you shouldn't. "Are you positive that you have the right dog, that this is really Eve and not some other spotted canine?" I hugged the sweet Dalmatian, who was snoring at my feet. How could I be so attached to this dog already?

"Come on, Eve," he called.

Eve got to her feet. She glanced back at me, then dropped her head and followed Mitch to the door.

"Sorry about kidnapping Eve," I said.

At the doorway, Mitch surprised me by turning around and almost smiling directly at me. His gaze sank deep into my soul as he said, "Don't be sorry, Bailey. It was fate."

He and Eve walked off down the hall.

I couldn't stand it. I called after them, "Mitch! When will fate strike again?"

"Ah, that's the question," Mitch hollered without looking back.

"Wait!" Barefoot, I raced down the hall after them. Ginny, one of our floor-mates, stuck out her head and yelled, "Dog on the floor!" like we sometimes yelled to warn "man on the floor," in case somebody happened to be streaking from the showers.

I slid past Mitch and knelt in front of Eve, blocking all forward progress. The big dog sat down and put her paw on my shoulder. She licked my cheek. I gazed up at Mitch. "I want visitation rights."

4

"Can you believe it?" I asked Amber. We were elbow to elbow at the bathroom mirror, getting ready for real dates. Eve sat in the doorway, watching us. I'd been babysitting her off and on for Mitch. He spent so much time in his film workshop, and I couldn't stand to think of his dog staying home alone. "Here we are at a university, getting ready for our big dates. And we both have boyfriends at the same time."

My boyfriend plan had worked, more or less. I'd gone to the right place and gotten the right kind of boyfriend. True, I owed it all to Eve and Dotty. I knew I'd gotten the magnificent Mitch simply because of a case of mistaken identity. But in the end, I had a boyfriend.

"Steve and I aren't exclusive, Bailey," Amber replied. "I keep telling you that."

"And Steve, no doubt."

She faced me. In two minutes at the mirror, that girl had put on her makeup, and it looked perfect. I had at least thirty more minutes to go.

She zipped up her little cosmetic bag. "I'm really glad you and Mitch are doing something fun tonight. If you ask me, that boy could use a little fun."

"Mitch is fun," I said defensively. "He just thinks about things more deeply than other people. That's all. If we all thought as profoundly as Mitch does about life, we'd have trouble being fun all the time, too."

"Then I'm glad I'm shallow," Amber muttered. "And I hope your play is as good as our movie is going to be. Sure you can't talk Mitch into doubling with Steve and me to the movies? It's that romantic comedy with the guy you used to have a crush on."

"I know. I want to see it. But Mitch is so excited about seeing this play with me. Lubinski is his favorite playwright. He wants to share him with me."

Mitch was passionate about filmmaking. I'd finally gotten a boyfriend who was passionate about something besides sex. He never flirted with other girls. And when I'd given him my little gecko talk and told him I'd only mate when I could mate for life, Mitch hadn't tried to change my mind. He'd just gazed into my eyes and said, "Deep."

"Well, hurry up. I want to see what you're going to wear to this play. I've got a couple of ideas for you."

We tried on every item of clothing in both of our closets, mixing and matching, and laughing until we collapsed onto my bed. Eve got into the act and jumped on the bed. I had to hold her down so she wouldn't lick off all my makeup.

In the end, we settled on a slinky, sleeveless black dress for me, short and tight. Amber wore black silky pants and a sleeve-less, electric blue turtleneck that made her eyes look like jewels.

"Can I wear your black shawl?" I asked, pulling on the three-inch spike heels Mom had bought in a garage sale and mailed to me. This would be the first time I'd worn them.

"You're welcome to the shawl, Bailey, but the temperature is supposed to drop tonight. Supposed to break a record or some-thing. I'm taking a heavy sweater."

"It can't get that cold. Besides, no way I'm hiding this," I declared, pointing to my fancy, sophisticated self.

The phone rang, and Amber answered it. "Sweet. Right there." She hung up and grinned. "They're both downstairs waiting for us."

We rode the elevator down. Better to make an entrance from an elevator than a stairwell. As soon as the doors opened, I heard a wolf whistle. We turned toward it, and there were our guys. Steve, looking like he'd won the Vegas jackpot, whistled again. He was wearing an oxford shirt and dress pants. "You ladies look fantastic!" Steve exclaimed, his gaze locked on Amber.

Mitch, not having given in to societal pressures, was dressed pretty much like he always dressed. Hawaiian snow boots—socks with sandals. Expensive jeans that looked worn out on purpose. And he'd added a tie to his T-shirt, which he did from time to time as "a statement." I never asked what he was stating with the tie because I didn't want to sound shallow. But I knew it was loaded with meaning.

"Ready to go?" Mitch asked.

We joined our men. I slipped the shawl around my shoulders, and Steve helped Amber with her sweater.

"Are you two sure you don't want to come to the movies with us?" Steve asked.

Mitch shook his head. "I'm boycotting the silver screen and those feeble attempts of bourgeois movies manufactured for commercial consumption."

"I'll take that as a no?" Amber said sweetly.

"But thanks for asking," I added. "Maybe next week?" I doubted it, though. I'd practically had to promise Wanda my firstborn to get her to give me a Saturday night off from Grady's.

I knew Amber and Steve and Wanda didn't like Mitch, but that was just because they didn't understand him. Mitch was almost universally misunderstood. And yet I understood him. I loved him. Sometimes I felt that nobody knew the real Mitch except me.

Steve offered to give us a ride to the Fine Arts Theater downtown, but Mitch stoically refused. So we walked the twenty-three blocks, much of it in silence because Mitch needed to get into the right mood to appreciate Lubinski.

Amber the Journalist had turned out to be a reliable weatherperson as well. By the time we made it to the theater, my teeth were chattering, and my blisters had blisters.

We were the first ones in line, where we had to wait for thirty minutes before the box office opened up. Only a handful of other people trickled in after us.

It was a classic theater, dingy with age. But you could still see the glory of the past in it. Thick, burgundy velvet curtains folded across a grand stage. A chandelier dangled above our heads. We took our plush velvet seats front and center. Mine kept going back too far, but I loved the wooden armrests. "What a great theater," I said. The room smelled musty with a hint of grease, but you got used to it.

Mitch reached over and took my hand. His fingers were long and smooth, an artist's hand. He whispered in my ear. "I've never shared Lubinski with a woman."

His breath, his voice, and this revelation made me feel closer to him than ever. I tilted my head and kissed him. He kissed me back. He was a great kisser.

Then he lost himself in the playbill we were handed on the way in.

I picked up my playbill and tried to read it in the theater's soft lighting. There wasn't much information about the play. A drawing at the top pictured a mouth, wide-open, uvula in motion, like somebody belting out a song, maybe. I would have loved to see a musical. I turned to ask Mitch if there'd be singing in the play, but his eyes were closed, and I was afraid to disturb him. He was probably meditating on the play's theme.

The only writing on the playbill listed *Life* as the title and Lubinski as the playwright. I already knew that.

Finally, the lights dimmed. I glanced around the theater, and the audience wasn't much bigger than it had been, no more than a dozen of us altogether. I thought about telling Mitch they needed to advertise more, but he was morally and ethically opposed to ads.

Instead, I reached over for his hand. His fingers interlocked with mine in this tight, intense way he always had, as if he wanted to share his desperation with me. I leaned in closer to him while the theater grew completely black. There wasn't even an exit light left on.

With no musical introduction of any kind, no warning to turn off cell phones and beepers, the curtain began to rise.

A scream rang out from the stage, and I jumped. The scream kept going, getting louder and louder as the curtain rose on a dark stage filled with trash. No actors were in view, but the scream kept going and going.

As the light onstage got brighter, more trash and garbage came into view. The scream shifted to the background, and a new sound flooded the theater like a rush of wind, a deep inhaling as the lights grew brighter and brighter.

Then the sound changed to a blowing rush of air, an exhale. Lights dimmed softer and softer as air was exhaled and the curtain lowered until, all out of air, the scream rang out again. Curtain closed. Scream stopped.

The end.

The whole thing took less than a minute.

"That was fantastic!" Mitch exclaimed. "What an experience!" He stood up, threw his arms in the air. "Genius!" He wheeled on me. "Lubinski is the next Brecht, I'm telling you."

"Yeah." What else could I say?

On the long walk back, Mitch rattled on and on about the lighting, the sound, the genius of production, how he'd give anything to be part of something that big.

My feet were beyond sore. I couldn't even feel them anymore. My arms and legs were numb. And my head hurt. I could have screamed and made my own play.

And then Mitch surprised me again, just like he always seemed to do at the right time, the times when I started wondering if we were too different after all. He stopped and turned to me, and he smiled. "Bailey, there's no one else in this miserable world I'd want to share that moment with except you." Then he kissed me and kissed me. They could have run two dozen Lubinski plays while we kissed under the stars in a shiver of moonlight that warmed me to my bones. At last, he said, "I love you, Bailey."

5

My musical career at Grady's Gas and Snack was giving me a bit of fame around campus. Almost every day somebody would walk up to me and ask, "Aren't you the singing Grady girl?" Sometimes they'd high-five me, or say nice things about my voice or style. Once somebody asked for my autograph. Wanda said business had picked up because of me.

Mitch never told me I had a great voice. But he stopped by Grady's sometimes. He taught me a few songs that came in handy for the late-night crowds, like "Eve of Destruction," and "In the Midnight Hour." Once he had his guitar with him, and we did "Where Have All the Flowers Gone?" for a guy frantically buying up pink carnations for his wife because he'd forgotten their anniversary.

Mom still e-mailed and texted, or called, every day, but her new job kept her busy on the weekends. Her boss didn't want her leaving town and missing a big real estate deal, and she didn't have any vacation days saved up. So, of course, she quit.

"Isn't that great news?" Mom said. "You and Amber won't come home to visit, so now I can pay you guys a visit!"

Summer school was almost over, but I knew how much this visit meant to Mom. I'd missed her, too. And Adam. "You have to bring Adam!" I said, getting into the spirit of the thing. "And you can finally meet Mitch."

"Exactly," Mom said.

Then I got an idea. "Mom, if you can make it this weekend, you can see Mitch's production!" Mitch's film workshop had finished their big project, an actual film, and they were showing it on campus. "Saturday is opening night."

"I'll be there," Mom promised.

"And don't forget Adam. I want him to meet Eve."

Friday afternoon Amber, Eve, and I waited outside on the dorm steps. Mom was late, as always. I knew she couldn't help stopping at garage sales on the way.

Soon as we saw her van, we ran out and flagged her into the visitors' parking lot. I think I was as excited about seeing Adam as I was about seeing my mother. The second she pulled into the parking space, I opened the van door. There were a chest of drawers, an old broom, and a box of stuff wrapped in newspapers—but no dog.

"Where's Adam?" I demanded.

"I'm sorry, honey." She stuffed her phone and wallet into her purse and climbed out of the van. "I just couldn't bring Adam."

I was so disappointed that tears blocked my throat. I had to swallow before I could talk. "But you promised."

"I didn't promise. I said I'd try."

Then I got a horrible thought. "Adam's sick, isn't he! Or . . . he's . . . he isn't . . . ?" I couldn't even say the words.

"No, honey. Adam's fine."

"Then why isn't he here?" I knew I sounded like a five-year-old, but I missed my dog.

Amber walked up and hugged my mom. "Hey, Big D. Great to see you."

"Thanks, Amber. You too." Mom turned to me. "Bailey, your dog has been eating us out of house and home."

"So?"

"So he's become king of the gas. Believe me, you don't want that little chubs in your dorm room. I drove him to the vet yesterday, and it almost killed me when he—"

"The vet?" I interrupted.

"Just to see why Adam's been gaining so much weight. The vet gave your dog a clean bill of health and put him on a special diet. With a special food at a special price, I might add. Sarah Jean's watching him for us. Besides, what if you get caught with a dog in your room?"

I hadn't exactly told Mom that I'd been babysitting Mitch's dog in my room. Eve, fed up with being out of the loop, nosed her way through to Mom.

"And you must be Eve." Mom stroked the dog's head. "She's so pretty. And big. Pleased to meet you, Eve." She glanced around. "Where's Mitch?"

"He couldn't come." Mitch hadn't said why. He wasn't into giving excuses or reasons for his actions. Mitch believed people should just "be," and other people should accept. I was pretty sure my mother wouldn't go for that explanation, though. "We're meeting him at this great pizza place."

"Okey-doke," Mom said. "You're the boss, Bailey. This is your world, and I'm just a visitor." She sounded like she'd rehearsed those lines on the drive up, but it was a nice thing to say anyway.

I leaned down and hugged her. "Thanks for coming, Mom. I can't wait for you to meet Mitch. He's a little nervous about his film debuting tomorrow. It means a lot to both of us that you'll be there."

"Are you kidding? Who would have thought I'd be going to a movie debut?" Mom locked the van, and we started for the dorm. "Are his parents coming? I'll bet it's going to be a really big night for Mitch."

I shook my head. "I don't think he invited them. And it's not exactly Mitch's movie." I glanced back at Mom. "It was a team effort with his whole class. Mitch thinks it would have been better if he could have directed the whole thing himself. I think he might be waiting to invite his parents to something he directs."

Mitch had let me view the film in editing with a couple of the guys in his film class. The movie was still pretty rough. I knew Amber and Mom wouldn't like it, but it wasn't totally weird, like Lubinski, or a gross-out or anything. I was reasonably confident that my mom and my best friend could fake enthusiasm for my sake.

"Wait a minute," Amber said as we skirted the sidewalk to the dorm's rear entrance, since we had Eve with us. "All week you've been telling everybody this was Mitch's show, that he was the director, right? That's what you said when you strong-armed our whole dorm, plus all your Grady's Gas and Snack fans, to go see it."

"I know. I sort of misunderstood that part," I admitted. I'd really thought Mitch was directing until I watched the editing session, not that it really mattered. "The film was more of a team project. Officially, Mitch was a grip."

"A what?" Mom asked.

"A grip. Like a movie grip? They always list the grips at the end of movies in the film credits. It's a real job, Mom."

"I'm sure it is, honey. And I'm looking forward to seeing the film. What's it called again?"

"*Earth*."

We showed Mom what we'd done with our dorm room. Then we walked around campus until it was time to meet Mitch at Shakespeare's Pizza. Mom filled us in on Millet gossip and the new job she'd be starting next week as church secretary and part-time hospice worker. "It doesn't pay as well as real estate. I even made more at my old dentist's office job, but the people I work with at the church are so much nicer than people with toothaches and root canals."

Shakespeare's Pizza was Friday-night busy. We waited twenty minutes for a booth, and Mitch still hadn't shown.

"Should you call him?" Mom asked after we'd ordered Cokes.

"Nah," Amber answered, handing Mom a menu. "Mitch is always late."

"He's not *always* late," I snapped. "He probably got held up."

"Besides, Amber," Mom said, "lots of perfectly wonderful people are frequently late."

I checked my cell. Two text messages, but not from Mitch.

Mom turned to Amber. "So, Amber, are you still seeing Steve?"

"Steve's great," she answered. "I think we'll always be really good friends."

"But he's not Travis," I added.

Amber's eyes sparkled when she talked about Travis. "You'll meet Travis tomorrow tonight. He's coming to Mitch's opening."

Mom smiled across the booth at me. "Are Mitch and Travis friends?"

"Not really." I was reasonably certain that Travis didn't like Mitch, although he was always polite. Mitch called Travis "the poster boy for the establishment" because he planned to major in business.

We waited as the restaurant filled. "Let's go ahead and order," I suggested.

"Great!" Mom eyed the menu again. "I'm starved. How about an extra-large meat-lover's with extra cheese?" She glanced up at us. "Or whatever else you want on it. Sky's the limit. My treat."

"No meat," Amber said. "Mitch doesn't eat animals."

Mitch finally got there just as our waiter set the big veggie pizza on the table. My boyfriend slid into the booth and kissed me. I couldn't help peeking at Mom, who looked a little shocked by Mitch or the way he was dressed—T-shirt and tie, shorts and sockless loafers.

I heard Amber whisper to Mom, "It's Mitch's statement on the duality of man."

Mom nodded. "Ah."

Only then did my boyfriend turn to my mother. "Mrs. Daley."

"Hi, Mitch. Good to meet you at last."

He narrowed his eyes at her. "You and Bailey could be sisters." Even though I'd heard that a hundred times, when Mitch said it, it made more sense. I hoped Mom could see that.

"We're sure looking forward to seeing your movie tomorrow night," Mom offered.

Mitch took a piece of pizza. "Film, not movie. There's an ocean of difference between the two, and only a handful of sand to tell that difference."

"Uh-huh," Mom commented, helping herself to a slice of pizza.

"Which theater will it be in?" Amber asked.

Mitch slammed his water glass so hard the water spilled. "The Rise Theater. Can you believe that?"

"What's wrong with the Rise?" I asked. Amber and I had gone there a couple of times to see old movies or cartoon fests. It was small, but the seats and floors were clean.

"What's wrong with it?" Mitch asked. I wasn't sure I'd ever seen him this fired up. "Do you know what drivel that theater usually shows? And get this. In their second theater tomorrow night, playing the same time *Earth* will be showing, is some vapid cartoon movie!"

I glanced at Amber and Mom, ready to kick them under the table if necessary. We *loved* cartoon movies. It was one of my life details I'd never confessed to my boyfriend.

Nobody spoke for a while. The pizza place camouflaged our

awkward silence with laughter and loud voices from other tables, clanging silverware, and a twenty-four-hour sports station on the big-screen TV.

"Anyway," Mom said, smiling at Mitch, who didn't smile back but did give her his full attention. "I can't wait to see your mo—your film."

No response.

Amber jumped in. "What's the weather supposed to be tomorrow?"

Grateful for a neutral topic, I tried to keep it going, even though I hadn't heard any weather reports for days. "I think it's going to be sunny. Really sunny."

"That's good," Mom said.

Mitch stared off into space, so I knew he was thinking deeply. "A day without sunshine . . . A day without sunshine is like . . . " He wrestled with the thought.

Mom, who could never stand to see anybody struggle with words or anything else, supplied, "Night?"

Still staring at the blank wall, Mitch repeated, "A day without sunshine is like night. Deep."

Mitch walked back to the dorm with us, picked up Eve, and went back to his apartment. Mom and Amber and I stayed up late popping popcorn and catching up on things. Amber and I wouldn't let Mom go back to the hotel room she'd reserved for the night. I gave her my nightgown and my bed, and I took the floor.

It seemed like I'd just fallen asleep when I heard a tapping. I waited. Then I heard it again.

"Who's that?" Amber whispered.

My brain finally deduced someone was knocking at the door. I got up to answer it.

"It's the middle of the night, Bailey," Amber complained, rolling over.

I kept the chain on the lock, but opened the door to see who it was.

Mitch stood there in baggy sweats, his hair disheveled, and Eve by his side. When the dog saw me, she scratched to get in.

I unlocked the door and slipped out into the hall so I wouldn't wake Mom. "Mitch, what are you doing here?" I whispered.

Mitch gazed into my eyes, his expression flat. "Why is life so long?" he asked, as if the fate of all humanity depended on the answer, and that answer had to come right then and there.

I sent Mitch back home to get some sleep. I knew he was worried about his film, no matter what he said. Maybe he had finally let me see through his defenses and into his soul.

Or maybe not.

6

On Saturday Mom, Amber, and I got up early and hit Columbia's garage sales. It felt like old times.

"There's one!" Amber shouted, spying our first sale of the day.

We came away with six vintage Mizzou drinking glasses, a more-than-slightly-used gold sweatshirt with a Mizzou Tiger still intact, and a black-and-gold tie, which Mom decided would be the perfect gift for the aspiring grip after his film debut.

In between garages I tried to call Mitch, but he didn't pick up.

"Still not answering?" Amber asked, catching me dialing again when we got back to the dorm.

"His cell's turned off. He's probably doing last-minute edits or meeting with the film team. I left him a text message that we'd meet him at the theater if he doesn't get in touch before then." I forced a smile and tried to act like it didn't matter that he was cutting me out of his big day. But it did. I was his girlfriend. If he was upset or nervous, I should have been there for him.

We played three-handed poker back in our room, but the time dragged.

"Bailey," Mom said, laying down her full house to beat my lousy two pair, "why don't you go over to Mitch's and make sure he's okay?"

I'd wanted to go all day. I just wanted Mitch to call and ask me to come. But that was stupid. I was his girlfriend. He needed me, whether he called to tell me so or not. I stood up. "Thanks, Mom. I'll do it."

It took about twenty minutes to walk to Mitch's apartment, which was more like a tiny room over Berkeley's Bakery in an older residential area of Columbia. Most of the buildings on the block had been torn down, leaving empty lots littered with glass and debris. Mitch seemed happy there—as happy as Mitch ever got anyway. But I worried about Eve. She was a big dog and needed a lot of exercise, and there wasn't any room to run around the bakery.

I climbed the back stairs and knocked. Eve barked from inside. "It's just me, girl," I called.

Eve hiked up the barking volume and scratched at the door.

"Mitch?" I called.

Nobody answered, except Eve.

I opened the door, which Mitch never locked on the principle that he didn't own anything. Eve bounded out, overjoyed at the freedom. She ran right past me down the fire escape and to the little patch of stones at the foot of the stairs. There, she did her business.

Mitch obviously wasn't home, so I closed the door and walked back to the dorm, taking Eve with me. I couldn't leave her. Mitch might not come back until the film was over.

When I got back to the dorm, Amber and Mom weren't there. Amber had left me a note saying they were going out for ice cream and I should join them. Instead, I took advantage of the alone time and called all my friends and classmates and favorite customers to remind them to come to Mitch's film showing.

By the time Amber and Mom strolled in, we had to rush to get ready for the big night. Mom and Amber both wore black dresses with sparkly jewelry. I'd learned my lesson. I wore tight jeans and a funky tunic top with a leather choker and slingback, one-inch heels.

"Bailey, are you wearing *that*?" Mom asked. Then, as if she'd remembered her mantra about this being my world and whatever I said went, she said, "Sorry. You look great, honey. I'm sure you know exactly the right thing to wear to a film opening."

She was being so sweet. For a second, I felt like crying. In a weird way, I think I was homesick. Here I'd gone all these weeks without being homesick—except maybe for Adam. And now that Mom was with me, I missed her? It didn't make sense.

I looked away fast, before she could see my face. "We better get going. I told Mitch we'd get there early and hold a seat for him."

Travis drove Amber, Mom, and me to the theater. A group of kids in cartoon character shirts hopped out of a van and ran into the theater like they were late for their own birthday party. A couple of middle-aged men I knew from Grady's trudged in like they were going to a funeral. It was pretty easy to tell which group was going to which movie.

The lobby was long and narrow, with a table of cartoon-movie souvenirs on one end and packaged candy bars and cookies on the other.

"Bailey, look," Amber called from the souvenir table.

Mom and I walked over to check it out. "It's a Goofy," Mom said, fingering the tiny ceramic dog. I'd started collecting Goofy after he'd sat with me on the park bench at Six Flags. I had stuffed animals and statues, some of them picked up in garage sales by my ever-vigilant mother.

"He's adorable." I examined Goofy's floppy ears to make sure they weren't chipped.

"Bailey!" Mitch called from the theater entrance and waved for me to join him.

"Just a minute!" I called back.

"I need you now."

Reluctantly, I handed Goofy back to the salesgirl. "Take good care of Goofy. I'll come back for him."

By the time I made it to Mitch, he was in the middle of an intense conversation with an older man. I couldn't believe it. Mitch looked fantastic in khaki pants, oxford shirt, and a corduroy sports jacket. No socks, but great loafers.

I eased under his arm for a hug. "You look amazing," I whispered in his ear. "You should have told me it was okay to dress up."

"Clothes mean nothing," Mitch said, taking in mine. I was the worst-dressed person there.

I stood by Mitch and greeted the people filtering in, all of them dressed a hundred times better than I was. On the other hand, some of these people had never seen me in anything but a Grady's orange-capped uniform, so I might have looked pretty good.

Mom pulled me aside on her way to our seats. "They're pretty cute together," she whispered, nodding to Amber and Travis. "Is he a good guy?"

"So far, so good." I liked that my mom was so protective of my friend.

Travis came over and shook Mitch's hand and wished him luck. I waited for Mitch to make some comment about the non-existence of luck, but thankfully, he kept his scorn of Lady Luck to himself.

I stuck around and made nice with theatergoers for about as long as I could stand. Then I took Mitch aside. "I'm going to find our seats. Are you coming?"

"I'll be there," he answered. He leaned in and whispered, "I have to check on Stan, our pitiful excuse of a film prof."

"I thought you liked him. You said he'd directed several plays and Sundance documentaries, right?"

"The man couldn't direct traffic," Mitch said. "Go ahead. I'll join you later."

Our seats were in the eighth row, as ordered by Mitch. I stopped and chatted with friends and customers as I made my way to our seats. Outside in the lobby, you could hear kids screaming and laughing.

"Must be the cartoon moviegoers," Mom observed as I climbed over her. She'd held a seat next to her for me, with a seat next to me for Mitch, who would end up dead center of the eighth row, the perfect viewing perspective, according to my boyfriend.

Mitch didn't take his seat until the last minute.

"I thought you weren't going to make it," I whispered as he climbed over Travis, Amber, Mom, and me and plopped into his seat.

"Shh-hh," he said, staring at the blank screen.

Mitch didn't mean to be rude—I knew that. I understood him. He was focused on his creation. Sometimes he had to shut out the world. And me.

Mom reached over and looped her arm through mine, like we'd done a million times at movies.

The theater darkened, and a scene appeared on the screen in black-and-white—a man's boots stuck in mud that went as far as you could see. Then the title flashed on the screen: *EARTH.* And the show began.

The audience watched in silence as earthy scenes replaced more earthy scenes. The camera angled up from the man's feet until his face appeared in shadows. This unnamed man was the main character of *Earth,* and we followed him back and forth through mud, snow, desert, and dust. Three other people had roles in the film. I'd seen the film once before, and I still had no idea who the characters were. They had lines, but they never spoke to each other. It was more like they didn't realize anybody else was there.

Mom yawned. When I glanced at her, she tried to hide it. Somebody in front of us had fallen asleep after the first five minutes. A few people sneaked out the back. But most of the audience paid polite attention.

I wished I understood the film better. From time to time I sneaked peeks at Mitch. The light from the screen fell on his cheek, and his eyes were wide with pride and awe. He looked beautiful, wholly enthralled.

The final scenes of the film were going to be the hardest on the audience. That's when the four characters finally got together and spat out hateful words. The last exchange went like this:

MAN 1: "I've listened to music from the East, and I can tell you there is no God."
MAN 2: "Then there is no God."
GIRL 1: "I told you so. I hate all of you."
GIRL 2: "I can die, then."

The actors disappeared, and the film credits rolled. Next to me, my mother squirmed. She muttered something to herself. Amber and Travis were whispering. Mitch was on the edge of his seat, watching the credits. I knew he was waiting to see his name roll by. Around us, people were getting up. Leaving.

I stood up. "Hey, everybody! Hang on a minute!"

"It's over," said a man, who made it sound like he'd just endured oral surgery.

"No! It's not! Look at the screen. Please?" I begged.

Most people stopped. I knew so many of them. They were my customers. They'd come to this depressing movie because I'd begged them to. I'd told them how much it would mean to my boyfriend and me if they'd show up and fill the theater. They'd *paid* to be here. "Seriously, everybody, thanks for coming. Hang on for one more minute." I loved them for stopping their mass exit, for looking at the screen, for wiping the frowns off their faces and smiling back at me. "You guys are the greatest!"

"There it is," Mitch said, his voice excited. "Right after the chief grips."

And then it came, Mitch's full name—Jonathan Randall Mitchell. And beside his name: "Assistant Grip."

"That's my boyfriend!" I shouted. I realized that at some point I'd climbed up on my theater seat. I wobbled, and Mom grabbed my legs to steady me.

Mom shouted, "Yippee! Whoo-hoo!"

Amber and Travis started the applause. Then people followed their lead—the apple man from Grady's, a girl in my French class, two guys Amber used to date. They clapped, and they kept clapping until every credit rolled by and the screen went blank.

"You guys rock!" I shouted.

"Now can we go?" begged Mr. Murtaugh, Wanda's father. He'd come because Wanda was holding down Grady's without me.

People trudged out of the theater. Only the remnants of the film class and our little group hung around.

"Congratulations, Mitch," I said, so grateful that my friends had pulled together for him. "I think they liked it, or appreciated it anyway."

Mitch frowned at me. "Do you think I care if spectators like my work?"

But I'd seen it. I'd seen how much he wanted to see the credit, his name on the screen. I'd seen the pride that filled him when people cheered. He *did* care. "So I got all those people to applaud for nothing?"

Mitch took my chin in his fingers and kissed me. Gazing into my eyes, he said, "Bailey, art is for art's sake."

Next to me, still in her seat, Mom breathed so heavily that I knew she was about to let it go. "Mitch," Mom began, her voice tight, controlled, "don't you care about the people who came to support you?"

"Why should I?" Mitch asked. "Nobody cares, really cares, about anybody."

Mom muttered something under her breath. The only part I could make out went something like, "Oh yeah? Try missing a car payment and see if anybody cares."

Mitch didn't know Mom, or he would have stopped right there, quit while he was sort of ahead. "Didn't you understand what was going on in that last scene?" he asked her.

"The God scene?" Mom scooted up in her seat and faced Mitch, talking in front of me. "What exactly was that about, Mitch?"

I didn't want them to fight. I wanted them to like each other. "Mom, it was just a film. Mitch didn't write it. He doesn't believe that stuff."

"But I do," Mitch insisted. "In twenty-first-century America, God no longer exists any more than—"

Now it was my turn to object. "Mitch, I've heard you go on and on about God and the Big Universe and even hell. So now you're saying you don't believe in God?"

"Of course not." He looked surprised, or amused, that I might not understand.

"How can you possibly have a dog and not believe in God?" I demanded.

Mitch narrowed his eyes at me. "Deep."

"Deep?" I repeated.

He nodded slowly. "Deep."

And right then I realized that Jonathan Mitchell had no idea what he believed. He wasn't deep. He was empty.

I shoved past him and down the empty row of seats. My mind was racing. I'd thought I understood Mitch. I'd thought I was the only one who did. But I had no idea what he believed and what he didn't. And neither did he.

Maybe I hadn't worn blinders in my relationship with Mitch. But I'd sure pulled out the rose-colored glasses.

Mitch caught up with me at the exit to the lobby. So did Amber and Mom. They circled behind me, my defense, my cheering section—something Mitch had never been.

"Bailey, chill," Mitch pleaded. "It's all cool, babe."

A calm came over me. "No, Mitch. It's not all cool. I thought it was, but it wasn't. It was my mistake." I laughed softly, remembering that I'd only met Mitch because I'd mistaken Eve for Dotty. "In fact, you know what? Our whole relationship has been one big case of mistaken identity."

Poor Mitch looked confused. He tried to run his fingers through his hair, but his hair was in a ponytail and his hand wouldn't fit through the band. "I don't get it. Mistaken identity?"

I nodded, almost feeling sorry for him. "Yeah, mistaken identity. All this time I thought you were a great guy and an ideal boyfriend. My mistake." I took his hand and shook it. "No hard feelings."

Then I walked out, with Amber and Mom, and even Travis, quietly cheering behind me.

We'd passed the souvenir table when I remembered the Goofy, one of Mitch's hated "capitalistic cartoon symbols." I turned on my heels and ran back. Plunking down twice the cost of the little Goofy figure, I told the girl, "I'll take it. And you can keep the change." It was worth every penny.

"Bailey?" Mitch called, scorn thick in his voice, like he knew I couldn't mean this. Like who could possibly want to break up with him?

I turned back for one last time. "And Mitch, since you don't own anything . . . I'm keeping Eve!"

WHILE I'VE BEEN TALKING about Mitch and Mizzou, my dogs have made themselves totally at home in Louie of St. Louie's. So have I. It strikes me that this *so* isn't how I'd imagined spending tonight, my big prom night. But it's been good to talk, to piece things together like this. My life is almost starting to make sense to me. "If you don't mind, I could sure use a refill of water."

"I'll get it," Colt says, setting down Adam and beating Rune up from the table. Colt, Rune, and Louie couldn't have been better listeners. The rain outside has evened to a steady downpour, a comforting clatter on the roof and windows, insulating our little group.

"So did Mitch ever try to get the dog back?" Rune asks, stroking Eve's head. She's curled up at his feet, her chin resting on his giant boot. I don't think Rune's moved his foot for the last hour.

"Mitch never came back for his Dalmatian," I explain. "Last year I ran into this girl who was in my summer school French class, and she told me Mitch dropped out of school. I think he got evicted from his bakery apartment before the end of summer for not paying his rent."

"Guess your mama was right," Louie says. "Somebody cared after all, just like she said." He stretches and twists in his chair as if his back is stiff. Or maybe his whole body aches.

I wish I could do something for him. "Louie, would you like me to make you some hot tea?"

He grins at me, and it feels like we've known each other for years. "Why, I thank you, Bailey. Can't remember the last time a customer offered to wait on me. I'm all right. Don't you worry."

Rune won't let go of Eve's story yet. "So that loser never even called to see what happened to his dog?"

"*My* dog, remember. Mitch never owned anything."

We laugh a little.

"Bet your mama loved having another dog to feed and walk," Louie muses.

I shrug. "She complained for about a week, but Mom and Adam both loved Eve right from the start."

"There you go." Colt sets down a tall glass of ice water in front of me and one for Louie, too.

"Thanks, Colt," I say, taking a long, deep drink. I close my eyes and think of the bright orange punch bowl I left behind at the prom.

"Earth to Bailey," Louie says. "Something wrong with that water?" His voice is teasing.

I take another drink and finish the whole glass. "Louie, this is about the best glass of water I ever drank. My compliments to your chef."

"That would be me, you know," Rune says.

"Hey, I'm the guy who got the water," Colt protests.

I feel like I've known these people forever. But it's almost three in the morning, and I must be keeping them from their real lives, their families. "I'm sorry I've gone on and on. I know you're staying here because of me. I should go."

"You can't leave yet," Louie says in that low, broken voice of his. He points to my dress. The dress is still damp, and scratchier than ever. I think it may be shrinking. "You still haven't explained that gown there. I believe that was the agreement."

Talking about Went and Mitch was fun. It almost felt like I was talking about another Bailey, like those events in my life happened so long ago, they happened to another person. But the closer the memories get to now, to *me* now, the more painful. I look around our little table, at kind Louie, sweet Rune, and adorable Colt, who's still a mystery to me. They've stuck it out with me this far. I guess they deserve the whole story. "Okay. But it's kind of a hard story."

"Love's hard," Louie says. "Yessir. It's not easy to find real love. And when you do, you got to hold on for dear life."

I smile at Louie. "Gecko glue."

"Wait just a minute." Rune pops up, and his chair tips over, waking up Adam. Shirley barks. "I need to make a phone call. Don't start without me. I want to hear how this turns out."

Colt sets the chair back up while Rune lumbers to the phone behind the counter.

"Good for you, Rune," Louie says. He leans on the table and whispers to Colt and me, "I think Rune's calling Fran."

"Who's Fran?" Colt whispers back.

"Rune's wife," Louie answers.

"Rune's married?" I hadn't pictured Identity-Crisis Guy married. I can't imagine any wife letting her husband leave the house with half a beard and half a head of hair.

"Fran's a sweetheart," Louie whispers. "Two great boys, too. Rune's a lucky man. I just wish he knew that."

Louie leans back in his chair and takes a sip of the water

Colt brought him. Colt and I grin at each other, like we're in on something together.

Rune's back is to us. His voice is low, but when we're quiet, I can hear his end of the conversation. "I know, Frannie . . . I know . . . I'm sorry, babe . . . And I mean it. About us having it good. Us and the boys . . . Yeah . . . Me too. I love you, Fran. That's what I called to say . . . Ah, don't cry . . . Listen, I'll be home later, when the rain lets up. You go back to bed. Kiss the boys for me . . . Fran? You still there? . . . Tomorrow, let's me and you and the boys do something together. Something family-like . . . What? . . . Six Flags? . . . Sure. We'll take the boys to Six Flags. Night, now. Hey, Fran? Fran? I been thinking. We need to get our boys a dog."

Rune hangs up, and the rest of us start an animated conversation about the rain and the Cardinals. When Rune joins us at the table, his whole face has changed, the lines softened somehow.

"Everything all right at home, Rune?" Louie asks.

Rune smiles at his boss. It's the first time I've seen the big guy smile. At least two of his teeth are missing. "Everything's real fine at home, Louie."

Shirley, my little brown-and-white Shih Tzu, barks again, at the rain, or at Rune, or at Adam, who's gone back under the table. I scoop up Shirley and set her on my lap. But the taffeta and pearls of my ballroom prom dress aren't soft enough for her, and she's squirmy. "Shirley, settle down. It's your turn, girl. Time for your story, so be good."

The poor little dog, her hair too long, too damp, looks like a drowned rat. I finally settle her on my lap and grin at my eager audience. "I guess you've been waiting for the final act of the

Adam and Eve and Shirley show, huh? Time for me to tell you how I ended up in Louie of St. Louie's on the biggest night of my life?"

"Why the biggest night of your life?" Colt interrupts. "Sorry. I mean, I guess a prom's a big deal."

"It is," I insist. "But it was only part of the plan for the biggest night of my life, if you know what I mean." I didn't really mean to get into *that,* but the words come out as naturally as if I'm talking to Amber.

Colt bows his head, looking adorably embarrassed. "Ah . . . I just thought maybe you were going to finish off with another bad boyfriend and—"

"Are you kidding?" I interrupt back. "Eric, a bad boyfriend?" I lean back and shake my head, remembering the first time I saw Eric, the first time we kissed. "Eric Strang is the perfect boyfriend."

"So our Bailey finally found the perfect boyfriend?" Louie says. "Mmm-mmm-mmm. I want to hear this story. Not that I haven't liked the first two stories. But I admit I'm partial to happy endings."

"Go on. Let her talk," Rune commands. I'm not sure if he's impatient for this story or maybe impatient to get home to Fran.

I take in my audience—three good dogs and three good men—and I recall something I left out of the story of my first fall. That day at Six Flags with Went, and without Went, while I was pouring out my heart to Goofy on that park bench, I remembered something my mom had said about men. I summed it up for Goofy that day: "Goofy, my mom told me once, 'Don't you listen when people say men are dogs. If only! Dogs love you unconditionally, just like you are. If you find a man who can love you like a dog loves you, you just might have found real love.'"

I haven't thought about that in years. Maybe I'm finally understanding what she was getting at.

Shirley squirms in my lap. I hand her to Colt, who looks like he's not sure what to do with the little dog. "Just hold her while I make a quick trip to the ladies' room, deal? When I come back, I promise to tell the story, the whole story, and nothing but."

COLT THE NEWSPAPER GUY

I WATCH BAILEY walk back to the john. We all do, three guys who've shared this diner most nights for the past couple of months. I don't have anywhere else to go since my folks moved to Florida and my roommate transferred to Berkeley. So I come here after my last class and do what I've always dreamed of doing. I sit in the corner of a St. Louis diner and read my article in the paper. *My* article, with *my* byline. *The University Beat by Colt Carson.* I've wanted to write for the *Dispatch* since I was five years old. It's all I've ever wanted to do.

Now I'm doing it, and it's not enough. I'm the first freshman at Washington University of St. Louis to score a front-page, top-of-the-fold feature like I had in today's *Post-Dispatch*. Reading my article tonight at Louie's should have made me feel like I had it all. But until that girl walked in here, I don't know if I felt anything seeing my byline above the fold. Maybe I haven't felt much for a long time.

It's funny. I didn't pay much attention when she walked in, even in that dress. People wear all sorts of crazy getups in this city, especially at night. I read the police reports and arrest columns, so I know what I'm talking about. Still, it was like the atmosphere in the room altered. Like we'd been sitting in water, and she walked in and made it carbonated.

I'm the word man, but I can't seem to put this into words. I went back to my paper. But when I finally looked up at her, I couldn't look away. Bailey Daley got inside me right then, I think. I'd never seen anyone like her. Except that once.

I might have recognized her right away when she walked in if it hadn't been for that dress she's wearing and her hair piled up on her head. Maybe not. But she hasn't changed much.

I haven't either. I've lived in St. Louis, Missouri, my whole life and never wanted to live anywhere else. My first job was as a paperboy. Then I worked at Six Flags.

I'm not sure when I realized I'd seen this girl before. I want to believe that I at least suspected it the moment she walked into Louie's. Or maybe when I pulled a chair up to her table. Or was it when she told us about Went, about his mother living in St. Louis? Did I start to piece things together then?

I know that while she was talking, while she took us with her to Six Flags, I knew then that this was the girl. I kept listening with a growing certainty as she talked about Went flirting with other girls—how could he possibly have noticed another girl with Bailey on his arm?

Then she got to the point in her story I'd been waiting for, when she sat on that bench and cried over a boyfriend who didn't deserve a girl like her. Until that moment, I'd hated my job at Six Flags. I shouldn't even have been in that Goofy costume. Every other day I was Sylvester the Cat. I only had that old Goofy getup because my grandmother had sewn costumes for Disneyland in the seventies. I snuck in that costume as a joke on my last day of work at Six Flags. I'd landed a job in the mailroom at the *Dispatch*. I thought it would be funny to show up at the park as Goofy. I was just going to tell the crew goodbye and pick up my paycheck . . . and then I saw her.

I listened with Louie and Rune as Bailey kept telling her story about seeing Went and Tweety Bird together, about crying and then feeling Goofy's arm around her shoulder. When she said that, when she actually remembered, I wanted to jump up and make her stop talking. It wasn't possible. I have never believed in coincidences. I'm a newspaperman. I deal in facts.

But there it was—bigger than any coincidence I've ever heard of. A God thing, a divine appointment. And I'm smack in the middle of it.

I was Goofy that day.

I was the guy in the costume who saw the beautiful girl crying on a park bench. I'm the guy whose arm she felt, the one she cried with, the one who cried with her from inside a Goofy costume. Watching Bailey leave the park, limping barefoot, shoes in hand, I couldn't believe any guy would leave her. I still can't.

So I'm sitting here again, feeling things I can't say any more than I could when I was inside that park costume. I used to pray every night I'd run into her someday. Now here she is, and I'm too late. She's found her "perfect boyfriend." So none of this really matters.

Bailey walks back to our table. She's carrying her shoes, walking barefoot like she did when she left me the first time. Her hair falls around her face as if she's spent hours making it do just that. She's the most beautiful person I've ever seen.

She sits down and smiles at us, warming the room. "Are you guys sure you want to hear this?"

We assure her we're not going anywhere until she finishes this.

"Okay then." She reaches over and pets Shirley, who's fallen asleep on my lap. "Here we go."

the third fall

shirley

1

"A gecko," I said, writing it down at the top of the list, under my heading: THE PERFECT BOYFRIEND.

Mom, Amber, and I sat cross-legged on the floor of my bedroom, Adam and Eve sprawled in the middle of our little circle. As she'd done every year since kindergarten, Amber was sleeping over on our last night before school started. Only this would be our last last night, our final year of high school.

Mom frowned at my list. "Tell me again why we're doing this."

"Because you may not have noticed, but in the past my boyfriends haven't exactly been perfect."

"We've noticed," Mom and Amber said in harmony.

"Okay." Amber sighed. "I'll play. How about *college bound* and *focused*?"

"Good one," Mom said.

"*Handsome,* of course." I added it. "And he has to think I'm hot."

"With extremely large breasts, perfect bod, and hair to die for?" Amber added.

"Exactly."

"Is *normal* out of the question?" Mom pleaded.

I started to object, then remembered Mitch and the Lubinski play. I wrote down *normal.*

"And *polite*," Mom added.

"Polite?" Again, I thought of Mitch, how he never helped me on with my wrap, the way Travis and Steve had done for Amber. I don't think I ever went through a door before Mitch did. I added *polite* to my growing list.

"*Respect*. I want a boyfriend who respects me," I said, writing.

"Excellent," Mom agreed. "You deserve respect, Bailey."

"*Considerate*," Amber added.

"Why couldn't he be rich?" Mom asked, trying to read over my shoulder.

"Mom, I thought you taught me that money isn't everything."

"And I meant it," she said. "Only, who was it who said it's as easy to fall in love with a rich man as it is to fall for a poor man? Besides, rich people have better garage sales."

I wrote down *rich*, but gave myself the option of crossing it out later.

"*Great dancer*." So far, the only boyfriend who'd liked to dance was my first love, Went. And he liked to dance with *everybody*.

"How about *real*?" Amber suggested.

Mom frowned. "Real?"

But I totally got it. "Absolutely! This time, no blinders or rose-colored glasses. What I see will be what I get. No mistaken identity. I plan to *know* this boyfriend."

"Not *know* in the biblical sense, right?" Mom said.

I ignored her.

Amber intervened. "Don't worry, Big D. Bailey gets it. She's back on our side now."

"And the side of the angels," Mom added. Her forehead

wrinkled. "Wait. What do you mean *back* on the side of the angels?"

"Mother!" I protested. Here I was entering my last year of high school, no doubt as one of the few remaining virgins in the Northern Hemisphere. And still I got no respect in my own home.

"He needs to believe in God," Amber said, further shoring up "our" side and the side of the angels.

I used to think that God and boyfriends inhabited two different worlds. I still wasn't sure how to make room for both of them, but I'd been thinking lately that it would be worth the effort to figure out. What I loved about God was that I could spill my guts to God. There had to be hundreds of verses in the Psalms that talked about crying out to God about life. Even Amber got tired of listening to me after boyfriend breakups. "Deal. God's in." I wrote *God*, noticing—not for the first time— the way *God* spelled backward is *doG*. "He has to be a dog owner. My boyfriend, I mean. He's got to have a dog."

"Great," Mom muttered. "All we need is another dog. Just so you know, I refuse to be part of a three-dog household."

I grinned at Amber. "Did she say 'three dog'?"

Amber threw a scolding glare at Mom. "You did, Big D."

I leaped to my feet. "Come on! It's a Three Dog Night, and it's time to dance goofy!" My mom had turned me on to this classic-rock group when I was five, Three Dog Night. She got me hooked because of the "dog" in the name, but it turned out they weren't bad.

I pulled Mom up, and Amber followed suit. Then I belted out our special song. I'd made up the lyrics, but the tune I got from Three Dog Night's "Jeremiah Was a Bullfrog" song.

"Jeremiah was a hound dog!

Dated him for a while.

He left me flat,

But I'm tellin' you that

Just rememberin' him makes me smile."

"Sing, you guys!" I commanded. "And where's your soul? Dance, wenches!"

Reluctantly, they joined in on the chorus:

"Boyfriends are fun.

I'm gonna get me one.

When he leaves in a poof, he

Always leaves me goof-y.

My prince is a frog,

But I still got my dog . . .

And he sure is a mighty fine dog!"

Amber and Mom, who's never been accused of singing on-key, started out slow and low. But by the end, they were totally into it, belting out lyrics as loud as I was, with Adam and Eve barking at us the whole time.

But the best part was this goofy dance we'd invented. I think we'd started putting it together after my breakup with Went. One night when Amber was sleeping over, I admitted to her and Mom that I'd known about Went hitting on them. After an awkward silence, Amber had walked to my dresser and picked up the little figurine she'd given me for my birthday—a statue of Goofy dancing. Without a word, Mom stoked up the music. And we danced the night away.

Over time, our "goofy dance" had grown into a synchronized routine to this one song. One song, but we managed to work in the twist, the swim, the mashed potato, the jerk, the boogaloo, the electric slide, a moonwalk, and a couple of slick disco moves.

Now, the night before our senior year, Amber and I showed Mom a couple of new dance moves we'd picked up at summer school, and we added them to the routine. When we were done dancing, we collapsed into a heap on the floor. Adam and Eve took turns pouncing on and licking us, while we laughed so hard it hurt.

As if an invisible conductor had lowered his baton to signal the end of our performance, we all grew quiet. Even the dogs stopped. For a minute, nobody spoke. I think we were all feeling it—our last night before school started for the last time.

Amber opened her mouth to say something, but Mom shook her head. "Don't say it. I'm going to start crying like a baby if you do."

"So we're all thinking the same thing?" I said, not wanting to go to the crying place. "This is the big one, right? Our last year . . . So that means . . ." I glanced from Amber to my red-eyed mom. "That means I have one last shot at finding the perfect boyfriend to take me to the prom."

2

"You know," Amber said as we elbowed our way through the halls of Tri-County High, "I'm proud of you, Bailey. Do you realize we talked on the phone for over an hour last night, and you didn't bring up guys even once?"

"Say it isn't so," I pleaded.

"And I know you won't admit it, but you like our advanced

creative writing class. I think you even like English Lit and French, too."

"Let's not get carried away." But the truth was, I loved those classes. In fact, two weeks into my senior year, I liked all of my classes, except World Cultures.

"Bonjour, mon amie!" Roni shouted as she and her goth buddies passed us in the hall. They were all dressed in various forms of black, but Roni had her own style—funky pink ballet slippers; straight black hair, but pulled into a ponytail; no makeup; no red lipstick or fierce eyeliner.

"Friends of yours?" Amber asked.

"Roni's cool. She sits next to me in French. She's really smart. I like her accent better than Madame Jones's."

Amber's grin was accusing.

"Okay. I do like French. Who knew that once you get past those conjugations, French really is a romantic language?"

"Who knew? Mediocre Mark. That's who."

"Funny. At least he's not in my class."

We got to creative writing early and took our seats in the second row, Amber's favorite location. Usually, I preferred the back, but I went along with Amber this time, mainly because of the view. I got to look at the back of Eric Strang, a well-muscled back at that. Topped off with a great neck and thick, sandy blond hair. He was without a doubt the cutest guy in Tri-County. He didn't play sports, although with his bod, he certainly could have. Eric was one of those rare hunks who are as brainy as they are built.

Suddenly, Eric swiveled in his seat and looked straight at me. *Caught.* But he grinned as if I hadn't stared holes through the back of his head. "Great story yesterday, Bailey. I couldn't get it out of my head."

"Yeah?" I said, ever quick on the uptake. This guy was movie-star handsome, and *my* story was in his head?

"Wish I could write like that." He turned back around before I could thank him . . . or kiss him . . . or volunteer to write stories just for him for the rest of my life.

Amber elbowed me. "See? Told you."

"Told me what?" I asked, still dazed.

"That your story was great, nitwit."

I'd had fun writing it, but I'd felt like hurling when Ms. Knowlton read it out loud to the class. I'd gotten the idea when Mom yelled at me about leaving my sandals in the middle of the living room for a week. So I made up a short story about a woman who lived alone in a high-rise in Manhattan—no friends, no boyfriend. It started to get to her. Then one day she noticed that she'd left the newspaper on her living room floor, and she thought, *If I don't pick up this paper, it will stay here forever. There's nobody but me in my world.* Years passed, and the paper didn't move. The woman kept her apartment clean, but left that paper where it was, stepping over it every day of her lonely life. Finally, she couldn't take it anymore, and she jumped out of her window and died. A rookie cop followed up and checked her apartment. He was about to leave when a headline in the old newspaper caught his eye, something about the St. Louis Cards being in last place. The cop went back, picked up the paper, scanned the article, and threw it into the trash. The end. When Ms. Knowlton finished reading the story, nobody said anything. I'd ducked out the second the bell rang.

Jeannette Martin walked into class and eased her slender self into the seat next to Eric. She had the kind of sophistication and class you almost never see in a public school. She flowed, while the rest of us chugged. She sat poised, we slumped. The

Martins were "old money" in Freemont. Freemont University had a "Martin Hall" and a statue of Clyde Martin, military hero.

Eric sneezed, and Jeannette whispered something to him. He whispered back, and they both looked worried.

Then she turned around to me. "Bailey, that was such a great story yesterday. You're really talented." The smile was real. Jeannette was impossible to hate, even though I wanted to.

"Thanks." I smiled back. Couldn't help myself.

I guess I didn't hear much of our lecture on self-editing. I was too involved imagining what it would feel like to run my fingers through Eric's sandy blond hair.

After school, Amber and I headed for the senior lot. Her dad had turned over his old car to Amber when he got a new one. The dealer hadn't offered to give him much for the gas-guzzling SUV with 182,000 miles. But Amber and I were glad to get it. Mom needed *our* car to drive to work—and drive home to walk the dogs, of course.

I stopped in my tracks. A couple of people bumped into me, but I barely noticed. A few feet ahead of us in the parking lot was Eric Strang. There should have been a law—or at least an all-school advisory—against anybody looking that good in khaki pants and a polo shirt.

Jeannette was with him, looking equally great, I had to admit, in crinkled linen. They never dressed alike, but you could tell they shopped at the same stores. Expensive, exclusive stores. Probably Strang Salons. Eric's father owned upscale clothing stores all over the United States.

Eric walked to the passenger side of his understated navy Volvo and opened the door for Jeannette. She slid in with the grace of a ballerina.

"Don't even think about it," Amber said.

"What?" I asked, as if my best friend didn't have the power to read my mind.

She led the way to Harper, her car, named after our fifth-grade teacher, who had never liked me much. She was right—Amber, not Mrs. Harper. Eric Strang was so far out of my league. Besides, he already had the perfect girlfriend in Jeannette Martin.

Amber turned the key, and the engine caught first try. She patted the dashboard. "Good, Harper." She glanced at me before pulling into the line of cars trying to exit the lot. "Want to come help me paint?"

"As tempting as the offer to help paint your house is, I have to say no. I'm working."

Mom's friend Sarah Jean had gotten me a part-time gig at Grady's Gas and Snack. Wanda's great recommendation to the higher-ups hadn't hurt either. So I was once again the Grady Girl. It had taken me a whole week, though, before I got brave enough to sing. People knew me in Millet. Sarah Jane went into shock the first time she heard me belt out "Lemon tree, very pretty, and the lemon flower is sweet" while I served up a lemon slushy. But it wasn't long before she was shouting for me to come up with a song for different customers. She didn't dance or sing like Wanda, but she did teach me more country western songs than anybody has a right to know.

The following week Amber and I were finishing our lunches in the school cafeteria when John Morgan, a senior in my cultures class, plunked his tray on our table and scooted his hulk of a body next to me. I knew what was coming.

"Wanna do something after the game Friday?" John asked, sticking three ketchup fries into his mouth.

"No thanks," I answered. It was painful to watch the mutilation of those fries.

"We could do something Saturday night."

"Sorry, John. No."

"Sunday? Or next weekend?"

I put my hand on his, blocking his reach for more fries. "John, don't waste your time on me. You're a great guy, but I'm not going to go out with you."

He jerked to his feet, almost tipping our whole table. "Fine. Like I care."

"That went well," I muttered.

"And what's wrong with John?" Amber asked, sounding curious but not disapproving.

"Can you imagine John Morgan in a tux?" The guy was a born fullback, a position he filled nicely for the Tri-County Tigers.

"Why would I want to imagine such a thing?"

"Because that's what my prom date will be wearing."

"To the prom that's half a year away?"

"Seven months, thirteen days," I corrected her.

"You're shopping for prom dates already?"

"You and Mom are always telling me to plan ahead," I reminded her.

"For *college*. Not for the prom." Amber shook her head. "So that's why you've been turning down dates? You're worried about the prom?"

"Not worried. Focused."

"You know you'll get a date to the prom. Not that the world would end if you didn't," she added under her breath.

"But that's just it!" I knew this would be hard to explain to Amber, who probably wouldn't care that much whether she went to prom or not. "I don't want just any date. Like, I don't want an imaginary prom date."

Amber grinned. "An imaginary prom date? Now that could be fun. If we double, could we ride in your imaginary Jag?"

"Not that kind of imaginary. I mean, where I drag in a friend of a friend, or some guy I knew from sixth-grade summer camp, or a son of Mom's old school buddy and pretend we're madly in love, the ideal prom couple."

"I get it."

"And I don't want a used or recycled boyfriend either."

"So Mediocre Mark's out?"

"Totally."

"And Mitch and Went," Amber added.

I nodded, but I didn't look at her. There was still an ember in my heart for Went Smith, and it sparked a little whenever I thought about him. Mitch too. I remembered being kissed by Mitch under a cold sky and bright moon, talking about art and music. . . .

". . . perfect prom date?" Amber was on a roll. "And all this time I thought you were finally getting into your classes."

"There's that, too," I said, pulling myself out of my memories. "I don't know how it happened, but my classes turned interesting. Teachers are better this year, too."

"Yeah. That's it, Bailey. Couldn't have anything to do with you, or the fact that you know what they're talking about in class because you're actually reading the assignments."

There was no question that not dating had given me more time to study. Several nights a week, Mom and I curled up on opposite ends of the couch and read for hours. I'd polished off novels that weren't even homework. Weird.

Lunch ended, and Amber and I worked our way through the crowded lunchroom.

"Ah, the drama," Amber said, glancing over the sea of noisy juniors and seniors. "Who will be the last date standing?"

3

I knew who I'd choose as my "last date standing." Eric Strang, the gorgeous, smart, kind—did I say gorgeous?—guy in creative writing. Every day I had to look at his strong back and sandy blond hair. How hot would he be in a tux?

I was still envisioning the handsome Eric in a tux as I plopped into my last-row seat in French class.

"*Bonjour, la classe!*" bellowed Madame Jones.

"*Bonjour,*" we muttered back.

"*Aujourd'hui, nous allons discuter quelque chose, et je veux que vous décidiez du sujet.*"

As always, I turned to my gothic French partner, "Mademoiselle Roni," to translate. She was wearing a red satin sheath dress, with leather half-gloves.

"She wants us to decide what to talk about today," Roni whispered.

"Not again." We'd done this before, and the kids who understood her were the ones who chose subjects like Napoleon or majoring in French in college. It was up to me. I raised my hand.

"Ah," said the surprised Madame Jones. "Mademoiselle Bailey?"

"*L'amour!*" I shouted.

My request was greeted with applause from half the class. Our teacher instructed us to come up with a list of French words relating to *amour*. She quickly, and wisely, excluded swearwords, slang, and coarse language. Even good ol' Mediocre Mark knew how to ask me to go to bed with him in English, French, and Italian.

Roni and I breezed through the easy words: *boyfriend, girlfriend, kiss, hug*. I allowed my goth buddy her unusual train of thought surrounding love: death, loss, sacrifice, torture. So I took a few liberties myself: tuxedo, prom, broad shoulders, sandy blond hair, Yale bound.

Roni stopped writing and narrowed her eyes at me. "Yale bound?"

I shrugged.

She smacked her forehead with the heel of her hand. "Don't tell me."

"What?"

"Should I add the name Eric Strang?"

"How did you know?"

"How many people in this school do you think are headed for Yale?"

"Two." I pictured Jeannette, her pale pink cashmere sweater (which cost more than my state-school tuition) tied around her shoulders as she strolled arm in arm with Eric across the Ivy League quad.

"Not you too," Roni said.

"Wait. What do you mean 'not me too'? Do *you* like Eric Strang?"

"Eeew! Gross!"

"Are we talking about the same Eric Strang? Because there is nothing gross about the Eric I'm talking about. In fact, he's the perfect *amour*."

She shook her head. "Not for me he isn't."

"Why not?"

"Bailey, Eric Strang is my brother."

"Your what?" I must have shouted because Madame Jones shot me a dirty look.

Roni fingered her necklace, which resembled a human molar on a leather strap. "Haven't you noticed the family resemblance?"

I took in her thin, almost emaciated build, the straight black hair, the . . . well, the goth. "Not exactly."

She dug into a black leather bag and came out with a driver's license that she stuck in my face. It was her picture, with the name Ronisetta Strang.

"Ronisetta?" I repeated.

She whisked the license away. "Don't ever call me that, or I'll rip your heart out."

"Fair enough."

I'd never thought about Eric having siblings. Or Roni. Maybe only children assume everyone is sibling-free unless proven otherwise.

Once her license was safely returned to her bag, Roni sighed. "I can't believe you have a thing for Eric. Got to say I'm disappointed in you."

"Why? What's wrong with your brother?"

"Nothing. Eric's perfect." There was zero sarcasm in her voice.

"Yeah? I mean, he looks perfect. He seems perfect."

"And what you see is what you get. My brother looks perfect because he is perfect." Roni said this with the emotion of a bored weatherperson.

"So why are you disappointed in me for liking Eric? From afar, of course."

She shrugged.

"Oh, I get it. Now I'm like every hopeless girl in this school. We all have crushes on Eric, but he's already got a girlfriend who's as perfect as he is."

Roni frowned. "Eric has a girlfriend?"

"Man, you guys really aren't close, huh? I figured he and Jeannette have been together since the beginning of time."

Roni laughed.

"What?"

"Eric and Jeannette *have* been together since the beginning of time, all right, since before they were born. Our mothers are best friends. We were country club kids."

"Ah." I'd always thought it would be romantic to have a childhood romance last through all eternity. "No wonder they're so close."

"Close, yes. *Amour, non.*"

I wheeled on Roni. "Wait a minute. Are you telling me—?"

"They're just friends, Bailey."

Just friends? Never had those clichéd words sound so fresh, so wonderful, so filled with possibility.

"*Trois minutes!*" Madame Jones announced, warning us that our time was just about up.

Roni turned back to our list and wrote a dozen terms, doubling our *amour* vocab list.

The good students discussed *amour*. The bell rang. The room emptied. And still I sat amazed, flabbergasted, astounded . . .

. . . and hopeful.

4

I was waiting for Roni the second school let out. "There she is!"

"She's traveling in a coven," Amber observed. "I'll wait for you in Harper."

"Roni!" I shouted, racing up to her. The black-clad pack of goths tightened around her. "Roni, I have to talk to you."

The pack turned to Roni. "Go on," she told them. "I'll catch up."

Reluctantly, they shuffled off, shooting surly glances back at us. Me.

"Make it fast, *mademoiselle*," Roni warned.

"I just need to ask you something."

"I'm betting it's not about French verbs. Okay. Five minutes."

"You promise that your brother and Jeannette aren't . . . aren't . . . ?"

"They're not. Eric doesn't think of her like that. Four minutes."

She was making it hard to think. People stormed past us as we held our ground on the step, pebbles in a rushing river. "So does he have another girlfriend?" I held my breath.

"No."

Yes! "Does he date?"

"Sometimes." She checked her watch. "Three minutes."

"Okay, okay, okay." My mind was spinning. Jeannette may not have been Eric's girlfriend, but she was still a problem. How could I get to know him—okay, flirt with him—with her around? "Are they always together?"

"Eric and Jeannette?"

No. Dracula and his bride. "Yeah. Doesn't Eric go anywhere without his friend who is a girl but not his girlfriend?"

She raised her eyebrows. I didn't think she was going to answer, and then she did. "Golfing. Jeannette hates golf."

"That's great! When does he golf? Where?"

She shouted to the goth pack, "There in a minute!" Then she turned back to me. "Every Sunday afternoon. Riverbend Country Club. With Eric Senior."

"Your dad?" My balloon burst. My bubble popped. "That doesn't help. Does he always golf with your dad?"

"Sometimes they pick up two more old guys and do eighteen holes." She tapped her wrist, and only then did I realize she wasn't wearing a watch. "Time's up."

Defeated, I watched Roni descend the steps into a pool of black. They moved off as one, but she turned back to me. "Saturday mornings. The driving range. Just him." She left, swallowed into the sea of black before I could offer her half my kingdom, my firstborn child, and my undying gratitude.

Saturday morning I was at the driving range forty minutes before it opened. Amber had refused to come with me on the flimsy grounds that she opposed the lifestyle of the rich and famous and upwardly mobile. Plus, she had to work for her dad on Saturdays.

I bought my bucket of balls and got first pick of the tee-box thingies. By the time I'd finished my first bucket, about half of the spots had filled up. I was the only girl and the only person under thirty. I had to lie to three people and tell them the tee next to me was already taken. With any luck, it would be—by Eric Strang.

I hit another basket of balls. And another. The sun grew hotter, and I was afraid I'd be sweaty by the time Eric got there, but I kept hitting little white balls. In fact, I was getting pretty decent at it. Stroke for stroke, I was crushing the middle-aged guy two tees over.

"Bailey?"

I looked up to see Eric Strang in all his gorgeousness. He put down his bucket of balls and set one up on his tee. "I've never seen you here before."

"Me either." I let that one hang in the air between us.

He lined up to take a shot, so I forced myself to look away and set up my own ball. I hit a few, without trying my best. Then I watched him. When his bucket of balls was empty, I said the line I'd rehearsed: "You have a great swing."

He smiled at me, a nice, friendly smile. I wanted to be so much more than friends.

"I'm really off my swing today," I said. "You want my golf balls? I'm wasting them."

"That bad?" He leaned on his club and watched me. "Hit a couple. I'll see if I can help."

"Okay." But the thought of being watched by Eric Strang made breathing nearly impossible. "Don't say I didn't warn you." I hit three balls without trying to make them good. What if he couldn't hit as far as I could? Femme fatale and all that. When I finished the fourth crummy hit, I turned to him. "I'm not usually this bad."

"I know," he admitted. "I saw you hit earlier."

"You did?"

He nodded. "Before I came out."

"Ah," said I on the outside. *You were watching me!* said I on the inside.

Eric took his club and lined it over his tee. "It's all a matter of leverage when you're driving. You get that by the lag, or the angle created by the club and your hand. See? The longer you keep the angle, the more energy you can release in the impact zone, so you get the maximum club head speed."

"Sorry. I don't speak golf."

He laughed—a nice, controlled laugh. "All right. Think of the golf club as a whip. You whip the ball and follow through." He did exactly that, then put down his club and walked over to me. "I'll show you."

I picked up my driver, and he put a ball on my tee. I took my stance in front of the ball and tried not to sweat as he walked up behind me, reached around, and placed his hands over mine. Instantly, I felt a deep attraction to him. We definitely had chemistry—at least, I did.

"Remember, just think of the club as part of your hand. Relax." He said this while squeezing his arms around me, resting his chin on my head, and gripping my hands. Not the ideal conditions for relaxation.

We hit three balls like that. Finally, my palms were so sweaty I couldn't grip. I let go of the club. When I turned, my face was inches from his. Greenish blue eyes, strong jaw, perfect nose. This was a face I could stare into for the rest of my life.

5

For two angst-ridden weeks, Eric and I saw each other every day in writing class, where I had perfect attendance. He even started saving me a seat next to him. Amber didn't mind. He was always friendly to both of us. So was Jeannette. I'd almost given up on getting out of the "friend" category when he finally called and asked me out.

"It's just a movie," Amber reminded me as I tried and rejected everything in my closet.

"No. It's a movie with Eric Strang." I held up a black tank top. "What about this with those jeans?" I pointed to the hip-huggers on my bed.

"Great, if you're trying to say, 'I'm slutty enough to sleep with you on the first date.'"

"Amber!"

"Okay. But Eric Strang has class . . . and, I must admit, a kind of magnetism." This was high praise coming from Amber. She dove into the pile of clothes covering my bed and came out with black Capris, a funky tank, and a green blouse that tied everything together.

"See, this is why you're my best friend," I told her.

Eric arrived exactly on time and rang the doorbell. The dogs barked like crazy. I hadn't finished my makeup, so I sent Amber. Mom had already gone with Sarah Jean to see her son, Rudy, in his school program.

I hurried, which made me get eyeliner on my cheek. By the time I got it off, Eric was already getting the tour of our eclectic collections. I was painfully aware of how crowded the room was. Eric was no doubt used to the palatial rooms in Riverbend, the exclusive community in East Freemont. "Hi, Eric. Sorry I'm late."

"No problem. We've got plenty of time. You look great, by the way."

"Thanks." He looked a hundred times greater than I did.

"I've been showing him Big D's war collection," Amber said.

"*Why?*" I mouthed to her behind Eric's back.

"*He's a guy,*" she mouthed back. "*They love war.*"

"This is real Depression glass," Eric said, staring into Mom's cabinet. "My mother loves this stuff."

"Really?" Who knew? Mom got hers at garage sales. I had a feeling that's not where Mrs. Strang got hers.

"One question," Eric said. "Why does your mom collect Goofy?"

Amber laughed.

"Did I say something wrong?" Eric asked quickly. "I mean, she obviously has great taste. There are some fantastic antiques here. Great Hummels. She has two Fabergé eggs and some great Murano glass. I just don't get all the statues of Goofy."

"You think this is something?" Amber said. "You ought to see Bailey's bedroom."

"I confess. The Goofys are mine." I could confess it, but I couldn't explain it. I'm not sure I knew myself why I kept collecting Goofy.

Eric put his arm around me and moved us to the door. "It's an interesting hobby," he said. "Just promise me you won't major in interior design."

"Promise," I vowed, feeling as if I'd promise him anything and happily keep the promise until death did us part.

Eric gave me a choice of three movies we could make easily. Amber and I had seen the feel-good movie, and I would have loved to see it again. But I had a feeling Eric wanted to see the foreign film.

"Let's see that Russian one," I suggested.

"The Czech film? You like foreign films?"

I started to lie and say that I did. Then I remembered Mitch and Lubinski and where faking had gotten me. "To tell you the truth, I've seen exactly one foreign film in my whole life, and I had no idea what it was about."

"Well then, pick one of the others, Bailey."

I shook my head. "Uh-uh. I really want to see the foreign one. I want to learn to like it." And that was the truth. I wanted to learn to appreciate all the things Eric appreciated. I even wanted to learn about Hummels and Murano glass, things I'd always made fun of until Eric admired them.

"Are you sure?" A passing car's headlights flashed across his face, and the image made me want to throw my arms around him.

"Totally sure."

Three hours later, Eric and I sat at a little table at a café in Riverbend, where Eric and Jeannette lived. I was bleary-eyed from trying to read the subtitles of the most boring movie I'd ever sat through. I was pretty sure this Czech film would have been boring in any language. At least the Lubinski play had been short.

"What do you want to eat?" he asked, handing me a menu. "They have great desserts here."

"Hmmm . . ." I was starving. I'd turned down popcorn in the movie because Amber said I crunched too loud. What I wanted was an entire chocolate cake with extra icing. I gazed around the café and spotted three rail-thin girls eyeing my date hungrily. I ordered an herb tea that tasted like sand and flower petals.

"You girls. You never eat. Don't know how you do it." Eric had some kind of raspberry flan. "So, what did you think of the movie?"

I couldn't tell Eric that I'd rather watch cattle being slaughtered. "I enjoyed it." And I did. I got to sit close to Eric for three hours.

"Really? That's great. There's an Italian director whose work I want you to see. We'll have to take in his films next month at the Riverbend Art Theater, okay?"

"Fantastic!" Eric Strang had just talked future with me. He'd said "we," as in Eric and *me*. I could hardly wait to tell Amber.

Eric drove me home, opened the car door for me, and walked me to the front door. Mom had defied the current energy crisis and left on enough lights to dock ships at sea. "I had fun, Bailey." He faced me, and I wished I were as tall as Amber so I could look into his eyes.

"I had a great time, too." I never wanted it to end. Except that I was starving. And I couldn't wait to talk to Amber.

"Could I kiss you good night?" His hands moved to my shoulders, which were melting. Every bone in my body felt like rubber. It was a miracle I was still standing.

"Okay." Had any guy ever come out and asked me for a kiss?

His fingers slid to the back of my neck, lifting my hair and sending tiny shivers to my toes. I closed my eyes and felt him move in. His lips brushed mine, and he kissed me. It was a good-night kiss, not a slobbery down payment promising he'd be back for more. Just a lovely, gentle kiss.

"Night, Bailey," he whispered. We separated into two distinct people again.

"Uh-huh."

I watched him drive away. My front door opened, and Mom stood there with an empty bowl of popcorn. "So? How was it?"

I gave Mom the abbreviated version while I raided the fridge. I found a half-eaten frozen cheesecake and took it, and a fork, to my room so I could eat and talk to Amber at the same time. She was up, waiting for the call. I gave a frame-by-frame description of the night.

"But you hate foreign films," Amber said when we got to that part.

"Well, yeah. Kind of." Amber's silence could be so annoying. "But I want to learn to like them. Eric isn't obsessed, not like Mitch. Eric's considerate. He would have been fine seeing a different movie."

"Then what?" she asked, after another silence.

"Then he took me to the coolest café in Riverbend." I took the last bite of frozen cheesecake and let it melt in my mouth.

"So?" Amber pressed. "You ate. He drove you home."

"*And* got out and walked all the way to my car door and opened it for me."

"Way to go, Eric," Amber commented. "And . . . ?"

"And he told me he had a great time." I knew what she was after, and I was going to make her work for it.

"Bailey, did he kiss you good night or what?" she demanded.

"He kissed me good night . . . and no *what*."

Again Amber went silent. Then she said, "Perfect."

We hung up, and I thought about what Amber had said. *Perfect*. The date *had* been perfect. Eric Strang was perfect. Now all I had to do was make him my boyfriend and get him to ask me to the prom.

6

Eric and I went out every weekend. We saw movies and football games and had dinners in real restaurants. I was starting to think Mom was right about falling in love with a rich man. There was nothing hard about it.

"Does my face look flushed?" Eric asked when he picked me up to go to a party at his friend's house.

I examined his handsome face by the car's dome light. "I don't think so." This wasn't the first time he'd asked me something like this. I'd asked Roni about it because I was afraid her brother might have some horrible disease he wasn't telling me about. I could have asked Eric, but I didn't want to pry.

Roni had laughed and said her brother thought he had every ailment he read about on the Internet, and this semester he was taking AP microbiology and studying all kinds of rare diseases. It had been a huge relief to know Eric was healthy.

Now, as I held his face in my hands and gazed into those dreamy but worried eyes, I wanted to help him stop worrying. "Want to know what Mom says about good health?" I asked cautiously.

Eric shrugged and started the car.

I kept my tone light. "Mom says good health is like buying an appliance at a garage sale. You do the best you can to make sure it's in good shape and then leave the rest to God."

"To God?" Eric asked, but it wasn't a real question. And I was already wishing I hadn't taken things in such a touchy direction.

"Funny how talking about God makes you nervous. Not *you*," I added quickly. "People in general, I mean." I had to stop talking.

Eric grinned over at me. "Perfect time for music, wouldn't you say?"

"Great idea," I agreed, relieved to see him smile again.

He found a soft-rock station on his satellite radio, and we listened to soothing music until we pulled up behind a line of cars in a long driveway. I started to get out.

"Not so fast," Eric said, his hand on my arm. He tucked a strand of my hair behind my ear, then let his fingers rest there, sending shivers all the way through me, down to my toes. He leaned in and kissed me, his lips soft but strong. And every anxious thought I'd had drifted far, far away.

Somewhere along the way, Eric Strang had become my boyfriend, and everybody knew it. His friends had become my friends. They didn't have names like Steffie and Buffy and Bunny either. Eric's friends were a lot like him—rich, polite, and nice.

As we walked toward the house, which was almost as big as Eric's, Eric held my hand, and I knew that every girl at the party would have traded her date for mine.

Fat chance.

A week before Thanksgiving break, Eric came over to help me fill out my Mizzou college application. We sat at the kitchen table, with Adam and Eve curled up under it. "I wish you hadn't waited so long to send in your application," Eric said, thumbing through the course catalog.

"Exactly," Mom chimed in. She was doing laundry, going back and forth from the laundry room and appearing at just the wrong times. "I kept telling her she needed to get that thing done. I just hope we're not too late to at least try for a scholarship."

Eric knew we didn't have money, but Mom didn't need to rub it in. There were still things Eric and I didn't talk about. The subjects simply didn't come up. Like my job. Eric knew I worked in retail, but that was about it. I wasn't sure a gas jockey fit the image of Eric Strang's girlfriend.

"You need to put down a major," Eric said, pencil poised.

"Um . . . interior design?" I joked.

He smiled, but didn't laugh.

"I don't know. I can't decide." Actually, I'd decided to be undecided. That way I could take different classes and see what I liked.

"But you must have a central interest, right?" asked Eric the Focused Boyfriend.

Mom set down the laundry basket of clothes. I could see my underwear in there. "Yeah. What's your central interest, Bailey?"

Great. Now they were ganging up on me. "Well, I like my creative writing class."

Eric frowned. "And you're a good writer. But you can't make a living writing stories."

"I love dogs. I'm good with dogs." I reached down and stroked Adam and Eve. They'd come to a truce with Eric. They left him alone, and he left them alone.

"I guess you'll just have to major in dogs," said Mom the Smart Aleck. "And if that doesn't work out, you can write about it."

"Don't you have dirty clothes to pick on?" I asked.

Mom took the hint and left us alone.

Eric smiled after her, but in a nice way, not like Went had. "I like your mom."

"Me too. Most of the time."

He put down his pen. "Bailey, it's time you met *my* parents."

Amber thought it was weird that I hadn't met Eric's parents, but I hadn't thought much about it. I liked things the way they were. What if his parents hated me?

"Why don't you come with me to my grandmother's for Thanksgiving dinner?"

"Really?"

"You could meet everybody in one fell swoop. My family and my dad's brother's family from Lee's Summit meet at Grandma's every year on Thanksgiving. She lives in Overland Park, Kansas, so it's a couple hours' drive. You should come with us. Wouldn't that be great? What do you say?"

"Are you sure? She won't mind?" I couldn't believe it. Thanksgiving with my boyfriend? In Overland Park, which was about the richest city in the Midwest.

"They're going to love you, Bailey." He hugged me, and I closed my eyes and almost believed him.

I waited until Eric left before I told Mom that Eric wanted me to go home with him for Thanksgiving. I was pretty sure she wouldn't be psyched about the idea. I was right.

"I guess you can go, if you really want to," she said, refolding a purple towel so she didn't have to look at me.

"We'll be back on Friday. And you and I and Eric can have our own Thanksgiving Saturday. Amber can come. We'll pretend it's the real Thanksgiving, okay?" I wasn't sure which one of us I was trying to make feel better. Mom and I had spent every Thanksgiving together since I was born.

All week I swung back and forth between excitement and dread. "What if they don't like me?" I asked Amber while we waited for writing class to start.

"Then they're all a bunch of rich stupidheads, I guess."

"This is my boyfriend's family you're talking about."

"Then what are you so worried about?"

"Who's worried about what?" Jeannette asked, sliding into her seat. She was wearing a straight wool skirt, a cream-colored blouse, and a pink sweater tied around her shoulders.

I panicked, just looking at Jeannette. "What will I wear?"

Amber groaned.

Jeannette wrinkled her classically high forehead. "What will you wear? When?"

"Thanksgiving! Eric's invited me to his grandmother's. I'm going to be meeting his parents and his whole family. And I have no idea what to wear."

"You're going to Overland Park for Thanksgiving?" she asked.

I nodded. "Have you met Eric's grandmother?"

Jeannette smiled. "She's sweet, Bailey. You'll like her."

"I'm not worried about me liking *her*. Seriously, Jeannette, what should I wear? I don't have anything that looks like . . . like that." I pointed to her skirt. "Sophisticated."

"I'm sure anything you wear will be fine. But if you want, you can come shopping with me. I'm going by the mall after school today. I need shoes."

"You're kidding! That would be great." She'd know exactly the right thing to wear to Eric's Thanksgiving. I couldn't believe she'd do this for me.

Eric arrived just as the bell rang. "What would be great?" he asked, coming in on the tail end of our conversation.

"Jeannette," I answered.

———

Amber bowed out of the shopping trip, so Jeannette and I set out for the mall in her BMW. I sank into the plush leather seat and wished we had farther to drive than across town. Her car matched her blouse. Maybe she had a car for every outfit.

We parked by Saks, only the most expensive store in this most expensive mall, where Mom and I had never done anything but window-shop. Jeannette weaved through the store like it was her second home. "Saks is pricey," she warned, "but they're having their semiannual sale. What are you looking for?"

"Something like you're wearing."

"Good idea. Keep it simple. A skirt. A couple of blouses."

We split up. Every price tag I looked at was in the healthy three digits.

Jeannette came running up with three skirts on her arm. "Bailey, you're not going to believe this! My skirt in three colors. And they're on sale!"

"On sale? Really?" Maybe there was hope for me yet.

"Twenty percent off! Try them on. I'll look for blouses."

I didn't look at the price tag until I was in the dressing room. I couldn't have afforded this skirt if it had been 80 percent off. But I tried it in navy, and it looked great. Maybe it was the fabric or the tiny tucks in all the right places. But it made me look thin, stylish, sophisticated. I had to have it.

Jeannette knocked on the changing room door. "Here. Try these." She handed me two silk blouses. One was as expensive as the skirt.

I tried them on and wanted them both, but I couldn't do that. I settled for one blouse and the skirt and the hope that something in my closet would work for a second outfit. I couldn't begin to pay for them from my checking account, so I did what I had to do. I slapped the whole lot onto Mom's credit card. She'd have to understand.

7

"You what?" Mom shouted.

"I didn't have a choice, Mom." I'd told her straight off what I'd done, charging her card. The honesty should have counted for something, but she was fired up. Adam and Eve took off to my bedroom to hide.

"That card is for emergencies only, Bailey. You know that."

"This *was* an emergency! Have I ever used that card when it wasn't one?"

That slowed her pacing down a step. "Not until today."

"Then you have to believe me. This felt like an emergency. I'm going to meet Eric's family, and I didn't have anything I could wear that wouldn't make me feel like I had no business being with Eric Strang."

"But an emergency is when your car breaks down."

"I don't have a car."

"Or you're kidnapped and locked in some maniac's trunk."

"And he takes MasterCard?"

I think that one made her grin. "This isn't like you, Bailey."

"I'm sorry, Mom. I'll pay you back."

"You bet you will. And before that bill comes."

"I'll work at Grady's every spare minute. I promise."

She nodded, and I sensed the worst was over. It was all systems go. I was on my way to meet my boyfriend's family.

———

Eric picked me up Wednesday morning so we could leave right after school let out. Amber was already at her locker when I walked up in my new skirt. "So?"

Amber shut her locker and eyed my outfit. "Very classy and sophisticated," she said without much enthusiasm.

"But—?" I knew her well enough to know there was a "but."

"It's just not you."

That hurt. "So my skirt's sophisticated and classy, but I'm not? Thanks. "

"Don't be that way."

"Well, you're wrong. Eric loves me in it. And in case you haven't noticed lately, this skirt *is* me."

Eric, Roni, and I set out for Overland Park before lunch, since classes would be dismissed at one o'clock anyway. Roni took the backseat, and Eric opened my door for me. Soon as he went around to his side, Roni leaned forward and said, "I still can't believe you're going to Gram's with us for Thanksgiving."

"Why not?" I snapped.

"Because *you* don't have to go."

We hadn't gotten more than twenty miles out when I spotted a dead animal on the side of the road. "Stop!" I shouted.

Eric punched the brakes. "What's wrong?"

"Dead animal. I think it's a coon, but it could be a cat!"

He sped back up. "You're kidding. You wanted to stop for that? *I* didn't hit it."

I stared out the back window. That animal would be there for weeks, months.

"You were serious, weren't you?" Roni said.

I nodded. I'd always made fun of Mom for stopping and burying roadkill, but I couldn't imagine *not* doing it.

Roni grinned. "I like that. There's still hope for you, Bailey."

The closer we got to the state line, the more nervous I became. "Your mother is going to hate me, isn't she?" I asked Eric as we entered Overland Park city limits.

He reached over and squeezed my knee. "She'll love you, Bailey. Everybody loves you." He was quiet, and I think we were all evaluating the truth of that lie.

Grandmother Strang's sprawling stone mansion loomed at the end of a long cobblestoned drive, lined with trees. Flowers still bloomed in artful shapes in front of the house. No butler opened the front door, at least. But the entry was straight out of a Disney princess movie. "Anybody home?" Eric shouted.

A thin woman in a white blouse and wide-legged, silky black pants rushed up to Eric. I shouldn't say "rushed," because she appeared to float or glide. She was beautiful—maybe fifty years old, but could have passed for thirty-five or forty, with extraordinarily large breasts, a perfect bod, and hair to die for.

She hugged her son. "You're late. I was afraid something had happened. Your grandmother is taking a rest." She turned to me. I'm not sure what I expected—an icy glare, a turned-up nose, maybe a sneer or an outright declaration that no son of hers would be caught dead in the company of a trollop like me. But I didn't get any of that. Instead, she gave me a hug. "And you must be Bailey. We've heard a lot about you." She stepped back and took a good look at me. "I can see my son wasn't exaggerating." She smiled back at him. "Can't you picture that gorgeous hair on top of her head in that Swedish style? Like Jeannette wore hers for the Anderson wedding?" She sized me up again. "Yes. Absolutely perfect, Eric."

I should have felt relief at those words. They were much better than "Absolutely a trollop." But my neck and back got tension knots in their knots.

"Hey, Eleanor," Roni called to her mother, easing past Eric. "I'm going to check out Gram's kitchen. I'm starved."

Eleanor Strang glared after her daughter, then smiled back at me. "Come with me. You must be exhausted after that drive." She led us across the polished marble floor, under a shiny chandelier, to a winding staircase with just about the best banister for sliding I'd ever seen.

No banister sliding, I told myself. But it made me grin thinking about it. My mom would totally have slid down that banister. Eric's room was in "the west wing" near "the master bedroom," and mine was above "the sunroom" in the east wing. I felt a little like *Masterpiece Theatre* meets Rebecca of Sunnybrook Farm.

Eric took me to "the study," and we waited for his father to get off the phone. He didn't look a thing like my Eric and might have been fifteen years older than his wife.

We exchanged a few words, and he informed us that we had tickets for the opera tomorrow night. I guess he was nice enough, but I wouldn't exactly have called him warm. When we left the study, Eric shut the door so softly I barely heard it click.

"What now?" I whispered.

"What do you say we get out of here?" Eric whispered back. This was evidently a house where smart people moved quietly and whispered. No pets here either. The "Do you have a pet?" question was one of the first I'd asked my Eric. Hard to believe that I had a dogless boyfriend.

"Eric," I whispered as he led me down the stairs. "I just figured out what to get you for Christmas."

"What?"

"A dog."

Eric burst into a laugh that echoed through the foyer.

Mrs. Strang appeared. "I'm glad to see you two are having such a good time."

"We're going out," Eric said. "Maybe have dinner at that new French restaurant." He put his arm around me.

I thought I detected a twinge of disappointment on his mother's face, followed by stoic acceptance. "That sounds nice. I was thinking we might have a late dinner here, but you young people go on ahead."

"Are you sure?" I asked, not wanting one strike against me already.

She smiled so convincingly that I thought maybe I'd imagined the disappointment. "Go. I want you to see the city, Bailey. Eric, your grandmother told us that *Money* magazine just rated Overland Park as the sixth-best place to live in America."

"Wow," I said, honestly impressed.

She smiled at me. "We're hoping Eric settles in the area when he takes over the family business. But I've kept you here long enough. Go along and eat."

"Do you want to come with us?" I didn't really want her to, but it felt funny leaving her already.

"How sweet. Thank you. But I have plenty to do to keep myself occupied."

"I'll bet," I agreed, realizing that we'd be eating Thanksgiving dinner with Eric's whole family in less than twenty-four hours. "My mom would already be going crazy. Thanksgiving is about the only real meal she cooks. The rest of the year, we use the oven for storage." They laughed politely, probably thinking I was kidding. "Maybe you need me to stay and help out in the kitchen?"

Eric's arm tightened around my shoulder, and immediately I sensed I'd said something wrong.

"Didn't Eric tell you? We have reservations at Mother Strang's country club."

"It's a great club," Eric said.

I couldn't imagine having Thanksgiving dinner in a restaurant. I wondered if Eric really liked the idea.

"So you see, Bailey," Mrs. Strang said, "my greatest concern preparing the meal is how to get Ronisetta into the dress I've bought her."

"Ah," I said, because I didn't know what else to say.

Eric drove me all over the city and bought me dinner at a French restaurant on top of a fourteen-story office building. City lights glimmered. I gazed around the candlelit room, with white linen tablecloths, waitresses who couldn't help staring at my dashing boyfriend, and waiters who didn't reveal the cost of menu items because it didn't matter. And I knew for certain that my life would never be the same.

8

On Thanksgiving Day Eric and I sat at a white-linen table full of Strangs: Eric's parents; his uncle and aunt; their grown daughter, Millicent; and Grandmother Strang, who had welcomed me politely and called me Jeannette twice, maybe on purpose.

I sat between Eric and Roni, who, the apparent victor over her mother, was dressed in a slinky black dress and a pink boa. "Great outfit," I whispered to her.

She grinned and flipped her boa. "What did you do to your hair?"

I elbowed her. "Thanks, *mademoiselle*." I'd worked all morning to get my hair into a version of Mrs. Strang's on-top-of-the-head hairdo, and I hadn't done a bad job if I did say so myself. It made me look older, and I was enormously pleased when both Eric and his mother complimented the style. But I suppose I secretly sided with Roni. I liked my hair down better.

The country club was even more amazing than Eric's, twice as big, with orchids and roses everywhere. On the walls were paintings by artists I'd flunked quizzes on in art class. Live orchestra music played in the background.

The waiter—one of an army of waiters—snapped my linen napkin and placed it over my lap. I thanked him. "What a great dance floor. I love to dance." I turned to Eric. "Can we?"

"I think we should at least dine first, dear, don't you?" Mrs. Strang said.

I didn't, but I wasn't going to argue with her.

"Bailey," Eric's grandmother began, "where will you go to school in the fall?"

Eric took my hand under the table and squeezed it. "We told you, Grandmother. Bailey is going to the University of Missouri."

"A state school?" she queried.

"They have a great journalism school," Eric countered.

"And you're majoring in journalism, Bailey?" Eric's mother asked. You couldn't blame her for thinking it.

"I'm not sure," I admitted.

"Bailey is an excellent writer," declared my boyfriend, as if someone at the table had accused me of being a lousy speller with poor penmanship.

Roni cleared her throat. "Doesn't anybody want to know what *I'm* majoring in?" She waited a beat, while nobody ventured a guess. "Fashion."

I laughed. Alone.

The table broke up into separate conversations until Mr. Strang raised his voice. "Where's dinner?" He glanced around for the first waiter in sight. "You, there! We have tickets to the opera. A little service, please?"

Suddenly I felt homesick. I missed Adam and Eve. And I missed Mom. I hated thinking of her alone on the real Thanksgiving. "Will you all excuse me for a minute?"

I got up, and so did all the men at the table.

In the ladies' room, I fished out my cell and dialed Mom. Nobody answered. I let it ring and ring and imagined Adam and Eve barking at the phone. I tried Mom's cell. Voice mail clicked on immediately. I stumbled through a message about having a great time and wishing she were here.

I hit Amber's number next. Her cell must have been off, so I texted her and then dialed her home number. Amber's mother answered on the second ring. "Yel-low." Her hellos had always sounded like the color yellow. I loved that. Amber's parents were older than our friends' parents. Amber had been a surprise.

"Hey. This is Bailey. Am I disturbing your Thanksgiving dinner?"

"Bailey! We're just getting to the pumpkin pie. Want me to put your mother on?"

"Mom's there?"

"She's reaching for the phone right now. Happy Thanksgiving, honey."

There was a scuffling sound. Then Mom got on. "Bailey? How did you track me down? Amber only talked me into coming over here at the last minute. How are you? Are they being nice to you?"

"Hi, Mom. I didn't track you. I called home and you weren't there, so I was calling Amber. I'm okay. I'm at a country club. And yes. They're nice."

"Guess what! Amber's mom promised to help me make stuffing for our Thanksgiving dinner. So we'll have real food. How 'bout that?"

We talked a little while. Then I wished Amber a Happy Thanksgiving. Finally, I knew I had to go.

I repinned my hair and walked back to the table, prepared to apologize for being gone so long. But nobody said anything to me. I don't think they noticed I was gone. Everybody had drinks and funny-shaped hors d'oeuvres on their plates.

Eric seated me, but he was deep in conversation with his mother. "It really sounds like frozen shoulder, except I have full range of motion. I was thinking it might be coccidioidomycosis. Remember? I told you about that. Except it comes from spores in the desert, and I haven't been to Palm Springs since that golfing thing last year with Dad." He rubbed his shoulder.

Secretly, I wanted Eric to drop microbiology. I hated seeing him worry so much when he didn't have to. Amber said teens who worry too much about their health could become full-fledged hypochondriacs and suffer their whole lives. "Maybe you just slept on it funny," I suggested, patting Eric's shoulder.

Roni laughed, spraying a mouthful of whatever she was drinking.

"Oh, Ronisetta," her mother said, not hiding her disgust with her daughter. "Are you ever going to grow up?"

Roni stood up. "Not here." She recovered her boa from the floor. "I'll take a taxi back to Gram's. You can give my opera ticket to a grown-up." She turned to me and smiled. "Happy Thanksgiving, Bailey."

Nobody said a word about Roni or her exit after she was gone. I felt awful for her. I wanted to run after her, but I didn't know what I would have said.

Conversation picked up where it had left off, and I couldn't stand it. "Eric?" I said, interrupting him as he was explaining health.com's top three viruses for the holiday season. "Do you think Roni's okay?"

He squeezed my hand. "Roni can take care of herself."

He was right. But I still wished she hadn't left.

The meal was fantastic, roast duckling and salmon. There wasn't any turkey, but it was a great dinner. "Can we dance now?" I begged Eric. "Do they ever play anything faster?"

He laughed, took my hand, and led me to the dance floor. I couldn't wait to be in his arms—all legal and everything, even with the whole Strang clan looking on. I loved slow dancing with the right guy, and Eric was definitely the right guy. We were the first couple on the dance floor, but two older couples followed suit. I put my arms around Eric's neck and snuggled in close.

"This is a waltz," Eric said, taking my hands and placing one around his waist and one out to the side. Every other guy I'd slow danced with had pretty much just held me and rocked back and forth.

"I don't know how to waltz, Eric."

"Just follow my lead."

I tried. He counted for me: "One, two, three. One, two, three." I managed to keep up with him and not fall down. And I think I got better by the end of the song—Eric said I did. But neither of us wanted to try it again. I promised myself I would learn to waltz with the best of them.

That night we went to the opera, and I pretended to like it, even though it was all I could do to stay awake.

Friday I woke up before dawn, showered, dressed, packed, and tiptoed down the hall to tap on Eric's door. He squinted out, his hair a mess, one side of his face wrinkly from sleep. I'd never been more attracted to him. I leaned in and kissed his sleepy head. He felt cuddly. "Happy Thanksgiving," I whispered.

Eric and I got a late start for Millet because his mother insisted we wait and have breakfast with Grandmother Strang, who chose to sleep in. I thought about inviting Roni to come home with us, but she hadn't come out of her room, and Eric said not to disturb her.

It was almost noon by the time Eric and I headed out for Millet.

When we got close, I directed Eric onto the old highway so we'd go past the town instead of fast-food row off the Interstate. "I'll bet you've never even seen the old town of Millet, have you?"

"I've driven by it."

"That's where I went to school!" I shouted, rolling down the window and pointing. A black dog was lifting his leg to a tree out front, and I couldn't help remembering little Adam the first day I saw him. And Went. "I think I fell in love for the first time right there." I felt so close to Eric. I wanted to tell him about Went, to share with him all I'd learned about love since then. Eric and I hadn't said the words yet, but I knew in my heart we loved each other.

Eric stared straight ahead. "So, have you heard back from Mizzou yet?"

"Man, talk about changing the subject."

He smiled over at me. "Sorry. I'd just rather talk about college than junior high or middle school, okay?"

"Eric, are you jealous of my first love? Because it was a long time ago and—"

"Don't be silly. It just doesn't matter now. Why go there? I'm sure you don't want me to bore you with stories about my old girlfriends, right?"

"I guess." He was right about my not wanting to hear about his exes, but it wasn't because I'd be bored.

"You and I, we're all about the future, Bailey." He reached over and squeezed my knee.

We passed the corner where Went and I had our first kiss. Then we turned onto Ukulele Lane.

Eve came running out at the car, barking. "Eve!" I shouted, remembering when I'd spotted the spotted dog for the first time and mistaken her for the firehouse Dotty. An image of Mitch sprang to mind. It wasn't that I needed to tell Eric the juicy details of my past. But not being able to tell him anything made my throat burn. I was afraid I was going to cry. Maybe the pressure of meeting his parents, of not being home on Thanksgiving—all of it had finally hit me. I was just tired.

Eric was probably right. Being part of his future, *our* future, was really all that mattered.

9

It was still daylight, but Mom had every light in the house on, plus all the outside Christmas lights—red, green, blue, and orange. "Just pull into the driveway," I told Eric.

"I won't be blocking the garage?" He turned in, but kept the motor running.

"We never park in our garage," I explained, fumbling with my seat belt. I couldn't wait to see Mom and the dogs.

Eric followed me at snail's speed while I ran inside, with Eve barking at my heels. "Mom! We're here!"

Mom came running out in her jeans and Missouri Tigers sweatshirt. She screamed and threw up her arms. I screamed and threw up mine, as if I'd been gone two years instead of two nights. We hugged and danced and yelled, "Happy Thanksgiving!" Adam and Eve galloped around the living room, barking and vying for my attention.

"How are my babies? I've missed you!" I dropped to the ground and let them pounce on me. Then I remembered Eric. He was still standing in the doorway. "Sorry! Kind of got carried away."

Mom walked over and gave my boyfriend a giant hug. "Happy Thanksgiving, Eric. I'm so glad you guys made it."

"Sorry we couldn't really be here on Thanksgiving," Eric said.

"Why, whatever are you talking about, Eric?" Mom shrugged at me. "This is a silly, silly man you've brought home with you for Thanksgiving dinner, Bailey Daley. Didn't you tell him that time is relative?"

I could barely speak because I was still dodging licks from Adam and Eve. "Time is relative, Eric."

We ordered pizza for dinner because Mom and I couldn't imagine our oven being responsible for meals two days in a row. The three of us sat in the kitchen to wait for the pizza man.

"Might as well get started on tomorrow's meal," Mom said. She walked to the fridge and pulled out a giant plastic-wrapped turkey.

I couldn't believe the size of that bird. "Wow, Mom! How much does that thing weigh?"

Mom grunted as she slid the monster fowl into the sink and tried to read its tag. "Um . . . I think he weighs twenty-six pounds, four ounces."

"Twenty-six pounds?" Eric asked. "Who else is coming for dinner tomorrow?"

"Just Amber, far as I know," Mom said.

"But—?"

"Mom always cooks a giant turkey and then gives most of it away to shut-ins and the homeless," I explained.

"Why are you taking it out now?" Eric asked. "Is that safe?"

Mom pointed her wooden spoon at Eric. "You are a smart young man. You may date my daughter." She turned back to the turkey. "I'm cooking Tom overnight."

"That's how Mom always does it," I added.

"And—not to worry—I set the oven thingy high enough so we don't all die of salmonella disease," Mom explained, "but low enough so I won't burn down the house."

"That's reassuring," Eric said, not sounding all that reassured.

"Mom, don't joke about a thing like that. It's not funny."

Mom looked stunned. "I'm sorry," she said, her voice a mix of surprise and confusion.

I hadn't meant to sound like I was scolding her, but I didn't want Eric to worry.

Mom had the bird in the oven before the pizza guy got there. We devoured the pizza in short order and played a few rounds of three-handed poker. Eric lost every game.

"Good move bringing a guy who's such easy pickin's at the poker table, Bailey," Mom said, raking in a pile of poker chips. We only played for chips, no money.

"Well," Eric said, joking back with her as he got up from the table, "you card sharks can play all night. As for me, I'm cashing in my chips and hittin' the hay."

"I thought you said this fella had culture, young'un," Mom said.

"You know the only real culture comes from . . ." I began.

"Bacteria!" Mom and I said together. It was an old, old joke, but we were always there together at the punch line. Then I wished we hadn't been. All Eric needed was another reminder about bacteria.

Eric went to bed in my old room, and I bunked in with Mom. We stayed up most of the night talking and laughing, then shushing each other so we wouldn't wake poor Eric. The dogs loved it. We let them try to sleep with us in our bed. I couldn't remember the last time I'd bunked in with Mom. Probably when I was little and scared of storms.

In the morning I made myself get up early with Mom to check on Tom. The whole house smelled glorious, like only Thanksgiving morning can. It took both of us to lift the roaster out of the oven, fighting off Adam and Eve, who must have been going crazy from the aroma of real food. They scratched at my legs and whimpered.

"No way this bird is under thirty pounds," I declared as we struggled to set the pan on the counter.

Eric came out to the kitchen, wearing cotton pajamas that looked like he'd ironed them. Mom and I had sweats and T-shirts. He yawned, and again his hair was all messy, and he had that sleep wrinkle on one side of his face. He looked so cute I had to go over and kiss him. "Morning, you."

He hugged me and kissed me again. "Morning, you. How's our friend Tom?"

"He got a little sick overnight," Mom called from the roasting pan. "Something about salmonella. He seems okay now, though."

"Not funny, Mom," I scolded, for real this time.

"She's just kidding. You know that," I whispered to Eric. I led him to the table and poured him a glass of juice. I imagined doing this every day of our lives, pouring my husband a glass of orange juice and getting a big morning hug and kiss.

Slow down, I told myself. *He hasn't even asked you to the prom.*

We hadn't slept together either—not that we hadn't wanted to. We'd get to that point where I felt I could get carried away. Then I'd stop us, or Eric would. We never talked about it, but I think we had an understanding. And anyway, Eric wasn't like other guys I'd dated. He had the money to take me to concerts and movies and things. So we had less car make-out time. The few parties we'd been to weren't the hang-out-and-make-out kind. Eric's friends were too classy for that.

"Tom smells good," Eric said bravely. "What time is dinner?"

"Whenever we get the food ready." I got out a stick of butter and ran it over the bird's back. "This is one of my very few kitchen skills."

———

Eric dressed up for our Thanksgiving dinner like he had for his family's. Since I didn't want him to feel overdressed, I dressed nice too, for me—slinky black pants and my new blouse. And I wore my hair up because Eric had loved it when I wore it up for the country club dinner.

"What's with the hair?" Amber asked, appearing in the kitchen in jeans and a Mizzou sweatshirt she'd picked up last summer.

"And Happy Thanksgiving to you too, Amber," I returned.

"That too," she agreed, still staring at my lofty hairdo.

Mom had all she could handle remembering to take side dishes—most of them ready-made—from the microwave.

"Love the dishes," Amber said, shaking out the jellied cranberries from the can onto a little plate with a turkey in the center. Mom had a whole set of turkey tableware she'd won in a contest.

"Where'd you get the centerpiece?" I asked. The ceramic turkey, occupying a square foot of space on the table, was pretty hard to miss.

"Garage sale," Mom answered.

We sat at the table, and Mom had us hold hands. I remembered so many Thanksgivings when Mom and I were the only two people at the table. We'd sat across from each other and held hands like this anyway. It wasn't that nobody had invited the single mom and daughter for Thanksgiving dinner. We'd wanted to have it ourselves. Sometimes we'd invite people we figured didn't have anywhere to go, like Old Ollie, who came in his farm overalls. Or Mrs. Jannis, the old maid third-grade teacher who hated me, and the feeling was mutual.

"We have a lot to be thankful for this year," Mom began, squeezing my hand.

I squeezed Eric's hand and smiled up at him. He looked like that deer in the headlights everybody talks about. Then I realized that his family hadn't said grace before meals. Now that I thought about it, their table conversation veered clear of anything controversial—no politics, no religion. And here we were, holding hands and ready to talk, not just about God, but to God. I wished I could have read Eric's mind. Or maybe not . . .

"Let's tell God and each other thanks for all the blessings this Thanksgiving. I'll start." Mom listed all of us by name, Amber's family, our dogs, her new job, Eric's family, her friend Sarah Jean, and the family of robins that had nested on our ledge.

Amber named a lot of the same people Mom had and added Travis—he'd stayed in touch from Mizzou—plus her job as editor of *Tri-County Rag,* our school paper.

I gave thanks for Eric and Mom and Amber, for Adam and Eve, for Eric's family, and for our senior year.

When it was Eric's turn, he cleared his throat. "Thank you for the blessings which you have bestowed and this meal you have put before us, along with the hands that prepared it."

It was a typical Daley Thanksgiving dinner, with Mom popping up every two minutes because she'd left potatoes, or beans, or gravy in the microwave. Or I'd get up and grab the butter out of the fridge or let the dogs out. Ours was a noisy feast. I hoped it wasn't too much for Eric.

At one point I caught Eric staring at my mother as she assembled her "Thanksgiving sandwich" without missing a beat in her conversation with Amber on freedom of the press versus investigative reporting of the school superintendent's DUI.

I felt I needed to explain Mom's sandwich. "Mom hates turkey."

"You're kidding?" Eric frowned as Mom took a big bite of her unique sandwich. "Then why—?"

"She says it just wouldn't be Thanksgiving if she didn't eat turkey," I explained. "So she puts the whole dinner between two dinner rolls—turkey, a heap of stuffing, potatoes, gravy, beans, a little cranberry sauce. And voilà! A Thanksgiving sandwich. And *that* she loves."

There wasn't a second of silence at the table during the whole meal or the hour after we finished the last bite of pumpkin pie and still sat around the table, laughing. We covered every subject from politics to Millet gossip to things Adam and Eve had done, like breaking into the neighbor's house and kidnapping their cat's rubber mouse.

I'm not sure when I noticed Eric wasn't talking. He was leaning back in his chair and holding his stomach. "Eric, are you okay?"

"I'm not sure." He put a hand to his forehead. "See if you think I have a fever."

I did what he asked. "Feels fine to me, sweetie."

"You're holding your stomach. Do you have a stomachache?" asked my mom the worrier.

"Sort of," he said, rubbing his stomach. "Abdominal pain. Or at least the beginning of it. I definitely feel gurgling."

"Gurgling?" Amber repeated.

Eric nodded, still frowning. "Peristalsis."

Amber sighed. "Eric, were you on your computer this morning?"

"What?" Eric asked.

"Amber," I warned, knowing where she was going with this. She'd heard Eric talk about his ailments at school after microbiology class a couple of times. Couldn't she just leave it alone?

"On the Internet?" Amber pressed.

"I was looking up a few things," he said to me, as if I'd asked the question.

"Like salmonella, for example?" Amber guessed.

"Salmonella?" Mom sounded horrified. "You think our turkey gave you salmonella?"

"No he doesn't," I said, trying to lighten the situation, while shooting Amber a shut-up glare.

"I've never heard of anyone cooking a turkey all night, so I thought I'd check it out," Eric admitted.

"I knew it," Amber said, letting out a little laugh that made me redouble my glare.

"It's not all that funny, Amber," Eric said. "Salmonella is the second most common intestinal infection. Fourteen in one hundred thousand people are stricken by it every year, and it's underreported. Only three percent of the cases are ever reported to a doctor." He didn't sound angry. I'd never seen Eric angry. It was more like he was lecturing a small child.

I knew from experience that Amber didn't like lectures.

"Eric," Amber began slowly, "you don't have salmonella. You have a bad case of cyber-chondria."

"What?" Eric demanded.

"People who Google diseases on the Internet can get cyber-chondria," Amber said. "Like hypochondria, only in cyber-space."

I started to laugh, then swallowed it. The last thing I wanted to do was laugh at my boyfriend. "Amber," I said, standing up and grabbing dishes, "help me clear the table."

Eric still seemed as good-natured as ever. He got up from

the table, but he didn't look at me. "Thank you for the lovely meal, Mrs. Daley. Let me help with dishes."

"No way," Mom said. "Maybe you should lie down for a while."

"Yeah, Eric," I said, eager to be sympathetic.

Still, he didn't even glance my way.

"If you're sure you don't need me," he told Mom, "I think I will lie down a bit. Thanks."

He was saying the right things, but it still felt like the closest Eric and I had been to a fight. I was a lousy girlfriend.

The rest of the afternoon Eric slept while Amber, Mom, and I cleaned up a million dishes and delivered turkey to the homeless shelter. We didn't mention Eric, but I agonized inside. I'd wanted him to have a great time at our Thanksgiving. I wasn't sure where things had gone wrong, but they had.

Mom dropped off Amber at her car, and she and I walked up the drive to our front door. The dogs were huddled together on the front step, and the house was dark.

"You poor babies," I murmured, letting them in and rubbing their cold fur. "Eric?" I called. He must have let them outside and forgotten about them.

"Eric?" I walked back to my bedroom and peeked in. He was asleep. I shut the door and joined Mom and the dogs in the living room. Eve was still shivering. I turned to Mom. "Eric didn't know they shouldn't stay outside. He probably fell asleep after he let them out."

"I know," Mom said as we both tried to get the dogs to settle down.

I figured the dogs must have scratched at my bedroom door

as soon as we'd left for the shelter. Then they would have started barking, and Eric wouldn't have been able to sleep, so he'd let them outside. "They don't have dogs," I explained, feeling like I had to defend my boyfriend.

"Believe me, I can tell," Mom muttered.

"Don't you like Eric?"

"I do, honey. I'm sure everybody likes Eric. Eric the captain of the swim team, Eric the captain of the debate team, Eric the student body president, Eric—"

"Eric my boyfriend," I reminded her. "So?"

She fiddled with Adam's collar and didn't answer for a full minute. Then she smiled up at me. "He's just not Eric the dog guy, I guess."

"He's *never* had a pet, Mom. What do you expect? In fact, I've been thinking that the only thing keeping Eric from being perfect is the fact that he's dogless."

"And a cyber-chondriac," Mom muttered. She grinned at me. "Being a dog owner *was* one of your requirements on your perfect boyfriend application, as I recall."

"True. And I'm already working on that one."

"Oh yeah?"

The idea born at Eric's Thanksgiving took root on ours. "I'm giving my boyfriend a dog for Christmas."

10

The weeks after Thanksgiving, I doubled my hours at Grady's.

"I don't understand why you're working so much," Eric complained when I had to work the second Saturday in a row. He'd called my cell just before closing, and I was crouched behind the cereal boxes to talk.

"I need the money, Eric." I had to pay down Mom's credit card, but Eric didn't need to know that one.

"But it's your senior year. *Our* senior year. Talk to your boss. He can't expect you to work Saturday nights." As far as Eric knew, I was working "retail," which to him might have meant selling jewelry. I never lied to him. He just hadn't asked specifics, and I didn't offer any.

"Bailey!" Sarah Jean hollered. "Where are you? Got a customer here buying a pack of smokes and a bottle of eyedrops. You're on, honey!"

"Gotta go," I whispered, and punched off. "Coming!" I shouted to Sarah Jean. This one was almost too easy. I pulled out my raspy, sexy Billie Holiday blues voice as I hurried up the aisle, singing, "You must realize / Smoke gets in your eyes."

"That's the ticket!" Sarah Jane said, laughing.

I knew all the lyrics because Mom must have watched Fred Astaire and Ginger Rogers dance to that song, "Smoke Gets in Your Eyes," about a hundred times in some old movie. "They asked me how I knew my true love—" I stopped singing. There, waiting impatiently at the counter for the Grady girl to ring up her purchases, was my boyfriend's mother.

"Bailey?"

"Mrs. Strang?" My orange cap never felt so heavy. I wanted to rip it off, but it was pinned on. My Grady dress felt scratchy and cheap. "Why are you here?"

She held up the eyedrops. "I . . . I'm on my way home from a Red Hat meeting."

I didn't know or care what that meant. We didn't say anything else as I rang up her pack of cigarettes and the box of eyedrops.

"Well," she said, her smile twisting and disappearing again, "have a—see you."

I watched her walk out, climb into her BMW, make sure her door was locked, then drive off.

Sarah Jane appeared beside me and put her arm around my shoulder. "What's the matter, sweetie?"

So I told her that my boyfriend didn't know I worked at Grady's, only now his mother did, and I was sure she already hated me.

"Don't you worry now," she said, wrapping me in her hug. "That woman's not going to tell anybody. Something tells me she's good at keeping secrets."

"What do you mean?"

Sarah Jean laughed and smoothed back my hair the way I'd seen her do for Rudy a thousand times. "Did *you* know she smoked?"

"She didn't light up over Thanksgiving."

"Not in front of you, anyhow. Something tells me she's not going to tell anybody she was in Grady's buying cigarettes."

I tried to hold on to Sarah Jean's assurance that Mrs. Strang wouldn't rat me out, or herself. But Monday at school I couldn't stop watching my boyfriend all during writing class to see if he'd changed toward me. But he hadn't. He acted normal. He even confided in Jeannette and me about his fear that he might have been infected with some germ when he pricked his finger in microbiology. So he obviously wasn't obsessing about Grady's Gas and Snack.

In French class, I couldn't wait to corner Roni. "Tell me the truth. Did your mother say anything about me last night or this morning?"

Roni wrinkled her nose, which had a tiny silver ring through one nostril. "You mean, like, 'Let's put a hit out on Bailey to keep her away from my son'?"

"I'm serious, Roni. I kind of ran into her last night."

"Let me guess. She went all the way to Millet to buy her cigarettes?" I guess I looked shocked because she explained, "We all know she smokes, but nobody says anything, and she never smokes in front of us. It's a Strang thing." Her eyes narrowed. "I get it. She bought her secret cigs in Grady's, right?"

"You knew I worked there?"

She nodded. "Some of my friends go there just to hear you sing."

"You're kidding. Have you been there?"

She shook her head. "I figured you didn't want us to know or you would have told us." She grinned. "It's a Strang thing."

I felt stupid. "I don't know why I haven't told Eric. I love my job, and I know there's nothing wrong with working at a gas station." I thought about it and tried to be honest with myself. "I guess I thought Eric would be disappointed in me. Do you think your mother will tell him?"

Roni shrugged.

For two days I obsessed about my Grady-girl secret. Amber had reached her listening limit. "Bailey, if you whine about this one more time, I'm telling Eric myself." We were sitting on the floor of my bedroom, Adam in my lap and Eve curled next to Amber.

"Maybe she's forgotten about it," I suggested.

Amber groaned. "That's it. I'm sure she's wiped the image of you in that cute little orange costume right out of her sophisticated, well-coiffed head."

"You're right!" I cried, feeling more desperate than ever. "Eleanor Strang would never let her son be with any girl in an orange uniform."

"Enough!" Amber grabbed a pillow and bonked me.

I figured she really had reached her crying-to limit. It was time to cry out to God.

God got right on it. I knew something had happened the next morning when Eric came running up to me at my locker. "Bailey!"

I braced myself. "What?"

"You know how I've been griping because you work so much and—?"

She'd told him. "Eric, I was going to tell you myself—"

"Well, what would you think about a job where you and I could see each other all the time, and it would be more like hanging out than working?"

"Wait a minute. You lost me."

"How'd you like to work at the Riverbend Country Club?"

"What?"

"I'll bet the pay's double what you're making now. It's a great job. I know dozens of guys on the waiting list to get in for a job there—any job. And you'd be on the social staff. You'll sign people in and help plan parties. What do you think?"

I couldn't think. I'd been sure he was going to break up with me. Instead, he was offering me a job? A really great job. "But why me? How did you pull it off?"

"It's all Mother. She had to call in a lot of favors to get you that job."

And then I understood. I could almost hear Roni whisper in my ear, "It's a Strang thing."

I knew Mom wouldn't be easy to convince, so I chose the middle of her favorite movie, *Doctor Zhivago,* to tell her about my new job.

"Do you really want to clean up after rich people every day?" she asked.

"It's not like that. They're my friends. Eric's and my friends. And anyway, I won't be a janitor." I explained it the way Eric had. "Plus, I'll make three times what I'm making at Grady's."

I could tell that one hit home. "It's your decision, Bailey. But you're the one who has to tell Sarah Jean."

I hated quitting on Sarah Jean, but she understood. She understood better than anybody, in fact. I had a feeling Amber wouldn't be so understanding, but I was wrong. She thought it sounded like a great job and even asked me to keep an eye out for an opening for her.

Only Roni voiced strong dissent. "I can't believe you'd give up your job at Grady's for that country club," she complained, after refusing to talk to me for two days.

"What exactly do you have against my new job, Roni?" I demanded. "Is it the lack of an orange uniform? The great hours? Or maybe the terrific pay?"

She sighed. "It's that you meet a much better class of people at Grady's Gas and Snack."

But Roni was wrong, and Eric was so right. I had the perfect part-time job. It didn't take long for me to pay off Mom's card, buy two new outfits and a pair of shoes, and still chuck some into my college savings account, which I thought of as my prom-dress account.

It almost took me until Christmas to convince Eric to accept the gift I wanted to give him—a dog. I think, in the end, I simply wore him down. He'd made a face like he'd just stepped in dog do-do, then resigned himself to the inevitable.

So, with only two days left before Christmas, Eric picked me up from my house, and we headed out to buy him a dog. "Where to?" he asked, turning on his windshield wipers against a light snow that had turned Millet, Missouri, into a wonderland overnight. "We haven't even talked about breeds. Are there any breeders in Millet?"

"Head for the old highway," I commanded. "We're not going to a breeder."

"Bailey, you can't always trust pet stores. They might say the breed is pure, but you never know."

"We're not going to a pet store."

"Okay, I give. Where *are* we going?"

"To the animal shelter, of course. We're going to rescue a puppy."

Eric tried to talk me out of it, but I wouldn't give in. "Don't forget—this is *my* Christmas gift to you. I get to be boss of it." I directed him to the shelter. Amber and I had been there a bunch of times. When we were about twelve, they let us walk the dogs and call ourselves volunteers.

Eric parked behind the building. "Why don't I just wait in the car?"

"No way! Dogs are members of the family. You have to help choose."

The animal shelter looked like an abandoned warehouse. But inside, it was pretty modern and smelled like bleach. A young woman at the front desk asked us to fill out papers, but all of her questions and comments were directed to my boyfriend. "You live around here?" she asked, fingering her beaded choker necklace.

"Bailey does," answered my helpful boyfriend, nodding in my direction.

She didn't give me so much as a sideways glance, which was understandable, since her gaze was riveted on Eric. "It's so wonderful of you to adopt a pet."

I shoved the adoption papers at her. "There you go. Maybe we could see those dogs now?"

The girl led us to a room packed with dogs in metal cages stacked on top of each other. At the first cage, a mangy dog limped to the front and whimpered. His tangled hair had bare spots where he'd probably been in a fight . . . and lost. But there was something about his soulful eyes.

"What about this dog, Eric?"

"You're kidding. My mother wouldn't allow that one in the house. Trust me."

It made me mad that his mom had power, even when she wasn't around. "You could keep the dog a secret." *Like your mom's smoking addiction.*

He put his arm around me and laughed. "Come on. Let's at least look at the other dogs, okay?"

We walked from cage to cage. I fell in love with every single dog, even the bulldog that growled at us. Why wouldn't he growl? There were no outside smells or sounds in this concrete echo chamber. And in a matter of days, somebody would take this dog and kill it because nobody wanted him.

Eric didn't like any of the dogs. I liked all of them. In the end, we just couldn't decide.

As we left the shelter, I tried to think positive. "Let's go look for dogs in Freemont. I've never been in their animal shelter, but it has to be pretty big."

"Tomorrow, okay? I promise." Eric grinned and opened the car door for me. "Right now, I've got a better idea."

Eric drove to Freemont, refusing to tell me what he had planned. He went straight to Riverbend and pulled into a BMW car lot. "Let's try some on for size," he said.

"Cool." Mom and I used to pretend we were car shopping. She'd let me pick any car on the lot, and then she'd ask to take it for a test-drive. We hadn't done that in years, but I was up for it.

Eric did the choosing, and I went along for the ride. I loved the new-car smell and the adventure of trying out cars with my boyfriend. Mom and I had never owned a new car. We bought our used cars from friends or out of the paper.

When we were done, I thought we'd head back. Instead, Eric motioned for the dealer. "I'll take this one."

"Eric!"

He flashed me his smile. "It's my Christmas gift and going-to-Yale present from my parents. I was pretty sure this was the model I wanted, but I thought it would be fun to try them out."

"You're actually buying this car?" I couldn't believe it. It was the coolest one we'd driven. Eric apparently shopped for a new car the way I might shop for a pair of new shoes—try it on, try it out, buy it. Even then, I never bought the shoes on the spot. I'd try on a dozen other pairs, then come back to the one I really wanted. I liked Eric's shopping style much better.

That night Eric drove me in his new BMW to a party at the

country club, sponsored by Jeannette's dad's company. We just sat around and talked and ate. I waited until I got Jeannette off by herself. "Jeannette, tell me the truth. Do you think it's a bad sign that Eric hasn't asked me to the prom yet?"

She laughed, but so softly there wasn't any sound to it. "It's so early. He probably hasn't even thought about the prom yet."

"Believe me, he's had to think about it. I bring it up every chance I get. Like, 'Look at that chandelier, Eric. That reminds me of the prom.'"

"You have nothing to worry about," Jeannette assured me. "In fact, I'd bet good money that you'll be prom king and queen."

"Get out." I'd been so focused on getting invited to my senior prom that I hadn't thought about prom court. But Jeannette had a point. Eric Strang was the most popular guy in school. Why wouldn't he be nominated for prom king? But me? No way. Our school elected couples. How could I not have thought of that? Who would vote for Queen Bailey?

No wonder Eric hadn't invited me to the prom.

11

Christmas Eve day I woke up to blaring Christmas music and Mom singing off-key from the kitchen. She was actually baking Christmas cookies (well, putting the premade, presliced circles of dough onto cookie sheets). "Merry Christmas Eve!" she shouted when I shuffled in. "Do you really have to go to Eric's today?"

"We're exchanging gifts." I'd been a little hurt that Eric and I weren't going to see each other on Christmas. Grandmother Strang was coming, and it was "just family."

"Don't forget to take him my gift, okay?" Mom had picked up a handful of books for Eric at a garage sale. "And good luck on finding the right dog this time."

I drove to Eric's so we could pick out his dog at Freemont's animal shelter and he wouldn't have to bring home his new dog in his new car. A light snow fell, but the roads were good. I sang along with radio Christmas music and tried to hold on to the Christmas spirit. Going to Eric's house always felt like the first day of school, when I knew I'd picked the wrong outfit and hairstyle.

The Strang mansion was outlined in white Christmas lights, everything tasteful and symmetrical and lovely. There wasn't a white light in the mix Mom had wound around our little house. This house didn't have a single icicle dangling from its roof. Our house had so many icicles that somebody could have mistaken it for a gingerbread house. But I knew we only had icicles because of poor insulation.

I checked the visor mirror before going in. I'd fixed my hair up again, French-braiding it, then tucking the end under and pinning. Eric's mother had complimented my hair twice when I'd worn it like this to work at the club. Both times it had given me a headache, but anything for beauty, right?

Slipping Mom's gift bag of books over one arm, I eased Roni's gift out of the backseat. I'd bought her two newts and everything they needed to live, which wasn't much. Eric had tried to talk me out of it, but I was pretty sure Roni would be psyched.

I was trying to figure out how to knock when the front door swung open and Eric rushed out. "Hey, you!" He took the packages and swept me inside. "Did the snow give you any trouble? I could have picked you up, you know."

I loved the way Eric looked out for me. "No problem. But we need to get going to the animal—"

Eric's mother glided up and gave me a stiff hug. "Merry Christmas, Bailey. Eric, where are your manners. Take your friend's coat."

His *friend*?

Eric took my coat, even though I tried to give him the signal that I wanted to go to the animal shelter *now*. "I have a surprise for you," he said.

"I do like surprises. Let me guess. Uh . . . I give up."

"Wait right here."

"I'm closing my eyes," I shouted as he left me in the foyer. I opened my eyes when I heard him come back. Eric was holding a little brown-and-white dog, its long hair tied up on top of its head with a red bow. It was some kind of exotic breed I couldn't remember the name of. "What a cute dog. Whose is it?"

"Mine, of course." Eric handed me the little dog. "Mother picked her out. You don't mind, do you? She can still be from you. I guarantee the only reason my mother bought this dog was because I told her we were picking one up from the shelter."

The poor dog shook in my arms, trembling even more when I tried to pet her.

Eric's mother stood a few feet away as if afraid of catching something. "*I* didn't select the dog. I have a friend—well, an acquaintance—from the club. She shows dogs and wins trophies and such. I asked her to select a small dog with good breeding."

"It's a Shih Tzu," Eric explained. "They don't shed. And the breeder promised that hers rarely bark—*never* if properly cared for."

I couldn't imagine a dog that didn't bark. I cupped the little dog in my arms and tried to calm her, but her eyes flitted from one of us to the other. "What's her name?"

"I have to check her papers," Eric said. "I think it's Balthazar's Imperial Belle."

"Not anymore it isn't." I stroked the little dog, trying to find a spot she liked. Finally, she turned to me when I gently scratched her stomach. Her big brown eyes begged for a friend. I felt bad about one more shelter dog not getting a home, but how could I not fall in love with this ball of fluff? "You're *my* gift to my boyfriend," I murmured. "*Surely* I can come up with a better name than the one you've got."

"What did you call her?" Eric asked.

"I just said, 'Surely I can—'" I stopped. *Shirley.* "That's it. We'll call you Shirley."

Eric laughed. "Shirley?"

"Shirley." It felt like the dog had named herself.

Poor Shirley had to stay in her kennel in the basement while the rest of us opened gifts. Adam and Eve would have barked us crazy, but she didn't whine or bark once.

Roni loved her newts and named them Curly and Moe, in honor of two of the Three Stooges. She gave me a black T-shirt that read: *Née pour danser!* "It's French for 'Born to dance!'" said Roni my interpreter.

I pulled the shirt on over my fancy blouse. "I love it!" I exclaimed, hugging her. She let me.

I felt rotten about not really having a present for Eric, thanks to his mother. So when nobody was looking, I ripped Mom's tag off her gift to Eric. "This is just something to take to college with you," I said, handing him the bag of books.

He unwrapped the aged copies of *The Old Man and the Sea,*

To Kill a Mockingbird, and *Doctor Zhivago*. "They're great, Bailey. Thanks."

Eric's parents had come out to watch the unwrapping. "How lovely!" Mrs. Strang exclaimed. "Are they first editions?"

I tried to laugh it off. "'Fraid not. Just old." I didn't know how much first editions cost, but I knew Mom had never been able to afford one.

"Ah," she said. "Well, they're very nice. I'm sure they'll come in handy."

Eric kissed me. "Thanks, Bailey. Now you." He handed me a large box wrapped in silver and gold, with a white bell for a bow.

I shook it. It felt like clothes. "It's too pretty to open."

"Go on!" Eric said. It was fun seeing him so excited about giving me a gift. If his parents hadn't been watching, I might have jumped his bones right there.

I unwrapped the package. Inside was an amazing dress. "Eric, it's beautiful!" I took it out of the box and stood up with it. The bodice, covered in pearl beading, was strapless, which I loved, and even the floor-length skirt was covered in crystal and pearl beading. It was classic and sophisticated, although I wouldn't have picked cream-colored or gone for the full skirt. "It's so elegant. I'm not sure where I'll wear it, but it's the most beautiful dress I've ever owned."

"I had help picking it out." Eric glanced at his mother. "It's supposed to be this spring's big color."

"Guaranteed," Mrs. Strang chimed in. "We can exchange if the size isn't right."

"No, it's perfect." It *would* be if I could lose ten pounds. It was a size too small.

"It's a Strang Unique," Eric said.

"You're kidding." Strang had three lines. I couldn't afford anything in the lowest end. And this was the designer end. "I don't know what to say."

"There's more," Eric said.

"More?" I dug below tissue and came out with an envelope. I opened it and read: "This card entitles you to 5 free waltz lessons. The "5" had been crossed out and "10" written above it. That was crossed out, and "15" was above that. I laughed. "I'm taking you up on this."

"Good," Eric said. "Because there's another card under there."

I reached around the box until I found one last card. I opened it. Inside, in Eric's beautiful handwriting, it said: *Bailey Daley is hereby formally invited to attend the Tri-County Senior Prom with Eric Strang.*

12

Mom and I had our traditionally great Christmas, waking at 5:00 A.M. to open presents under our lighted tree. We'd wrapped treats and balls and bones for Adam and Eve, who tore at their gifts while Mom and I went after ours. I saved a handful of treats for Shirley.

I'd gotten Mom tickets to the *Antiques Roadshow* in Kansas City, where people took their junk and experts appraised it on television. "This is the best thing you've ever given me!" she squealed, hugging the wind out of me. "I'll take those wooden angels. I'll bet they're worth a fortune! And that dish I got in the flea market last week!"

Mom outdid herself on my gifts, too. She'd picked up three

Goofy figures I didn't have. She must have been looking for them all year. Amber came over, and we exchanged gifts and ate Mom's cookies and Amber's Christmas brownies for lunch. Then the three of us, with Adam and Eve, built a Christmas snow-woman and a little snowdog.

I was having a great Christmas, but I missed Eric. We'd texted on and off all day, but I couldn't stand not seeing him on Christmas. Finally I broke down and phoned him.

"Hey, Bailey." He sounded glad to hear from me.

"Eric, I'm claiming my Christmas gift. I want my first waltz lesson."

He laughed softly. "Sounds great, honey. I just don't know if I can sneak away."

"Well, you have to. A gift is a gift."

"Good point. Be there as soon as I can."

"And Eric! Bring Shirley."

It was dark when Eric arrived, carrying Shirley out in front of him like she was a football ready to be drop-kicked.

I kissed my boyfriend and took his dog. "How's my Shirley?" I rubbed her tummy, and she licked my nose. "I missed you."

Eric took off his boots and coat. "You only met the dog yesterday, and already you're attached? What is it with you and dogs?"

I couldn't explain it. I nuzzled Shirley. She knew. "You have to sleep over here sometimes, Shirley."

"I'm not sure that's such a great idea."

"Why not?"

"You are a great influence, Bailey. But your dogs are another story."

"What's the matter with my dogs?"

"I'm sure they're great dogs. I just don't want Shirley to pick up any bad habits."

"From Adam and Eve? They don't have any bad habits."

"They bark."

"Dogs are supposed to bark."

"Not this one."

Mom came in and spotted the little dog. "Well, you must be Shirley." She took the dog out of my arms and snuggled her. Adam and Eve came running. Adam barked at the intruder, but Eve lunged at Mom, trying to get a good look at Shirley.

"Come on, guys." Mom walked away, with Adam and Eve trailing her. I heard the kitchen door open and the dogs go out.

"What did she do?" Eric asked.

We scurried to the kitchen and crowded at the storm door to watch all three dogs in the snow. Shirley stood like a statue while Adam and Eve danced around her. They sniffed every inch of the newcomer. Finally, Shirley thawed and pranced around the backyard with the other dogs. They nose-dived into the soft snow.

"She's going to get dirty out there," Eric said.

"Well, I hope so," Mom muttered.

It was a week before I could convince Eric to bring Shirley over again. We were up to waltz lesson number three. Our second lesson had been on New Year's Eve at the country club. We hadn't danced much because I was working, but Eric hung around and gave me my kiss at the stroke of midnight.

"So," Mom said, plopping down on the couch. "Waltz already. I want to see if these lessons are paying off."

"Me too," Amber said, crashing beside Mom.

I put in Mom's *Doctor Zhivago* CD and punched up "Lara's Theme"—the "Somewhere, My Love" song—and started waltzing with my boyfriend. We'd barely gotten going when Adam and Eve burst into the room, barking and chasing each other in circles. Little Shirley trotted behind Eve, silent as ever.

Eric stopped dancing and shut off the music. "Whoa. Sorry. Too many dogs for me."

"Too many dogs?" I asked. "How many is too many?"

Amber laughed.

Eric frowned. "Uh . . . apparently, three."

Mom groaned. "Bailey, no."

I nodded to Amber, and we pulled Mom off the couch. "You, sir, may take a seat in the audience," I told Eric. "This is a Three Dog Night."

He laughed, but he had no idea.

"Hit it!" I shouted.

Amber changed to the third CD slot, where we always kept our special music. "Let's get goofy!" I cried.

The music blared. Over the soundtrack, we sang out our own words: "Jeremiah was a hound dog!" I messed up some of the lyrics, but we danced our routine with perfect synchronization, if I do say so myself.

When we were done, Eric gave us a standing ovation, but with less enthusiasm than Adam and Eve and Shirley were showing us.

Amber and Mom took the unspoken hint and disappeared with the dogs to another part of the house so Eric and I could finish our dance lesson in private. After he played the part of instructor and showed me some fancy waltz moves, I decided I was tired of his version of slow dancing.

"My turn," I told him, popping in a soothing Norah Jones CD. "Now, here's the correct position." I inched as close as I could get to him and reached my arms around his neck. "Your arms fold around me like this." Eric played along. I rested my head on his chest and felt his head on mine.

"Now, none of that fancy stepping. Just lean side to side. That's the way." This was how boys in Millet danced, in a moving hug.

"How am I doing, coach?" he whispered, his hand moving up and down my spine.

"You, young man, are a quick learner." I loved being held by Eric. We moved together, pressing closer. I felt his lips, his breath, on my head, my cheek. Still wrapped in each other's arms, we kissed. I'd felt passion for Eric every time we were together. But this was something more. My heart was racing.

Eric ended the kiss, and I sensed his whole body sigh. "Bailey?"

"Mmm-hmmm?"

"I want to be sure of something."

"Anything."

He smoothed my hair and whispered, "When I'm moving like this with you . . . are we traveling around the Virgin Islands?"

I gulped. I knew exactly what he was asking. With my face buried in his chest, I nodded. I knew this would happen. It always did. It was amazing it hadn't before now.

"I thought so," he said.

I pulled away from him. "Why? Why did you think so? It's not like I haven't had boyfriends before." What did he think? That nobody had ever wanted me?

"Hey, I respect that, Bailey. I'm glad you haven't sailed off the Virgin Islands with anybody else."

I relaxed a little. "You are?"

He smiled down at me. "Of course I am."

I studied his face, his eyes. He meant what he said. Was it possible that I'd finally met a guy who loved me and respected me for waiting? "It's not that I don't want to."

"I get it, Bailey. I do. Your first time is so important. You want to be sure, right?"

"Right." I also wanted to be married. But the vortex pulling me in to Eric Strang kept me from saying anything more. All I could do was agree with him.

"And when you're sure," he said, pulling me back into his arms, "I just want you to know that I'm here for you. And I hope you'll let me be your first."

13

In a way, it was good that I had four months to prom. I needed to lose at least two pounds a month to fit into my prom dress. And I needed all of my waltzing lessons. The weeks flew by in a flurry of senior year activities. Amber and I were reduced to texting each other because she was always slaving on the school paper, and I spent so much time working, or playing, at the country club.

Eric and I, on the other hand, spent more and more time together. The subject of "Virgin Islands" didn't come up again. I wanted to know what Eric was thinking, but I wasn't about to pry it out of him.

It was early March when Roni begged me to come over and

check on her newts. Eric was off with the debate team, and nobody else was home. The first thing I did was free Shirley, who spent way too much time in the basement kennel. The little dog was so glad to see me that I decided I'd take her home with me for a couple of nights.

"This way," Roni said, leading me through her enormous bedroom to her private bath. I'd never been in her room before. Her bed was made, and she had nature prints on her walls.

"So where are the daggers tacking up posters of Dracula?" I asked.

"Shut up!" she called from the bathroom. "And get in here." Her bathroom was as big as my bedroom. "I'm scared, Bailey. I'm not even sure Moe's alive."

The two newts, slimy, shiny black lizards, were sprawled on rocks at opposite ends of the aquarium. They weren't moving. "Which is which?"

"Don't be so *bête*. Curly's female, and Moe's male. I thought they'd get together by now and have a baby, and I'd call him Larry. Then I'd have all three stooges."

"I don't think they do it that way, you know? One lays eggs, and the other fertilizes. I don't think they ever touch each other."

"No sex?" she asked. "No wonder they're so sad."

I glanced at Roni and wondered if she'd already had sex.

She caught me studying her. "No, I haven't," she said.

"What?" I asked, as if she hadn't read my mind.

"You and Eric haven't either, right?"

"How did you know? Did he tell you?"

"Are you kidding?" She laughed.

"So, do you think it's weird that we haven't?"

"No!"

"Well, do you think that it's weird we don't even talk about it?"

"Eric? It would be weird if you did. Not a great talker, my brother."

"Are you kidding? Eric can talk to anybody about anything. There's a reason he's captain of the debate team."

"That's because they don't talk about anything past layer three." She reached into the aquarium and stroked Moe with her fingertip. The newt moved. "Look! He's okay."

"Wait a minute. Explain 'layer three.'"

Relief spread over Roni's face. She really cared for the slimy creatures. "What? Oh. Layer three. Like, out of ten. It's my personal onion theory. See, it's like we've all got layers on layers, going deep inside, to layer ten, that place where we're spiritual and private. But we don't show those deep layers. Strangs, for example, can live their whole lives on the top couple of layers. We don't like to dig into others or ourselves."

I thought about the way Eric had cut off my conversation about old boyfriends. And the couple of times I'd mentioned God, he'd changed the subject pretty fast.

"Peeling onions can make you cry," Roni said. "Did you ever see Eric cry?"

I shook my head. And Eric had never seen me cry either. Amber, Mom, and I had seen each other cry—cried together— more times than I could remember. I don't think I'd ever seen Eric sad. But so what? What was so wrong with not crying?

"Come here, you." Roni lifted Curly out and eyed her. "I love you, Curly."

"That's because Curly doesn't have layers two to ten," I

teased, trying to convince myself that the onion theory was just another of Roni's quirks. "So Curly never cries. See? Made to order for a Strang."

Roni didn't laugh. She set Curly down again. "No judgments until you've walked a mile in my shoes, Bailey," she said softly. "So far, you've only walked a few hundred yards."

Roni's onion theory might have had some truth to it. Maybe Eric and I were staying on those top layers of the onion, but they were fun and wonderful layers. I loved working at the club. Eric dropped by all the time. Jeannette too. They both helped out when I worked on retirement parties, debutante balls, and spring galas. Even our own senior prom got shifted from the Tri-County gymnasium to the Riverbend Country Club, thanks to Eric's mother. Tickets would cost more, but most of the kids seemed fine with it.

Not Amber, though. "I mean it," she complained at lunch when she heard the news about the prom changing locales. "The only good thing about a stupid prom is being able to transform a gym into something cool. Now that's gone!"

"Come on," I reasoned. "No way could you turn the gym into anything as cool as the club will be."

"The *club*," she muttered. "Eric's mother is behind this, isn't she?"

I shrugged. Eleanor Strang had used her influence at the club and on the school board to pull this off. She'd bragged about it to Eric and me. More than Amber needed to know.

"I can't wait to write my editorial in the *Rag*. I might throw in something about a link between prom buffets and salmonella," she muttered.

"Will you give my boyfriend a break? Anyway, he's got a point about salmonella. Did you know that in St. Louis last year—?"

Amber didn't want to hear it. "I'm boycotting the prom if it's at a country club," she vowed.

"Amber, you are not."

"No? Well, you just wait and see."

The rest of our senior year flew by.

Amber kept her word about boycotting the prom. She'd already invited Travis, but two weeks before the prom, she half uninvited him. Instead, they made big plans to watch TV and dog-sit for Mom and me on prom night. Eric's mom had roped my mom into helping chaperone the prom. Like Jeannette, Mrs. Strang was convinced that Eric and I would be on prom court, and she couldn't imagine Mom not wanting to be there to see it. She'd even given Mom a dress, a Strang original (though not a "Unique"), to complement her own. Problem was, our school colors were orange and black. And Mrs. Strang's chaperone dress was black.

"I look like an undergrown pumpkin in this dress," Mom complained when she tried it on for Amber and me. Adam and Eve barked at her. Shirley, who'd spent the night, hid under the couch.

"It's nice, Big D," Amber said, obviously fighting off hysterical laughter.

Mom swatted at the poufy skirt as if she could close it like an umbrella. "Do you know that the woman actually had the nerve to tell me she'd picked this one especially for me because she thought I could wear the thing again?"

Amber's floodgate of laughter broke. "Sure, Big D. Like to Candyland."

"Stop it, Amber," I said. But I was laughing, too. The dress really was hideous.

"Plus," Amber continued, "you never know when they'll have tryouts for *Gone With the Wind*."

Mom threw couch pillows at us. But she was a good sport and promised to wear the Strang dress to the prom.

The week before prom couldn't have gone better if I'd scripted it myself. When the student body voted on the prom court, not only did Eric and I make it, but so did Jeannette and Glen, her date and one of Eric's best buddies. I knew I was just there because everybody loved Eric. But it still felt great, almost like I was living somebody else's life.

Prom morning was picture-perfect, with the sun shining in a clear blue sky. Amber promised to come over later and help me get ready. I'd had my hair appointment at Mrs. Strang's favorite salon lined up for two months.

Mom was studying the classifieds for garage sales when I came out to the kitchen. "Morning," she said. "I can't believe this is your senior prom, Bailey."

"Know what you mean." I let Adam and Eve and Shirley outside and watched them in the yard. Shirley loved staying with us. I strongly suspected that on Shirley-sleepover nights, Mom tried to teach the little Shih Tzu to bark. Once I'd caught Mom on hands and knees outside, barking into puzzled Shirley's little face. Shirley romped around with the other dogs, but she still didn't bark.

"Are you going over to Amber's?"

"I have prom court rehearsal this morning, remember?" Mrs. Strang had insisted that all five couples rehearse the promenade and the "Royal Waltz," even though it would only be danced by the king and queen. Eric and I had stopped our waltz lessons around number seven, but I knew the basics.

"That's right." Mom sighed. "Eleanor wanted *me* to be there. Tell her . . . tell her I didn't have anything to wear to rehearsal."

"Mom," I scolded.

"Hey, I'm sacrificing my dignity and wearing a pumpkin to the ball for you, my dear daughter. A tiny white lie is the least you can do for me."

Rehearsal was worse than I thought. Jeannette was sweet as ever, but the other girls snapped at each other. "Jeannette!" Cara Weyland shouted, storming up behind her. "You're standing on my spot. Michael and I are supposed to be there."

"Sorry," Jeannette said, retreating to the rear with Eric and me.

"What's with Cara?" I didn't know her very well. She was a cheerleader, and her parents didn't belong to the country club.

"I think the competition's getting to everybody." Jeannette smiled at me. "Like they don't know there's no competition here."

Eric put his arm around my shoulder. "Jeannette, you don't know that. You and Glen have as good a chance as anybody."

Jeannette narrowed her eyes at him. "Anybody but you guys."

I knew Eric expected us to win as much as his mother did. I'd be lying if the thought of being prom queen to Eric's prom king didn't make me light-headed. But the whole campaigning thing wasn't something I'd thrown myself into. Eric had, though. And so had all his buddies, which had made me feel bad for Jeannette. They were her friends, too. And Glen's.

I watched Jeannette walk gracefully back to her date. "Do you think Jeannette likes Glen?" I asked Eric.

Eric frowned down at me. "Of course she likes him."

I grinned up at my perfect, but dense boyfriend. "I mean *likes* him, as in romance?"

Eric swung his head around and stared at Jeannette as if I'd just clued him in that she was on fire. Then, seeing no flames, he relaxed. "No way. Jeannette and Glen?" He shot them one more look, longer this time. "Don't be crazy."

"What's crazy about Jeannette and Glen together?" I couldn't explain it, but I felt the old jealousy creeping back in. Why should Eric care if Glen and Jeannette were more than friends?

Before Eric could explain, his mother clapped her hands and called us to attention. "Now, some of you have been to debutante affairs on this very dance floor. I expect more of you in the promenade. After all, *prom* has its root in *promenade*."

She made us walk from the stage down the steps and across the length of the room on the arms of our escorts two times before switching to the "Royal Waltz." A few kids from the junior class watched us as they set up tables and decorations.

I was losing confidence with every step. "Eric," I whispered, "I think I forgot how to waltz."

He put his hand firmly on my back and raised his arm to waltz position. "Relax. Just follow my lead."

Mrs. Strang had booked the club's favorite orchestra for our prom and made them agree to give us an hour during rehearsals. I knew most of them, especially Billy, the sax player. They started with a familiar waltz tune, but I couldn't remember the name. I couldn't remember anything. I felt Eric's mother watching me, hating every step I took, as Eric tried to move me around the floor.

"Stop! Everybody stop!" Mrs. Strang shouted. "Flow, people.

Don't stomp. One, two, three. Glen, raise your arm. Don't expect Jeannette to lead. Again."

We stopped and started for an agonizing half hour. Finally, Mrs. Strang lost it. "All right! Eric and Jeannette, come out here and show them how to waltz."

They tried to object, but they were no match for Eleanor Strang. The music started, and Eric and Jeannette took the stance. Then they danced. They flowed together as if they didn't have to think about it. They were part of the music. I don't think I'd understood the waltz until that moment.

And I understood something else. When they swept past me, Jeannette had the most joyful, and painful, expression on her face. And in her eyes—I recognized it because it was the same way I looked at Eric—in her eyes was love.

14

When Jeannette and Eric's waltz ended, we applauded. Even the musicians stood up and clapped for them. After that, Mrs. Strang made each of the couples practice individually, without music.

But how could I waltz with Eric after that? "Eric, I'm too tired to waltz."

"We can use the practice," he said.

We'd inched close to the musicians, and I could tell Billy the sax player was eavesdropping. The rest of the guys were slumped in their seats awaiting orders from Eric's mother. Mrs. Strang shouted something over to them.

"What did she say?" asked the trumpet player.

"She wants us to play again." The drummer didn't seem too pleased.

I grinned at Billy. "Do you know Three Dog Night's Jeremiah bullfrog song?"

"The what?" Eric asked. "Bailey—"

But Billy was on my side. "'Joy to the World,' key of C!" he shouted.

The others came to life.

"Funny, Bailey," Eric said. He turned to Billy and the band. "Forget it, guys." Eric sounded as forceful as his mother.

The musicians laid down their instruments.

Eric put his hands on my shoulders and grinned down at me. "What am I going to do with you, Bailey Daley? Man, you can be so goofy sometimes." Then he kissed my forehead. "Now, let's waltz."

We waltzed to beautiful music, but Eric's words circled in my mind, echoed in my ears: *You can be so goofy.*

Those words didn't go away all afternoon. They hung like a swarm of gnats, following me to Eleanor's exclusive hair salon, where the girl knew exactly how to fix my hair up.

While I waited at home for Amber to help me get ready, I could still hear Eric's *Man, you can be so goofy.* I tried on my Strang Unique prom dress. It fit perfectly. I stood in front of the long mirror and studied myself in that elegant dress, my hair piled on top of my head in subtle curls, the way Eric liked it best.

"I am eighteen years old with a perfect bod and hair to die for, and I can be so goofy.

"I am eighteen years old with a perfect bod and hair to die for, and I can be so goofy.

"I am eighteen years old with a perfect bod and hair to die for, and I can be so goofy."

I turned off the light and sat on my bed in semidarkness

until I heard voices from downstairs, filtering up like static. Amber and Travis had arrived. The dogs—at least Adam and Eve—were barking at them.

You can be so goofy, Eric had said.

And inside I was whispering, *"Can I?"*

Amber thundered up the stairs, burst into my room, and turned on the light. "You look great! Okay. To be honest, that dress isn't you. You've totally lost your funk. But still—wow! Why are you sitting in the dark?"

I shrugged.

She shut the door and sat beside me. For a minute she didn't speak, but she didn't need to. It felt like a deep layer of my onion was talking to a deep layer of hers, only without words. We both teared up a little. "I'll never understand them," she said quietly.

I knew she meant guys. "Or us," I added.

"So true." She lowered her voice. "Guess who called me last night." I didn't guess, so she told me. "Steve. Remember him from summer school?"

I did remember the tall basketball player who'd fallen for Amber the minute he saw her. But they'd lost touch during the year. "What did he want?"

"He says he's never gotten over me. That's why he stopped calling. He thought he could get me out of his head, but he can't. Bailey, he says he loves me."

"Wow. What about Travis?"

"Nah, I don't think he loves Travis. Not his type."

"Funny. How do you feel about Steve?"

Amber plopped back on the bed and stared at the ceiling. "We talked for two hours. And I'm telling you . . . when he started in on how he'd never meet anyone like me again, I felt like telling him I wanted to see him again."

"So why didn't you?"

"Your mother. You know what she always says about going back to an ex-boyfriend."

I knew, all right. I'd heard it a million times. "It's like buying your own garage sale rejects."

"No. Not that one. I was thinking about the cow thing. About how hanging on to an ex-boyfriend is like chewing your cud until somebody drops a fresh bale of hay in front of you. Or something like that. She's *your* mother."

"Ah, Mom. The woman does have a way with words."

"Yeah. And she's probably right about ex-boyfriends anyway. Do you ever think about any of yours?"

"Sometimes," I admitted. "Went."

"Your first."

"And Mitch."

"Oh, Bailey! Not moody Mitch."

We talked about old times for a while. Then she said, "Well, you finally did it."

"Did what?"

"Landed the perfect boyfriend."

I pictured Eric, his smile, his great bod, the way everyone admired him and admired me when I was with him. Eric Strang's girlfriend.

Amber bounced up off the bed. "Where's that list?"

"What list?"

"You know!" She ran to my desk. "The 'Perfect Boyfriend' list."

I laughed. "I forgot all about that." I joined her and rummaged through a stack of old papers. Finally, I found it in my top dresser drawer. I unfolded the paper and read to Amber: "THE PERFECT BOYFRIEND will be:

"*A gecko.*"

"Check," Amber said. "I've never heard of Eric Strang even looking at another girl. And I am a newspaper reporter, don't forget."

I went on with the list. "*College bound and focused. Handsome. Thinks I'm hot.*" Amber nodded, and I agreed. "*Normal. Polite. Respects me. Considerate. Rich. Great dancer.*" I frowned over at Amber. "Does waltzing count?" She nodded, and I forged ahead.

"*Has to believe in God.*"

"Strangs go to church, right?" Amber asked. "That big one in Riverbend?"

I nodded. I was sure Eric did believe in God. He just wasn't comfortable talking about God. Too inner-onion.

"Is that it?" Amber asked.

I finished the list. "*Real. No mistaken identity.*" I grinned. "Roni told me once that with her brother, what you see is what you get."

"Check."

"*A dog owner.*"

"Check," Amber said. "Although you did kind of rig that last one."

"So that's it, then," I said, folding up the list. "I did it. I have the Perfect Boyfriend."

"And the perfect prom date," Amber said.

"Hey!" Mom stuck her head in. She held up her orange dress. "Isn't anybody going to help me turn into a pumpkin?"

My boyfriend arrived right on time, in a limo. He looked so handsome in his tux. He might have walked off the cover of one of the Strang Unique catalogs. Plus, he smelled like Italian leather with a hint of lime. And he brought flowers for me and for my mom and told us we both looked beautiful.

I couldn't believe the change in the sky as Eric and I dashed to the limo. A cool breeze had swept in dark, bottom-heavy clouds. "Looks like we're in for a storm," I observed, ducking into the plush row of seats. "That's going to put a hitch in our after-prom plans." Our class had rented the park center, with mini-golf and batting cages.

Eric scooted closer. "I have some alternative plans I want you to consider." He wrapped his arms around me, and I snuggled in. "I've rented a suite at the Hilton."

"You what?"

"Don't say anything yet. I'm not pressuring you. It's your decision. I just want you to think about it. I love you, Bailey, and I want this to be the *perfect* night, a night you and I will remember for the rest of our lives."

15

Eric and I sat at the prom court's special dinner table at the club. I think I was the only one not touching my food. Eric was downing everything set in front of us, with no questions about how safely food had been prepared. More than anything, I wanted to call Amber and talk to her about Eric's "alternative plans." But I'd left my cell home because it wouldn't fit in my bag. "Eric, could I borrow your cell?"

"Didn't bring it," he said, finishing off his chocolate cake.

"You're kidding." He always had his cell.

He leaned into me and whispered, "I didn't want to make

it easy to track me down after the prom." He reached over and squeezed my knee. I still felt that shudder of pleasure whenever Eric touched me. He was a magnet, or a spinning vortex, drawing me in. I knew he meant it when he said this was my decision. I could say yes or no. But how could I say no to Eric? Somewhere along the way it had become almost impossible to say no to Eric Strang.

I really had to talk to somebody. I looked around for Mom, but she'd only promised Mrs. Strang to be there when the dancing started.

All around us, lights twinkled, and tables glowed. The room smelled like a garden. The other tables had turned in their ballots for prom queen and king. Behind the scenes student leaders and faculty volunteers were tallying up the votes.

Conversations around our table seemed stilted. Jeannette, who looked elegant in a short teal gown, kept a calm smile on her face, but even she wasn't talking much to Glen or anyone else. I thought about talking to Jeannette about Eric, but I couldn't do that to her. I knew how she felt about him.

Eric's mother came to our table. "This is it, everyone," she said. "I need you to move backstage so we can make the announcement. Don't forget. The king and queen make their speeches *before* the waltz." Babbling more instructions at us, she herded us behind the curtain, where we stood like sheep waiting for slaughter.

Mrs. Strang sneaked up behind me. "You really shouldn't bite your nails."

Unaware that I had been, I dropped the offending hand. "Sorry. I always eat myself when I'm nervous."

She didn't laugh. Neither did Eric. Outside, thunder rumbled and shook the stage.

Mrs. Strang shushed us, and we could hear Brad, the junior class president, welcome everyone to the Tri-County Senior Prom. "Remember, no losers tonight," he said into the mike. "We'll start with the fourth runner-up."

"Eric, I can't do this," I whispered.

"Don't be silly. You're just nervous." He took my hand.

"I don't mean *this*. I mean all of it."

Eric dropped my hand. "Are you talking about after the prom?"

Was I? Or was it something more?

"Cara and Michael!" shouted Brad.

Cara groaned, then painted on a smile and walked out through the curtains with Michael as the crowd clapped politely.

"Listen," Eric said, putting his arm around me. "Everything will be perfect. You'll see. Just leave it to me. I know you want this as much as I do."

"How can you know that?" It wasn't a challenge. I really wanted to know.

"What do you mean?"

"Because you don't really know me, Eric." Maybe I was finally admitting Roni was right about her onion theory.

"How can you say I don't know you?" He laughed, but it didn't quite work. Was the vortex slowing down? "Come on, Bailey. This isn't you."

"No, *this* isn't me." I pointed to myself, finally beginning to understand what was so wrong. "Eric, I hate my hair this way." I yanked at one of the plastered curls that was already giving me a headache. "This is a gorgeous dress, a fantastic dress—just not on me."

"Bailey, you don't know what you're—"

But I was just getting started. "I don't like to waltz. I hate that bow your mother puts in Shirley's hair. And it makes me sad that Shirley can't bark. I love desserts. I stop for roadkill. I am a born Grady girl! I worked at Grady's Gas and Snack, Eric. You never even knew that."

He backed up a step, braced to defend himself. "I'm sorry. I didn't know—"

"Of course you didn't know! How could you? I didn't let you know. I wanted to be perfect for you. I wanted to be the person you wanted me to be. It wasn't your fault. That was *my* mistake."

My mistake?

"Oh, man. I guess this *was* another case of mistaken identity," I explained, more to myself than to Eric. "Only this time it was *my* identity that was mistaken." I laughed, feeling free and right and honest—and me again—for the first time in a long time.

Eric glanced nervously at his mother, who was glaring our way. "Keep your voice down, will you, Bailey?"

"No." I laughed and said it again. "No can do. This is me— loud and obnoxious, like Adam and Eve." Eric had called my dogs that once—loud and obnoxious. "And I'd give just about anything to help Shirley be loud and obnoxious, too."

Eric threw up his hands. "Now you've totally lost it." He looked over at Jeannette, and I wished I could have read his mind.

Two more couples had been called onstage as runners-up. Jeannette and Glen were the only ones backstage with Eric and me. I wondered how much they'd overheard.

From the other side of the curtain, Brad boomed into the mike, "And our first runner-up couple is . . . Jeannette and Glen!"

Applause broke out from both sides of the stage. Jeannette called over to us, "Congratulations, you two!"

Eric's mother was right there, pushing us to follow Glen and

Jeannette. "I knew it. Congratulations. Now remember every-thing I taught you about the waltz."

Eric and I walked to center stage and were crowned by last year's king and queen. I felt the tiara on top of my piled-up hair. It was not a good fit, not in any way. Eric waved to the crowd, but I just couldn't. He walked to the mike and started speaking, thanking everybody.

I looked around for a familiar face, and the first thing I saw was a splotch of orange, with arms waving at me. I grinned at my mom. Then she pointed to the side of the club, where doors led to a patio. I followed her gaze and saw Amber cheering for me. Travis crouched beside her, struggling to hang on to Adam and Eve's leashes. Amber. I should have known she'd sneak in to see if I won.

Eric's speech was winding down. Any minute it would be my turn. What on earth could I say?

"Bailey?" Eric said. He backed up, and the mike was mine.

I dragged myself to the mike. My too-tall heels clunked, and when I stopped at the mike, my breath was amplified like a rush of wind. "Um, thanks. I mean, I know you just voted for me be-cause you love Eric." I heard polite laughter, and I laughed, too. My tiara tottered, and I reached up and pulled it off. "This thing is a lot heavier than it looks." I grinned at Eric, but he wasn't smiling. "I don't think anybody here questions the fact that Eric Strang is the perfect prom king."

"Whoo, Eric!" a girl shouted in the back of the hall. Other kids laughed.

"I agree. On the other hand, come on. I am so not a prom queen." Nobody laughed. "Eric is the perfect boyfriend, too. I've looked a long time for a perfect boyfriend. The only thing is that until a few minutes ago, it hadn't occurred to me that to have the perfect boyfriend, I had to be the perfect girlfriend. And I'm no more that than I am a perfect prom queen." I glanced over at Eric again. He shook his head, but he didn't look angry anymore.

The only voice I heard was Eleanor Strang's whisper from behind the curtain, "You're ruining everything!"

"Eric Strang," I went on, "you are a prince. And a prince deserves a princess." I laughed softly. "I am a frog. You could kiss me for the next twenty years, and you still wouldn't turn me into a princess. Not even a classier frog." There was nervous laughter, but I'd tuned out the audience. I wanted Eric to understand. "I'd still be a goofy frog because, guess what, I like being a frog."

Mom apparently couldn't hold it in any longer. "I love frogs!" she shouted.

"Me too!" cried Amber. She and Mom had come together and now stood in the center of the dance floor, just below stage.

"You go, *mademoiselle!*" someone in the back shouted. Roni, dressed totally in black, gave me a thumbs-up. A couple of her fellow goth party crashers stood with her.

I don't think most people had any idea what was going on. I faced the audience. "So thanks for voting. And you got it half right. Eric is the perfect prom king." I walked over to Jeannette and put the tiara on her head. She tried to stop me, but I won. And that crown was a perfect fit. I went back to the mike. "See? She's the perfect prom queen. And you guys just wait until you see her waltz. So . . . I guess that's it then."

The room grew silent, a horrible silence. A deadly quiet. People were whispering and staring back. I don't know what they expected. But I couldn't seem to move.

Then I heard a little, off-key voice. "Jeremiah was a hound dog!" *Mom.*

Amber, in jeans and letter jacket stopped staring at Mom, turned to face me, and belted out, "Dated him for a while."

I laughed out loud. Stunned silence reigned in the country club. I hurried down the steps to join Mom and Amber, singing, "He left me flat, but I'm tellin' you that . . ." They joined in for the rest of the verse as we lockstepped into our rock 'n' roll routine.

Billy the sax player picked up on the chorus and struck up the band. They played, and we sang and slid into our synchronized dance steps. Before I knew it, people were clapping, then racing onto the dance floor to join us. People in gowns and tuxes were doing the twist and the swim and every other old move they knew. Roni bumped into me. She was doing the cha-cha with Glen. It was crazy.

Suddenly Amber stopped. "Listen!"

"I know," I said. "They're loving it!"

"No!" Amber said. "Not that! This." She unzipped her jacket, and there was little Shirley.

"Amber, how did you—?" But I stopped. Because I heard it too now. It sounded like a squeak. Then it grew to a *yap, yap.* And it was coming from Shirley.

"She's barking!" Mom shouted.

Little Shirley had found her voice at the prom—just like me.

"Eric's mother will be so pleased," Amber said. "Looks like you guys got yourselves another dog."

Mom shook her head. "Three dogs."

"Come on!" I shouted. "Let's get out of here."

Mom and Amber took off, and I started to run after them. Then I turned to see where Eric was. He and Jeannette were sitting on the stage, watching, talking. I waved until they saw me. It struck me that I really was walking away from the perfect boyfriend. It might be a very long time before I got another boyfriend. I'd probably be spending a lot of time with just me. But maybe it would be okay. I didn't mind me so much now.

Jeannette shrugged, palms in the air, then waved back. I think she shouted, "Thanks!" but I couldn't hear her. Everybody was singing now.

Eric kept staring at me, but I didn't read hate there. He was looking at me as if he were seeing me for the first time. Maybe he was.

I stared back and hoped he could read half of what I was feeling. I knew he didn't understand, not everything. But I prayed he'd understand enough to be okay. Maybe Jeannette could help him get there.

Amber and Mom were outside with Travis and the dogs when I ran out. A light rain fell, and Adam and Eve were already soaked. Shirley wouldn't stop barking. Amber let her down, and she pranced in mud puddles, showing off.

"What now?" Travis asked.

I turned to Mom. "Good question. I don't really feel like hanging around here."

"Me either," Mom said, hiking up her orange gown. "Bailey, we're going to St. Louis! I've always wanted to see what kind of garage sales they have in that city."

"A road trip! Good for you guys!" Amber cried, snuggling closer to Travis, who put one arm around her and held on to Adam and Eve with his other hand.

Thunder rumbled in the distance. "What about the dogs?" I asked.

Mom grabbed Adam's and Eve's leashes out of Travis's hand and took off for her car. "They're coming with us!"

"Well, come on, Shirley!" I yelled, running as fast as I could, with the dirty little bundle of dog on my heels. "On to St. Louis! No dog left behind!"

ST. LOUIS — The Present

"LOOK! THE RAIN'S STOPPED." I stare out the big front window of Louie's of St. Louie. The sun is coming up. We can't see it yet, just the light it promises.

"Well, I'll be," says Louie.

Far away that stone city arch comes into focus as a fog lifts. "Louie, you can see the Arch from here!" I exclaim. I grin at my three new friends around the table. They're staring outside like they've never seen that world before.

Colt turns back to me. "So you and Eric . . . ?"

I shake my head.

"You're not with him anymore?" he says, something real in his voice, like it matters to him.

"Nope."

"Nice save," Rune says. He gets up from the table and stretches. Tattoos dance on his arms. "I better get on home, see if I can get me a couple hours' sleep before chasing my boys all over Six Flags."

"Good for you, Rune," Louie says.

Rune smiles at Louie and nods, some understanding passing between them. Then Rune stares down at me. I don't think he knows what to do with me. I reach up to him, and he leans over

MY BOYFRIENDS' DOGS

and gives me an awkward hug. His big arms close around me so gently that tears, good tears, spring to my eyes. "I'm glad you and these here dogs ended up at Louie's tonight," he whispers. "You're gonna be just fine, Bailey Daley." He stands up and almost stumbles over Eve. Rune takes the dog's face in his hands. "And you, Eve ol' girl, you take care of her."

Eve's tail thumps the café floor, and the dog makes whimpering sounds for more attention.

"Yeah," Rune says, his face close to hers. "I'm gonna miss you, too, girl." He glances at me, maybe including me in this conversation. Maybe not. "I think I'll get my boys a firehouse dog just like this one. Might even call her Eve the Second."

"Eve the First would be honored, Rune. Have a great time at Six Flags."

Rune nods to all of us. "I'll do that." And then he's gone.

Louie lets out his low laugh that turns into a cough. "Well, you kept your bargain, Bailey. Guess we know why a young lady with such a fine gown graced our premises in the middle of this night."

I glance down at my Strang Unique, covered by the gaudy green sweater. Eric's mother would have a heart attack. "I can't wait for the stores to open so I can get something else to wear." I smile over at Louie. He looks older and more wrinkled in the dawning light, and more beautiful in his own way. "I want you to meet my mother, Louie."

"I'd like that."

"Of course, you'll have to wait until she can get something to wear besides the pumpkin dress." I laugh, and so do Louie and Colt. When we stop laughing, I know it's time for me to leave. But I love it here. It's helped me to talk to them, helped me in ways I can't explain, like telling the stories made the pieces fit.

That makes me think about when I first walked in. The dogs had shaken off rain all over the linoleum floor. I stand up. "I want to mop your floor, Louie. The dogs and I messed it up." I turn toward the door, but all the water has dried.

"Don't you worry about that." Louie gets to his feet, but it's obviously an effort, his body straightening by bits and fits. "I reckon it's time for me to think about opening. It's a brand-new day out there."

"Do you need some help?" Colt asks, scooting back his chair. Shirley, still in his lap, wakes up and barks for good measure. "With Rune gone and everything?"

"I'll be fine, thank you, Colt. Sunday's a light day. I'll manage just fine. Got me a girl who comes in for the lunch crowd." Louie smiles across the table at me. "You'd best get on back to your mama before she wakes up and finds you missing and brings all of St. Louie down on my little café."

I know I have to tell him goodbye. How could it be so hard after so little time? I dash around the table and wrap my arms around the old man. He folds his stiff arms around me and leans his head against mine. I can't hold back the tears. I didn't cry once during my whole story about falling three times from love, and yet here I am crying like a baby, saying goodbye to a wrinkled old man I've only known for a few hours. "I'll never forget you, Louie."

His arms close tighter on me. "Me neither, Bailey Daley. Me neither. Love, that real and right love, it's right around the corner. You mark my words."

I finally let Louie go, and turn to Colt. He's holding Shirley and has Adam and Eve on their leashes. It makes me laugh, and I'm grateful for that.

"Can I walk you back?" Colt asks.

"I think you're going to have to. My dogs like you too much to leave you here."

We step outside, and the wet streets smell like spring. The sidewalk's wet, and trees drip on us when we pass under. A car slows as it passes, and the driver does a double take.

All three dogs hover around Colt's feet as we walk.

"Do dogs always like you?" I ask him.

He squints, like he hasn't thought about this before. "Yeah. I guess they do."

"They like me, too," I tell him. "I'm not sure why."

Colt smiles over at me. He has a wonderful, rich smile and a tiny gap between his front teeth that makes him adorable and handsome at the same time. "I have a theory about why dogs come to some people and run away from others," he says.

"I'd like to hear that theory." I'm not looking where I'm going. So when we get to the corner, Colt holds his arm out in front of me to keep me from crossing against traffic. It's a tiny gesture, but he's so not conscious of doing it that my heart beats a little faster, like he saved me from oncoming traffic without a second thought.

"I think dogs prefer people who don't chase them," Colt begins. "People who don't try too hard to get them to come. You know? Then they get to come on their own, in their time."

The light changes, and we cross the street. I have Eve's leash, and Colt has Adam's and Shirley's. "You're right," I tell him. "I don't ever try to get dogs to love me."

"They just do, right?"

"Right."

I don't say anything else, but he has to be thinking what I'm thinking. Why did I chase my boyfriends? Even when I didn't scare them off, did it start love out wrong? Put us on a course that could never be as natural or as real as it might have been?

"You know what a beautiful young girl told me once?" Colt asks.

He grins at me, and there's something weirdly familiar about him. Maybe I felt it the first time I really looked at him in Louie's. I shake my head, and I am riveted. I can't take my eyes off this guy.

"This girl told me that when people say men are dogs, they don't know what they're talking about. She said dogs love unconditionally. If you find a man who can love you like a dog, you just might have found real love."

A shiver rushes through me, down to my toes. It's exactly what I said to Goofy that day. "*Who* told you that?" I didn't tell that part of my story back there in Louie's. I'm sure I didn't.

"A beautiful, but sad, girl told me that. Actually, I think she was quoting her mother."

"Colt! How do you know that?" The only time I ever said that to anybody, except Amber, was years ago on a bench in Six Flags in St. Louis.

Colt is calm and cool, but his grin spreads over his whole face. "Just call me Goofy."

"No way! You're not saying—! You're not trying to tell me *you*—. That's not possible." Maybe I'm dreaming this. Maybe I dreamed the entire night in Louie of St. Louie's.

"I wasn't even supposed to be Goofy that day. I was quitting my job at the park. Then I saw you on that bench." He stops walking, and so do I. We stare at each other for a minute. "I don't think I ever got over that day, Bailey."

People walk past us and stare. Maybe it's the dress. Or the dogs. I don't care. "You're Goofy."

Colt shrugs and nods. "Soon as you talked about going to Six Flags, I had this feeling. I already thought I'd seen you before. Then when you told us about being at the park with Went, I knew, even before you got to the Goofy part."

I shake my head. I'm a little dizzy.

"And by the way," he adds quickly, "Tweety Bird—the real Tweety, not the park's version—is definitely a boy. Everybody knows that."

I crack up then. I can't stop laughing at the wonder of this. It's too big to be a coincidence. I wouldn't believe it if anybody else told me this story. But I was there. And we're here.

Shirley is barking nonstop. Adam and Eve are doing their business, synchronized in the middle of the sidewalk, to the frowns of people passing us in wide arcs.

Colt slips his two leashes to his left hand and puts one arm around my waist. "I think we better get out of here."

We run, breathless with laughter and the morning's crisp air in our lungs. We don't stop until we get to the hotel.

"You're coming up with me." It's a statement. I'm not asking. "You've got to back me up on this whole story with Mom. She's not going to believe you're *the* Goofy, the reason I have two hundred Goofy figurines in her overstuffed garage."

My dogs lead us to the right hotel room. "I don't have a key," I say, patting the sides of my prom dress.

"What?" Colt acts shocked. "Are you telling me the designers of Strang prom dresses forgot to put in pockets?"

"And they think they're so clever," I agree. "Guess I better knock." I'm about to when the door flies open.

Mom, dressed in her bright orange gown, is standing in the doorway. When she sees me, she stops fidgeting with her belt and puts her hands on her hips. "Bailey! Where have you been?"

"Didn't you get my text message?"

"Safe and warm and not kidnapped? Yes, I got that one. Still, I woke up an hour ago, and you and the dogs . . ." Her voice trails off as her gaze fixes on Colt. "Well, where did you get him?"

Colt sticks out his hand. "Colt Carson," he says. "I'm really glad to meet you, Mrs. Daley. I've heard a lot about you."

Mom lets her hand be shaken, but it's clear she has no idea what Colt's talking about. "You have? You've heard about me?"

"From Bailey." Colt smiles over at me. "Great dogs you guys have, too." He reaches down and scratches all of them.

Mom raises her eyebrows at me. I can tell she's not mad anymore, just intrigued. "Well? Is anybody going to fill me in?"

Colt and I exchange grins. "It's a long story," I say.

"A very long story," Colt agrees.

"On the other hand, we've got time," I add.

Colt turns his charm on my mother, but there's nothing fake about this charm. "I have an idea. Why don't Bailey and I fill you in while I show you guys the sights of St. Louis?"

"The sights?" Mom's still thrown, but she's recovering nicely, grinning at Colt, narrowing her eyes at me.

"Just the highlights. The Arch, of course. Six Flags absolutely. And garages."

Now Mom perks up. "Garages?"

"I've lived here my whole life. I know where all the best garage sales are."

Mom steps inside the room for her purse, and Colt turns to me. "We need to stop by my apartment and walk Sam first."

"Sam?"

"My dog. I'd like you and the dogs to meet Sammy."

"You have a dog?"

"Of course."

I can't explain why this fact makes me feel like I want to dance.

Mom comes back out with her purse and shuts the door behind her. "First we buy clothes."

"I know some great rummage sales," Colt says, leading the way. The dogs trot happily among us.

Mom glances at me over her shoulder. "Who *is* this boy?"

"Mom," I answer, moving in closer to Colt, "you wouldn't believe me if I told you. At least, not until you've heard the whole story."